# Exposing Casey

Also by Deanna Lee:

*Undressing Mercy*

*Barenaked Jane*

"Abundance" in *Sexy Beast IV*

# *Exposing Casey*

## DEANNA LEE

APHRODISIA

KENSINGTON BOOKS

http://www.kensingtonbooks.com

APHRODISIA BOOKS are published by

Kensington Publishing Corp.
850 Third Avenue
New York, NY 10022

All Kensington Titles, Imprints, and Distributed Lines are available at special quantity discounts for bulk purchases for sales promotions, premiums, fund-raising, and educational or institutional use.

Special book excerpts or customized printings can also be created to fit specific needs. For details, write or phone the office of the Kensington special sales manager: Kensington Publishing Corp., 850 Third Avenue, New York, NY 10022, attn: Special Sales Department, Phone: 1-800-221-2647.

Aphrodisia and the A logo Reg. U.S. Pat & TM Off.

ISBN-13: 978-0-7582-1487-4
ISBN-10: 0-7582-1487-1

First Kensington Trade Paperback Printing: April 2008

10  9  8  7  6  5  4  3  2  1

Printed in the United States of America

# Contents

# Watching Casey

# 1

I watched in silence as Connor Grant moved across the large open gallery space that dominated the first floor. He'd never told me he loved me or even that he liked being with me, for that matter. He'd told a million lies with his actions and his body. How could a man give a woman so much pleasure and also give nothing? I knew he was from Great Britain and that both of his parents were dead. He had a law-enforcement background that he could not talk about and no siblings. That was it; and I'd gotten that from his personnel file.

It had been my rule for years not to get involved with a man I worked with. I'd broken that rule with him and I was paying the price. Every time I saw the bastard, my knees got a little weak with the memory of him. As a lover, he'd been the perfect combination of demanding and giving; it was just too bad that he was a motherfucker in the vertical position.

He was moving toward me, smiling and weaving his way through the crowd of people I'd put between us. After dumping his ass, I'd taken a two-week vacation. Fourteen days in the U.S. Virgin Islands had given me new sense of self and a fantastic tan. I took a drink from my glass and pursed my lips as he came to a stop in front of me.

"Casey."

"Mr. Grant." I tried to keep my voice cool and neutral.

I watched shock and then anger drift across his face in equal measure. "Back to that, are we?"

"Seems like we never really left it." I glanced around the room for a way to escape.

"I'd like to talk to you."

"I'd like to forget you exist." I tried to move past him but he took my arm to stop me. His grip was firm but not painful. "Let go, Connor. You've made it abundantly clear what you can offer me and what you never will. Frankly, I can buy a dick in a store."

"We have a good thing."

"No, we had an empty and physical thing. Now, we have nothing." I looked to his hand. "Let me go."

His hand fell away and he sighed. "I'd hoped you'd be over this by now."

"You just hoped I'd still fuck you," I murmured softly and cleared my throat. "We're way past that."

At least, I was damn positive we were past that. Connor was attractive in a truly British kind of way. He'd worked for the Holman Gallery for over a year and had been the head of security for nearly four months. We'd been fucking for just over five months when I realized through no admission of his own that he never wanted anything serious with me or any other woman. It's true that he'd never made promises to me. He'd also never told me how much the idea of marriage or even a committed relationship freaked him out. If he'd had his druthers, I still wouldn't know.

He caught up with me in the staff hall that led to the administrative area. I stopped, turned around, and glared at him. "What?"

"You can't just dismiss what we are to each other."

"No, but I'm very capable of realizing of what I'll never be to you." I pushed my finger against his chest. "I deserve more."

"I can't argue with that." He grabbed my hand and pulled me to him. "Case, I've missed you."

I stilled myself against the small thrill it gave me to hear him say it. But, I knew deep down he really didn't mean it. "You miss putting your dick in me."

He slid one hand around me, pressed against the small of my back until I was flush against him. "True. I miss talking to you, hearing about your day. Where have you been?"

"I went on vacation. That's no secret."

"Three months early and you didn't tell anyone where you were going."

"I'm a grown woman." I pulled briefly but sighed when his grip tightened. "I'm entitled to a private life."

"I thought I was a part of that private life."

"You don't want to be." I shoved at his chest and sighed at how weak I was about it.

The truth was, being in his arms felt great and just about as right as I could imagine. A year ago, he'd walked into the gallery and I'd spent the day in damp panties. His cool blue eyes, dark hair brown hair, and tight body had put more than one woman in the gallery on the edge of orgasm.

My body was already a jangle of raw nerves and I winced as my nipples started to tighten against his chest. "Just let go."

"And if I can't?"

"You don't have a choice," I snapped. "Go find another woman; it won't be hard."

"You can't tell me that you don't want me."

He covered my mouth with his and I responded before I could think better of it. Parting my lips to his questing tongue was as easy as breathing. His big hands slid down my back and pulled me closer. My body was screaming, "hell, yes," but my mind wasn't having it.

I fisted my hands in the lapels of his jacket and jerked my mouth from his. "Don't."

"Case."

I sucked in a deep breath and closed my eyes against the sudden tears. "I can't do this."

"Do what?"

I met his gaze and tears slid down my cheeks. "I can't be your fuck. I can't be that woman you call in the middle of the night when your bed is cold or you can't sleep. I need something you can't give me and I'm begging you to leave me alone."

He released me and took a step back; concern softened his eyes but his own displeasure was still very evident. Connor wasn't used to women dumping him. He'd been furious two weeks ago when I'd left his apartment and that fury still lingered.

"I don't make it a habit to hurt women."

Well, I doubted seriously he set out to do it, but I was confident I was the most recent in line of women who didn't get what they wanted from him.

"You never made promises to me." I wiped at the tears and sucked in a deep breath to steady myself. "And I realized that they were never coming. I'm just disappointed. I'll get over it."

"You mean you'll get over me," he muttered.

"You never let me get close enough to get attached. I'm not one of those women who confuse sex and love." I crossed my arms over my breasts and shook my head. "Look, the others will speculate but they won't ask questions. In a few months, they won't even care about what happened between us."

And maybe in a few months I could look at him and not be angry. I turned and walked quickly to the end of the hall and pulled open the door to the office area. At my desk, I pushed off the high-heeled shoes I'd donned for the party and stared at the blank screen of my computer. It had been just a little over a year since I'd taken the promotion that'd pulled me off the sales floor and into the administration area.

Jane Tilwell, my boss and mentor, had thrown a lot in my lap from the very start, but I was confident that I'd proven myself.

The door opened and the click of high heels on the floor told me that one of the women from the party had followed along to see how I was. I glanced up and smiled softly for Mercy Rothell-Montgomery. She was the director of the gallery and one of my favorite people on earth. Gloriously redheaded, strong-minded, and very pregnant, she looked a little out of sorts.

"What did he do to you?"

My mouth dropped open briefly but I shut it quickly. "What? Nothing."

"Don't give me that. You're sitting at your desk, crying in the dark. He did something." She crossed her arms and glared.

I wiped at my damp face, startled that I was still crying. "We just don't work, that's all. He didn't do anything *to* me." I glanced toward the door as it opened again and Jane came through it. Great, I had my doubts about being able to fend them both off. "I'm all right."

Jane came to a stop beside Mercy, took off her shoes, and pursed her lips. "He's at the bar with a scotch neat, and you're in here in the dark. Sounds like you're both just doing great. He looks so miserable I couldn't even lecture him for drinking on duty."

There were plenty of security guards at the party; in fact, Connor hadn't planned to work it at all. However, I'd never known him ever to shirk his duty.

Jane waved at me with her shoes as she continued. "Are you crying?"

"No." I glared at Mercy when she started to speak. "I wouldn't cry over a man." I reached down to pick up my own shoes and shook my head. "Look, you guys, I'm fine. If you two don't go back to the party, your men will come looking for you, and, frankly, if I wanted to be on display I would have stayed at the party."

"The party is over and the men know better." She pointed toward her office. "In there, right now."

Sighing, I stood up and stomped toward her office. "Fine, but I'm not talking about him."

Being made a liar really sucks. I snuggled down in the over-stuffed chair in Jane's office and sighed. The two of them had spent the last hour listening to me bitch about Connor's commitment issues, but I hadn't even skimmed the surface of my real problem.

Jane was on the couch and Mercy was in a chair that matched the one I'd claimed. They both looked irritated, but were at a loss as to what to say to make me feel better. I looked at Mercy's swollen belly and bit my lip.

"I'm thirty years old."

"And?" Jane frowned at me. "I'm thirty-two."

"I'd planned to have a baby by now and I haven't even come close to marrying a man, much less having a kid." I stood up from the chair. "Look at me."

Jane did; her serious gaze took me in. "You look like a living, breathing Barbie doll."

That was true enough, but I wanted to give her the finger anyway. Being two inches shy of six feet, with blond hair, green eyes, and a set of tits like many women pay to get wasn't always the advantage that she assumed. "Yes, and that's how men treat me. That's how I've *let* men treat me. Well, I'm done with all of that."

"Nothing wrong with a little harmless sex," Jane said with a sigh. "You know relationships are overrated."

I laughed. "So says you." Picking up my shoes, I sat down in the chair and put them on. "I'm going home."

"Get a security guard to walk you to your car," Mercy said as she scooted to the edge of the chair and stood up as gracefully as she could muster.

I nodded, but already knew I wouldn't ask. The last thing I needed was to spend several minutes in the company of one of the men who worked for Connor. None of them had ever treated me as if they even knew I was fucking their boss; but honestly, I just wanted nothing to do with another man for a while.

Out at my desk, I plucked my coat from the chair and grabbed my purse. One day back on the job and I was already sincerely missing the beach and the pretty boy who'd brought me drinks on a little tray. Now, that's when looks like mine pay off.

I got all the way down the stairs and halfway to the staff's side exit before a security guard appeared out of nowhere to escort me. Startled and in an increasingly bad mood, I cast a glare at the man and didn't say anything as he opened the door for me. Self-preservation must have kicked in, because he fell in a few steps behind me and didn't say a word.

Being an hour behind schedule, I'd had to park on the second level of the parking deck. He cleared his throat once when I started toward the stairs but followed along dutifully. By the time I was sliding into my car, he was gone again. I wondered if they'd drawn straws to see who *had* to see me out to my car.

It was probably paranoid and vain to assume that the security staff had nothing else but me to think about.

I made it across town to the small grocery store across from my apartment in record time. However, the moment I entered the place I realized that for the first time in months I was shopping for one again. What a fucking depressing thought. I'm not one of those women who need a man to live. I'm fine without one.

I can take care of my own sexual needs and I certainly don't need a man's money. Deciding to break things off with Connor had been difficult and painful. He was a good lover and he made me feel like a million dollars when we were together. Sex has its place, of course, but being at someone's beck and call for sex had been demoralizing.

So, I'm shopping for one again. It's not a big deal. Who needs a man raiding their fridge at three in the morning and eating all of the cornflakes? I made my selections quickly, paid, and trucked back out into the night resolved to never wear the shoes I was wearing again. I'm a slave to fashion, but I refuse to be a beaten slave to fashion. Both arches were aching and all of my toes were numb or close to it.

I live in a small building that housed two apartments. The two apartments share a front door and a small foyer. The woman who had lived across from me since I'd gotten the apartment had died, and I'd been waiting a respectful period of time before I approached her family about purchasing it. However, her grandson had moved in a couple of weeks after her death. I'd seen him briefly in passing a few times but I hadn't gotten a chance to really talk with him. The man, Shawn Tranner, was superfine but since I'd been stupidly invested in Connor, I hadn't given the man much of a shot.

I may be a horrible person, but I'd started saving money several years ago to purchase the apartment once it was available. Lavone had turned one hundred years old the week I'd purchased the apartment next to her, so it wasn't like I was rushing her into a grave or anything. She figured her days were numbered and I agreed. I may go to hell for it.

In the foyer of the building, I put my bags down and searched through my purse for my keys. It wasn't a long search since I was carrying a "party" purse that hardly qualified as anything more than a small square of beaded material and a string.

"Good evening."

I screamed like a girl and jerked around. Six and half feet of man was lounging in the doorway of the other apartment. *Shawn.*

My whole body tightened at the mere sight of him. "You scared me."

"Sorry."

He didn't look like he meant it. In fact, he looked to be amused by my reaction. I let my gaze drop to his bare chest, over a finely rippled stomach, to the low-riding jeans that covered the bottom half of him. He was beautiful. Rich, dark brown skin covered a well-muscled frame that wasn't overworked. Men who work out too much had always turned me off. He had the face of an angel, smooth, angular, and classically handsome. I met his gaze and flushed at the knowing look in his black eyes. I'd never met anyone with black eyes before, and for a few seconds I just stared into them as my panties quickly dampened.

Shortly after he'd moved in, he'd asked me to dinner. At the time, turning him down hadn't been difficult, but as I looked at him, I wished I'd given him a chance.

"Can I help you with your bags?"

I started to say no, but he left his doorway and walked across the short distance to pick up the bags. "You shouldn't leave your door unlocked. The front door hasn't closed properly for years. Pull it closed. I have my keys in my pocket."

I did and hurried to open my door. "Thanks."

"No problem, doesn't look like you bought the store out."

I blushed. No, there really hadn't been any need to. But, then, even when I had shopped for two, the groceries had normally gone to Connor's place. "How do you like the place so far?"

"My grandmother hadn't had a repairman in the place in years, so I've spent the last couple of weeks repairing the stairs, replacing floorboards, and talking to plumbers. I'm sorry I scared you. I've actually been looking for you to return so that I could get with you about the front door." He put the bags on the counter and glanced around the kitchen area. "Same floor plan."

"Yes." I motioned upward. "I use my loft space for storage

just like your grandmother did." I pulled off my coat and over-looked his raised eyebrow at my dress. It was short and reveal-ing and I'd worn the little blue bit of silk as a petty little dig at Connor. It felt even more petty now. "So about the front door?" "I'd like to have it replaced and put in an alarm system. I've gotten four quotes from companies so that we could go over it together. If it isn't in your budget, we can work out a payment plan of some kind." He looked me over again and then met my gaze.

I'd meant to ask him about it when he'd first moved in, but my impromptu vacation had interfered with that.

"No, I can handle it." I had quite a little bit of savings that wasn't going to go into buying Lavone's apartment after all. "I tried several times to talk your grandmother into getting a se-curity system, but she always refused. Since we shared that space, I couldn't do it without her. Not unless I went to court, and I really didn't want to bully her."

Shawn laughed. "I imagine she was a pain in the ass to live with."

I frowned at him. "You shouldn't talk about your grand-mother like that."

"Unfortunately for us both, Lavone and I never actually met." He leaned against the counter. "She disowned my father when he married my mother."

"That sucks."

"Yeah." He nodded and shoved his hands into his pockets. "I tried to meet her once, but she refused. After that, I just left her alone. She was an old woman and I couldn't bring myself to bully her any more than you could, I guess."

"Stubborn and unreasonable were some of her better quali-ties," I admitted. "And she left the apartment to you?"

"To my father, actually. The family took a vote and because I was living in a rental, I got the *privilege* of taking over the apartment and cleaning it out." He shoved his hands into his jeans and looked around. "I hired some movers to help me get rid of stuff before I could even move in myself."

I laughed softly. "Well, at least it's paid for."

"Yeah." He slid the tip of his tongue across his bottom lip and let his gaze drop down slowly over me. "I figured I was going to be living next door to an old woman, so seeing you before your disappearing act was a pleasant surprise."

"I feel old, if that counts for anything." I leaned against the counter and tried to relax. It had been a long time since a man's interest had made me nervous.

"Hardly detracts," he admitted. " I collected your mail while you were gone. It's in a box by my door."

"Thanks." I blushed. Christ, I hadn't thought of anything but me and my dog when I'd bailed on Connor and Boston in general. "I took a vacation. It was a sudden decision."

"We all need a little time to ourselves now and again. What do you do?"

"I'm a sales and purchasing manager for Holman Gallery."

"That charity art place downtown?"

"One and the same."

"Nice. I took my niece through there about a year ago; she really enjoyed it."

That's what I get for leaving the sales floor. Eye-candy watching had been cut to practically nothing. "I'm proud to be a part of something that offers so much to the city. What about you?"

"Much to my mother's distress and my father's shock, I'm a cop. I've worked robbery/homicide for about eight years now."

"I take it you weren't following in his footsteps?"

"No, he's an accountant. I have two older brothers . . . one is a lawyer and the other a psychologist."

"No sisters?"

"My mother couldn't have gotten that lucky. She's been outnumbered for nearly forty years."

We both jerked when the phone started ringing. I figured it was Mercy or Jane; but when I got to it, it was Connor.

Picking it up with a sigh, I rubbed my forehead carefully. "Hey."

"Can I come in?"

I frowned. "Come in?"

"I'm outside in my car."

*Fuck me running.* I glanced at Shawn and bit down on my lip. "How many drinks have you had?"

"I sat at the bar with one and stared at it. I'm sober, Casey. I just want to talk to you."

"Okay, but not long. I've got an early morning." I disconnected and looked at Shawn. "I'm about to have company."

"I heard." He tilted his head slightly. "So, did that dress make him as uncomfortable as you'd hoped?"

I laughed. "I don't know."

"Okay, well, I'll be across the hall if you need me."

"Thanks and you can just pick the best bid for the door and let me know what my half is." I walked with him to the door and opened it. Connor was standing there. "Hey, come in."

Connor glared at the two of us and backed up a step to let Shawn by. My new neighbor had barely closed his door when Connor spoke. "Who the hell is he?"

"My new neighbor." I shut my door and glared at him. "A cop and my old neighbor's grandson. What's it to you?"

"He comes out of my woman's apartment half-dressed, it's my concern."

I glared at him briefly and shook my head. Taking off my shoes, I walked toward my bedroom to get into some comfortable clothes. "Look, Connor, I realize that you aren't used to being left by a woman, but you aren't going to turn into a psycho on me, are you?"

"No." He glared at me from the doorway of my bedroom

and frowned. "Look, you walk out on me after a great evening, disappear for two weeks, and then come back only to act like you barely know me."

I grabbed a T-shirt and a pair of flannel pants from a drawer and glared at him briefly before slipping past him to go into the bathroom to change. When I emerged he was standing, waiting. "Great evening? We fucked all night and then I woke up, came into the living room, and found you on the phone with God-knows-who talking about me like I'm a piece of ass off the street."

"You misunderstood."

"The hell I did." I pushed my finger into his chest. "*No, man, she's just a good time. You know me, I can't get tied down.*" It hurt to even repeat the words; hearing them the first time had been devastating. "I know nothing about you that matters and now I don't want to know."

"I respect and care for you, Casey. You have to know that. Men say stupid shit to their friends."

I wanted to smack his face. "Care for me? Respect me? A man that respects me wouldn't have told his friend that I was just a *good time.*"

That night, I'd left his apartment and cried the whole way home. I'd never felt so dirty or used in my entire life and a part of me hated him for it.

"I never promised you anything serious."

"That's right." I glanced over my shoulder briefly before going into the kitchen. "You didn't promise me a thing." I emptied out the grocery bags and he stood there silent. When I couldn't take the silence anymore, I turned to him and sighed. "We really don't have anything to discuss, Connor. We fucked for a while and now that is over."

"I like being with you."

"But I hate myself for even thinking about being with you,"

I spat out before I could help myself. "I let you use me. You certainly aren't the first man and I can't even really blame you. Hell, most men wouldn't turn down pussy with no demands."

"I've never seen you as just a piece of ass."

"Do you love me?"

He jerked as if I'd hit him.

"Do you see a future with me?" I demanded. "How about babies?"

"Oh, for the love of God, Casey. Aren't you a little old for fairy tales?"

"No, I'm a little old for sex games." I tossed the perishables onto the first empty shelf of the fridge and slammed it shut. "I'm too old to get a three a.m. phone call from a man who just wants his dick sucked."

"Fuck you, I never asked you for that."

I laughed at his indignant tone and expression. "No, I don't suppose you did. But you certainly didn't turn it down."

"Well, I'm not daft. Just a little stupid when it comes to women." He sat down on the couch when I sat down in my favorite chair. "I don't think I'm built for love, Case."

He'd called me Case for so long in his clipped British tone that it *almost* made things feel normal. As if I'd never heard him talking on the phone that night.

"You just aren't built to love me," I whispered softly; relieved that I'd never come close to being in love with him. "We're using each other and it's got to stop. It has to go away, Connor. I can't take it."

He stood, walked to me, and knelt on the floor in front of me on both knees. I glanced down at my hands as he took them and kissed the palm of each one carefully.

"I'm sorry."

"For what?" I asked softly.

"For not being the man you need or deserve."

I leaned forward and kissed his forehead. "We just aren't

good for each other. But we can move past this and it can be like it was before we went to bed together."

He laughed softly. "Don't be naïve. I'll never look at you without remembering you spread out on my bed waiting to be fucked."

"Dirty boy." I grinned and relaxed. So, maybe things could get back to somewhere civilized.

# 2

My new neighbor is a *jogger*. The kind of jogger women plan their mornings around. I encountered him, sweaty and wearing a pair of little red shorts, when I was leaving for work. He'd held the door for me, told me I looked great, and disappeared inside. For the love of God, I had no idea how I was going to get anything done, ever again.

By the time I'd gotten to the gallery, I'd managed to push Shawn and Connor both out of my mind enough to actually think. The few looks I'd caught from people told me that everyone was curious about my sudden departure and return; but the only people that needed to know why knew and even understood. I glanced toward Jane's office. The blinds were open and she was staring at her computer screen like it was cursing her out. She looked out at me and motioned me to come in.

Great, she was going to share the pain. I grabbed my handheld and went into what most of the staff considered the lion's den. Jane was a great boss, but she was also something of a taskmaster and some people found her difficult to please. I pulled the door shut behind me and sighed.

"Inquiring minds?"

"No questions as yet." I walked to the grouping of chairs in front of her desk and picked one out. "What are you staring at?"

"Kenneth Victor."

Yuck. I hated that guy. "No."

Jane chuckled. "He's good money for the foundation and you know we can't ignore him. James wants him in here for a special focus show at the end of summer, which means, being the anal-retentive person he is, he will be here tomorrow to measure the space he has and make plans with us for it."

I could feel it coming and I wanted to get up and bolt from the room before she had time to say it. I slouched down in the chair. "Just say it and get it over with."

"He's requested to work with you while he is here."

Sorry bastard. Of course he had. He'd done two other shows with the gallery and both times, I'd had to work with him at his request. Keeping a high-ticket artist like Kenneth happy kept the foundation in money. Since the Holman Foundation funded an arts academy, a halfway house for abused women, a cancer hospice facility, and several youth centers throughout the city of Boston, I couldn't very well do anything to damage its chances of making money.

"This sucks."

"I know, and I'd do it myself but he's such a diva when he's crossed. You don't have to have contact with him outside of the gallery, and if he tries to even hold your hand you're to report it immediately." Jane pursed her lips. "I don't like it, you know. I realize that Milton forced you to play hostess to him and you can tell me 'no.' He'll make do with me or Mercy."

"You know he won't." I frowned. "I guess I can take one metaphorically for the team. But if he touches me, you'll know about it from the wails of pain you hear."

"Understood."

She didn't look comfortable; and I knew she wasn't very happy with herself for even asking me. It made it easier to think about doing. Because at the very least she was as angry about it as I was going to be in the morning. Kenneth "barely human" Victor had a reputation for being irrational and very difficult to work with. Anybody that didn't jump to the snap of his fingers was *working against him* and that was his most charming quality.

"Men don't take rejection well."

"No one takes rejection well," Jane corrected. "I take it you had another conversation with Connor?"

"Yes, he came by my apartment. I guess he was hoping to talk me out of it." When I'd first started working directly for Jane, I called her Ms. Tilwell, and never got personal with her. Now, a year and a half later, she knows just about everything. She's one of those women who inspire trust and faith without even trying.

"You'll both move past it eventually."

"Well, I had two weeks alone to think about what I wanted in my life. He spent the last two weeks trying to figure out what he could say to make things right again." I shook my head and stood. "I need to clear out my schedule for tomorrow."

"Give me anything you can't pass to the admin staff."

"I sure will." And I was going to start with the ladies'-club luncheon I'd agreed to attend. We all hate them, and I'd drawn the short straw last month when we'd decided who would go. "The club luncheon is tomorrow."

She sat up straight in her chair. "You're kidding me."

"Nope." I smiled sweetly and walked to the door. "At least the food will be good."

"Who could enjoy food with all of those rich ancient socialites?"

I left with that question unanswered. Jane had her issues with the profoundly wealthy and it was a subject we'd disagreed on in the past. I grew up with my maternal grandparents, and I'd grown up much the same way as those rich old socialites we all hated to dine with. They might be drowning in money, but most of them were generous and thoughtful with it. Back at my desk, I found a message from Shawn about the security system. The phone rang a few times before he picked up.

"Detective Shawn Tranner."

I smiled. His voice was nice and made me a little warm, which was irritating. I wasn't about to jump into another empty physical relationship with an emotionally unavailable man. "Hello, this Casey Andrews."

"Ah, yes, my mysterious neighbor. I've made an appointment with a security firm to install the system. They'll need access to your apartment."

"When?"

"Thursday at one p.m."

"I'll put in on my calendar." I picked up my handheld and tucked the headset between my shoulder and neck. "Detective, huh?"

"I got my gold badge about two years ago."

"So you don't work the street?"

"Only as an investigator."

Not as dangerous, I thought. I glanced toward Jane Tilwell. Jane had been a cop in Georgia until she'd been shot in the line of duty. "Well, I was thinking I could bring home something for dinner and we could get to know one another."

"Sounds good. I'm on shift until about six."

"Pizza or Chinese?"

"Chinese is good."

I relaxed a little in my chair and smiled. "Good. I'll see you then."

Ending the call, I began to self-lecture. The sexy jogger neighbor was off limits sexually. He had to be. I can't jump from one man to another like some woman on a cable show. Well, I *shouldn't* jump from one man to another. My sexuality had always been both a hindrance and an asset for me. I enjoyed sex and liked to have it, a lot.

I figured that ending my relationship with Connor, such as it was, would have some rather frustrating repercussions. However, my body was not in charge of my life and I was finished with heeding its call over my better judgment. Detective Shawn Tranner was my neighbor and would remain just that.

Rearranging my calendar to accommodate Kenneth Victor was as irritating as just about anything can be. Kenneth was a talented artist and worked in many forms. He had several homes and one was in Boston. Since he'd only just finished a run in New York, I'd figured it would be six to eight months before he'd come back to Boston for another show. I'd been mistaken, and it was irritating. He'd never done a small special-focus show so I hadn't anticipated that interest. It would allow for a smaller, more limited, collection and it would require more of my attention.

The first time I'd met Kenneth he'd asked me out. Milton Storey had been the director of the gallery at the time and had insinuated strongly that I should do anything to make the artist happy. I'd told them both to shove it. Milton hadn't been stupid enough to fire me for it. Thankfully, that troll had been gone from the gallery for quite a while.

"Kenneth Victor?"

I looked up from my computer. Mercy was standing there. "Yes?"

"The last time he was here he asked for you specifically. This time he's asking that you personally handle not only his arrangements but also his show."

I flushed bright red with embarrassment. "I've done nothing to encourage his requests."

"I realize that."

"We all do things we hate for the sake of the foundation."

"Yes."

"If he gets out of line, I'll take care of it."

"Just keep me informed." She frowned and crossed her arms. "I don't like it at all."

"I appreciate that." I smiled and almost laughed. "I really do. I can take care of myself, promise."

"The guy from last night?"

I shoved my chopsticks into the rice in front of me and picked up the little box it was in. "Well, we had a relationship. It's over and he didn't exactly agree."

"Men don't appreciate having their supply cut off."

I glared at him briefly and then started to laugh. "Very rude thing to say."

"I've gotten a good look at that body you're hiding in that big T-shirt. Can't see how I can blame the man for being a little pissed about losing you."

I couldn't help but preen a little under the warmth of his gaze. Shawn Tranner was the kind of man who made a woman feel sexy and feminine with just a look.

"He never really had me." I grabbed a pack of soy sauce for the rice and met his gaze across my coffee table. "How about you? Got a girlfriend, militant ex-wife, or a side piece?"

"No, yes, not right now."

"So why did you get divorced?"

"I wanted children and she didn't. I thought we could talk about it and she took a surgical option to prevent accidental pregnancy."

"Nice."

"I came home from a conference and she was recovering from having her tubes tied. Stunned barely covered my feelings on the subject. She'd altered the course of our future without even giving me a choice. I filed for divorce."

"I take it she wasn't happy?"

"No. She considered our divorce a failure and Dana doesn't do failure. By the end of it, I'd forgotten why I ever loved her in the first place."

"Ouch." I sat back against the couch and poked that rice a little before snagging a piece of chicken out of one of the containers between us. "How do you like the neighborhood?"

"It's interesting. Everyone I met was happy to have a cop on the block."

I had no doubts. The neighborhood was full of widows and single women with children. I'm sure half of them had spent the morning loitering on their front steps to watch him jog around in his little red shorts. It had occurred to me that I should warn him about that, but it would also be sort of amusing to watch the women chase him around. I could even get some cookies or brownies out of it. Lois across the street made amazing peanut-butter cookies.

"Tell me about your job."

I glanced up from my food and smiled. "You'll find it boring."

"I promise to at least pretend to be interested in it."

"Okay, I'll remember that. I'm a buyer and negotiate the re-sale of fine-art pieces for the Holman Gallery. The gallery is the cornerstone of the Holman Foundation. It's also my job to supervise the administration staff for the gallery and work as Jane Tilwell's assistant. So, I wine and dine artists on occasion as well."

"And Jane is?"

"The assistant director of the gallery." I snagged a piece of broccoli from a container near him and shrugged. "The foundation is a nonprofit organization dedicated to helping children and families in Boston. We use the money we make with the gallery for the arts academy and the shelters."

"It must be very rewarding to know that every day you help someone else have a better life."

Yeah. That was pretty awesome. "A world without art would be a boring world." I tilted my head and looked over his face. He didn't look like he was pretending. "So, what about you? Why are you a cop instead of an accountant?"

"Well, math was not my favorite subject in school. I studied criminal justice in college with the intention to go to law school." He shrugged, but I could tell the question had made him tense. "Four months from graduation, I decided that law school was not in my future. Nothing extraordinary happened . . . I had the grades and had already been accepted into three schools. I just didn't want it. With the degree I had earned, I had a few options. Law enforcement satisfied my sense of justice and would allow me to put my degree to some use."

"And your parents?"

"They were upset at first, but they love me, so they got over it and even managed to throw one hell of a party when I graduated from the police academy."

"Good." I couldn't say the same. My grandmother had been absolutely furious when I'd left California and moved to Boston. She didn't speak to me for a year, and still resented that I hadn't returned when she'd demanded it. "Having family support is very important."

"What about your parents?"

"I believe that they would be proud of what I'm doing. They both died in a car accident when I was three. My grandmother raised me."

I rarely discussed my family. So it was a bit surprising that I'd answered his question without even thinking about it.

"The two of you don't get along."

I jerked and raised one eyebrow at him. "What?"

"The moment you mentioned her, your whole body tensed up. It's my job to read people and their reactions." He leaned back against the couch and picked up his water. "You didn't live up to her expectations?"

"She wanted a doll." I sighed. "As I child and well into my teen years she picked out my clothes and basically ran my life from the moment I woke up to the moment I went to sleep. She would have structured my dreams if she could've. My mother hadn't done what she'd wanted. She'd married the wrong man, had the wrong child, lived the wrong life, and died the wrong death. My grandmother was never abusive, but she cut herself off after the loss of my mother."

"So, she had your life all planned out?"

"Oh, yes, even picked out a man." I rolled my eyes. "If you could call him that. He was a mama's boy through and through. He didn't cross the room without asking his parents if it was okay. Have you ever met a grown man that allowed himself to be called 'Scooter'?"

He laughed softly. "No, saw a few on TV."

"Right." I shook my head. "It's disgusting, and I could just imagine what kind of life I'd have with him. She thought she could control me all of my life, but the day I turned twenty-one I inherited the money my parents had put in a trust for me."

"And you came to Boston?"

"I finished my degree and yes, moved to Boston." I put down the chopsticks and grabbed my water. "She was unhappy at first, now she's just bitter. I guess she figured she could keep me under her thumb with her money. But, I want to think that even without my parents' money I would have come here and started the career that I wanted."

I'd been telling myself that for years and I still wasn't even sure I bought it. It was certain that I resented her dominant presence in my life, but would I've come across the country to escape her without any money? Dwelling on it would only lead to a sleepless night, so I pushed it aside.

"And now?"

"We exchange cards on the holidays and talk once a month."

"It's a shame."

"You're close to your family?"

"Yeah, we're a big rowdy bunch but it's fun. The holidays are always loud."

It sounded almost foreign. In my grandmother's house, I hadn't even been allowed to speak at a function without being addressed. She was of that school of thought that children should be seen but never heard. Honestly, I'm surprised I came out of it at least halfway normal.

"So you've broken up?"

The casual tone of the question caught me off guard and I paused to consider my words. "We want different things. I want to make a life, have children, and grow old with someone. He's more interested in the world and exploring all it has to offer. I doubt he'll stay in Boston another year. I thought in the beginning that I could make him want those things, with me. If he wants to marry one day and have children, it became very obvious that he didn't consider me the one." I shrugged and glanced around my apartment. "I guess eventually I might want a house outside the city, but maybe not. Nature is sort of overrated."

He laughed and shook his head. "So, no walks in Boston Common for you?"

"Maybe when Harvey comes back from the vet."

"I wondered where the little pug I saw earlier in the month went." He inclined his head. "And his name is Harvey?

"Yeah." I pursed my lips and then laughed. "When I first brought him home he slid around the floor a lot because it was so slick. He hit walls a lot."

"Harvey Wallbanger."

"Yeah."

He chuckled. "Cute."

I liked his face and his smile. It was *way* too soon to be thinking about another man in my life. I glanced around the table at our mess and then stood up. "Well, we made a mess."

Shawn stood as well and helped me gather the boxes and

plates. "I'm going to have a home security system put in tomorrow when the guys are here setting up the security door. Would you like one installed as well?"

"Yes, that would be great. Can you call me when they are here so I can come home?"

"Not a problem."

I snagged my purse from the countertop and rummaged through it to find a card. I pulled out the little silver case and flipped it open. "This has my cell phone number on it in case I'm not at my desk."

He tucked the card into his front pocket and nodded. "So why is Harvey at the vet?"

"I'm getting him fixed."

Wincing, he shoved his hands into his pocket and sighed. "That's horrible."

I laughed. "Not really. It's important to keep unwanted births down and he has gotten out a few times to try and visit the people across the street. Of course, they have a female Great Dane."

"He's ambitious."

"Indeed."

Shawn checked his watch and sighed. "I gotta run. I need to go in early in the morning so I can take the afternoon off."

I followed him to the door, resisting the urge to find another conversation to have that would keep him with me. Foolish thoughts flitted around in my head. "Thank you for handling this security thing. I really appreciate it."

"It's no problem. I'd feel better about you being here alone once we have the security door set up."

"I can take care of myself."

"I'm sure." He reached out and almost touched my face before he apparently thought better of it. "But why should you have to?"

Great question. I had no answer, so I smiled. "Next time you see your mom, you tell her she raised a nearly perfect man."

"Nearly?" Shawn asked and tried to glare.

"Yeah, I'm pretty sure there is something wrong with you; I just haven't figured it out yet." I inclined my head and looked him over. There *had* to be something wrong with him.

"Let me know when you do." He glanced toward the front door of the building and then focused on me. "Make sure to put your chain on."

I nodded, but frowned. "We've never really had problems with crime in this neighborhood. I mean, some jerk tried to take your grandmother's purse about two years ago, but she laid him out with her walker."

His eyes widened. "You're shittin' me, right?"

"No." I laughed. "It was a sight to behold. The guy was begging for the cops to take him away by the time they got over here. He tried to get in the cop car before he was even hand-cuffed to escape her. It took me a half hour to talk her into coming inside. As I said, Lavone was a stubborn woman."

"Yes, she was."

"Make sure to check your back door before you go to bed as well."

The back door led to an alleyway and a Dumpster. I only used it when I had to take out the trash, but I nodded and agreed to check it before going to bed.

Once I shut the door and pulled the chain into place, I leaned against it and started to go over the reasons that I could not allow myself to tangle up with another man so soon. There was no real way to tell if Shawn was just as unavailable as Connor had been. True, he'd at least tried marriage once, but it could have left him bitter about commitment. I doubt he trusted women all that much, considering what his ex-wife had done.

I made quick work of turning out the lights before I went down the hall that led to my bedroom and the narrow back door that led outside. Just short of the small utility room that the hallway spread out into, I paused. I hadn't taken out the trash since I'd returned from vacation, but the back door was ajar. Slowly, I backed up a few steps and glanced around. If someone was in the apartment with me, I hadn't heard them. Fear slid over me and rooted me to the spot momentarily. I heard about home invasions all the time on the news, but those stories had almost always seemed so surreal to me. The thought of it happening to me had never crossed my mind. Forcing myself to back up, I resisted the urge to turn and run. I wanted to see what was coming at me and I was relatively sure if the burglar was still in the apartment that he was in front of me instead of behind me.

The moment I realized I was wrong, my world came to a stop. In one horror-coated second, the wood floor behind me groaned softly under the weight of another person and I was shoved against the wall. I screamed, but he cut me short with a sharp jab in my side.

"Shut up."

The whisper was fierce and determined.

"I don't keep anything valuable here. There is a laptop in my bedroom and some cash in my purse. Just take it and go."

"I'm not here for *things*, Casey."

Oh, God, anything but that. Despair clouded around my heart and I squeezed my eyes shut. "Please don't kill me."

"No, I wouldn't dream of destroying something as beautiful as you."

"Casey!"

I jerked at the shout of my name and the man behind me yanked me back against his chest and covered my mouth with one gloved hand. "What happened to the old bitch who lived next door?"

It had dawned on me already that this man knew me, even if I didn't recognize the voice.

"Casey!"

There was a loud snap of wood breaking and the man released me.

"Shawn, hurry!"

The intruder shoved me to the floor and darted out. The back door slammed behind him.

Strong hands were suddenly pulling me from the floor. "What's wrong? I heard you scream!"

I pointed toward the door with shaking hands. "It was open. Someone was in here."

"Stay here." He released me and pulled a gun from the back of his jeans as he ran toward the back door. "Call 911, ask for a unit, and tell them there is an officer on the scene that needs assistance."

# 3

"No, I'm positive that door was locked before I went on vacation." I stared at the uniformed officer. "I took my dog to be boarded, arranged for him to be fixed while I was gone, and came back here. I checked all of the windows and the alleyway door before I left."

"And you haven't opened it since you've returned?"

"No."

"Does anyone besides you have a key?"

"Not that I'm aware of. I don't give out keys to my apartment."

"How long have you lived here?"

"Nearly five years." I glanced at Shawn, who was talking with a plainclothes cop who had arrived shortly after the uniformed officer.

"Was anything out of place when you returned?"

"No. I checked on my dog and came home."

"And that was Saturday?"

"Yes. On Sunday, I slept in, did some laundry, and went to a formal event downtown at the gallery where I work. I came home."

"And your ex-boyfriend showed up?" The detective asked as he came to stand near the cop who had been questioning me. I pursed my lips and glared at Shawn, who had turned to hear the answer to that question. "Yes. He did. We talked and then he left."

"Don't look at me like that. They can't help you with this if you don't give them all of the details," Shawn said evenly.

I glared one more second and then focused on the detective who had sat down on the couch in front of me. The uniformed officer slid away. "His name is Connor Grant. He's the lead on the Holman Gallery's security contract and it wasn't him."

"How can you be certain? You said yourself that you never even got a look at the man." Detective Martin asked softly. I was pleased that I'd managed to remember his name in the twenty minutes that had passed since he'd introduced himself.

"I've known the man for over a year. It was *not* Connor."

"I will be contacting him to ask him a few questions, just to cover my bases."

I nodded. "Fine."

"You said the intruder spoke to you."

"Yes, he told me to shut up when I screamed and punched me in the side." My hand went to my ribs briefly and then I straightened. "Then I tried to offer him money and my computer. I figured he was here to rob me."

"His reaction?"

"He said, '*I'm not here for things, Casey*.'" I cleared my throat. Repeating the words hadn't made them any less scary. "I asked him not to kill me and he said he wouldn't."

"Do you remember his words exactly?"

I snorted. "*I couldn't destroy something so pretty* or something close to it. It all happened very fast."

"So, you started down the hallway to check the back door as Detective Tranner had requested and you see that it's ajar."

"Yes."

"And he comes at you from behind?"

"Yes."

"He was in your bedroom?"

I scrunched up my nose. "Yes, apparently."

"Do you remember if you went into your bedroom when you returned home?"

"Yeah, I went in and changed clothes."

"You opened the closet?"

"No." I swallowed hard. "He was in my closet?"

"Evidence seems to support that he spent some time in your closet. He could have been here when you got home."

I wanted to throw up. This could not be happening. I just wasn't the kind of woman who found herself in a situation like this. "He knows my name but he isn't someone I've spent time with or anyone I work with."

"How do you know that?"

"He was surprised by Shawn. I think he thought that Mrs. Tranner still lived next door to me."

"Shawn, why did you suggest that Ms. Andrews check her back door?"

Shawn sat down on the loveseat with me and picked up one of my hands. Casually he rubbed warmth back into my fingers. "The front door doesn't have security on it, the back doors on both apartments are in need of repair. When I was out in the alley earlier in the afternoon I noticed that people seem to use it a lot as a shortcut. It occurred to me that it would be easy for someone to come through the alley and into one of our apartments. I doubt anyone would consider someone walking into or out of that alley as suspicious activity."

"The door wasn't forced, was it?"

"No." Shawn shook his head. "It wasn't."

"Did you get a look at the guy?"

"No, he was gone by the time I got into the alley. I checked the street. The traffic was pretty tight out front and everything looked normal. He either had a car waiting for him or he lives nearby."

Neither one of those options really had appeal. I pulled my fingers gently from Shawn's and cleared my throat. "I'm going to pack a bag. The uniformed officer offered to drive me to a hotel for the night."

"You can't take anything from your closet."

That hurt. "Are you taking my clothes into evidence?"

"Right now, forensics is testing the clothes for fluids and hair. Everything that doesn't have any kind of biological matter on it will be left. The rest will unfortunately be put into evidence for the case file."

Biological matter. That sounded particularly disgusting. "Okay."

"You'll let me in this damn door right now or I'm going to wake the Mayor."

I jerked at the sound of Mercy Rothell-Montgomery's voice. "Mercy?"

She slipped past the uniformed cop in the doorway and hurried toward me. "Casey, what the hell is going on?"

I accepted the embrace and curled my fingers briefly against the soft fabric of her blouse. "What are you doing here?"

"Mathias and Jane were having dinner with us when his beeper went off. When he called in he found out that you'd had the police called to your residence." She touched my face with gentle fingers. "You aren't hurt?"

"No, I'm fine." I looked toward the entryway and found Mathias Montgomery and Connor Grant standing there. "Hey."

Shawn came to stand beside me.

Mathias entered first and offered Shawn his hand. "Mathias Montgomery. My men heard the call come in over the police scanner." He turned to me. "Where is your security badge?"

I paled and my mouth dropped open. It hadn't even crossed my mind. Turning, I went into the kitchen. The badge lay where I had dropped it. "It's here."

"Your handheld?"

"In my purse." I pulled it from my open bag and offered it to him.

Mathias glanced toward the cops and shook his head. "Did you bring home any paperwork, contracts, or other secure documents in your briefcase?"

"No. I left my briefcase at the office, actually." I blushed. Since I'd made plans to have dinner with Shawn, I'd left work at work.

"You can't stay here with the front door broken."

I glanced toward Connor and nodded. "I know."

"You'll come home with us." Mercy looked at each man in the room as if she expected one of them to disagree with her. "Jane went to the gallery to check on the security team and make sure everything is secure, or she'd be here as well."

"Do you think this is related to the gallery?" I asked softly.

"Since his interest was centered on you, I somehow doubt it. Otherwise he would have grabbed you elsewhere, perhaps near the gallery so he could force you to let him in."

That was not a comforting thought. "Okay, so it was personal." The statement dropped in the room like a lead balloon.

Mercy took in a deep breath. "Let's go. We're about the same size, so you don't need to pack anything."

I turned to Detective Martin. "Should I come down to the station with you?"

"No, your statement from tonight will work for the report. Just be careful and watch yourself."

"I'll call you tomorrow about the security company," Shawn said softly.

"Yeah, thanks." I touched his arm briefly as Mercy ushered me toward the door. "I gotta pick up Harvey in the afternoon; but I'll be straight home after that."

He nodded and after a brief nod in Mathias's direction followed along after Detective Martin as he went down the hall. A part of me would have preferred to stay with him, but that made me feel foolish. I barely knew Shawn Tranner.

I was sitting in a huge red chair in the corner of Mercy's living room when Connor finally got me alone. He pulled up an ottoman and sat down in front of me.

"How are you?"

I shrugged. "I'm okay."

"You've been holding your ribs since you got here. Are you hurt?"

"He punched me." I lifted my hand from my side and pulled my legs up into the chair. "It's sore, but I don't think anything is broken."

"The cop neighbor of yours is protective of you."

"Shawn's been nice to me." I glared at him when he raised an eyebrow. "Look, just because you use "niceness" to get in women's pants doesn't mean every man does it."

He laughed. "At least your attitude is still intact."

"I'm fine."

"Don't lie to me, Case." He stared at me for a moment and then lowered his gaze to the floor between us. "I didn't do a very good job of making sure you were safe."

"It's not your job to protect me."

"As a matter of a fact, it is my job to protect you. At least while you are at the gallery. And I should have checked your doors and locks at your apartment."

"The back door wasn't broken. The cops think he used a key." The thought was a pretty scary one and not one I'd allowed myself to dwell on too much. "He knew my name."

"His voice wasn't familiar?"

"Everyone sounds the same when they whisper." I rubbed my face with both hands. "Where's Mercy with that wine she promised me?"

"I think she's waiting in the kitchen." Connor glanced over his shoulder. "Look, I know we've had some problems lately . . ."

I laughed softly. "Problems?"

"Casey."

"No," I whispered and glanced toward the kitchen door. I figured Mercy was lurking with her husband behind it. "That part of our relationship is over. One day we can be friends. But, right now, no matter my circumstances . . . we're done. I don't need or want a man to come to my rescue. I also don't want to be party to a testosterone festival . . . so I suggest you check your ego."

He laughed and shook his head. "You win."

"I know."

"For now."

*Bah.* He stood up and walked away from me. Mercy came through the door just then with a smile. "Perfect timing."

She flushed and shrugged. "I had a hard time with the cork."

"Whatever." I took a deep drink of the wine and huddled in the chair.

She sat down carefully on the ottoman and looked over my face. "Do you want a shower?"

I nodded. "Yeah, after the wine."

"Jane wants to know if she can come over."

"Yeah, after the shower." She laughed and glanced briefly at her husband, who nodded and walked away. I assumed he went to call Jane. "I'm okay."

Her eyes brightened with tears and I reached out and grabbed her hand. She sucked in a deep breath and blinked once or twice. "It scared the hell out of me. I can't imagine how you felt."

"Well, it wasn't a good time," I murmured. It was distressing to realize that my brush with violence had reminded her of her own past. "Thankfully, Shawn managed to hear me."

"Yes, he seemed pretty protective." She raised an eyebrow and I laughed out loud.

"He's a nice man." I pursed my lips. "I wonder how long that asshole was in my apartment."

"He didn't make any noise?" Connor asked from his place on a couch.

"No. I came home, put the food in the kitchen, and went into my bedroom. I changed clothes, and by that time Shawn was home." I flushed when his gaze hardened, but continued. "We ate in the living room and he left after about an hour. I went down the hallway and realized that the back door was open." I stopped then. I couldn't repeat it. Not so soon.

I brought the wineglass to my mouth and finished it off in one uncouth swallow. "He must have sat in there and listened to us talk the whole time."

"And your new *neighbor* didn't realize you had another man in the apartment?"

I glared at Connor. "As you might remember, men don't get invited into my bedroom."

He flushed and stood. "I'll go down to the gallery and brief the security staff. If you give me your keys, I'll retrieve your car and bring it over here."

"Thanks." I picked my purse up off the floor and rummaged through it.

Mercy watched him retrieve the keys and leave before she turned to me. "I take it the two of you are pretty far from being friends."

"He just didn't like it when I cut off his supply of pussy." I blushed when her husband Shamus busted out laughing. "Christ, I'm sorry. I forgot you were here."

"No, it's fine." Shamus came to me and held out a hand for the empty glass. "Do you want some more?"

"No, thank you."

I waited until he left the room. "I don't have any underwear."

"Oh." She was silent for a moment and then turned slightly. "Honey! Would you go to the store for Casey?"

"Oh, my God!" I shook my head. "I can't send your husband to the store to buy me panties."

She frowned. "Don't be silly. Honey!"

"What?"

"Will you go to the store and get Casey some underwear?"

"What?" He came out of the kitchen and raised an eyebrow.

"Well, she didn't bring any of her things with her." She pursed her lips. "And while you are there you could get me and the baby a candy bar."

He snorted. "I see you operating."

"Really, you don't have to go to the store." I'm not sure I could survive if he went and bought me underwear.

He frowned. "Well, she's about your size, right?"

"Well, yeah, about seven months ago." She glared at him as if at the reminder of her past waistline.

He nodded and then walked toward the stairs and went upstairs to their bedroom. Men are such odd creatures really; I can't imagine what he was up to. When he reappeared with a gift box, I flushed.

Shamus cleared his throat. "Well, I bought these for you for your birthday but then I figured since you were having my kid you deserved diamonds."

"You're damn straight I did." She grabbed the box, pulled off the lid, and sighed. "Great taste darling."

She handed me the box. Dark blue panties and a bra were nestled in the tissue paper. I doubt I'd ever owned lingerie as pretty as what I was holding. "I can't take these."

"Please." Mercy chuckled. "Maybe your new neighbor likes blue."

"Oh Christ." I grabbed the lid and closed the box. "Thank you. I'd like to reimburse you." I looked toward Shamus.

He laughed. "No way. It's not often that I get to buy that kind of thing for a beautiful woman who isn't my wife."

"Men," Mercy muttered.

"So, how are you?"

I stared at the ceiling for a minute and turned my head to look at Jane, who was sprawled out beside me on the pull-out couch. It had been comforting when she'd insisted on staying with me, but I'd pretended to be exasperated.

"I'm mad."

"Good."

"I bet that asshole touched all of my clothes. Everything will have to be cleaned."

"You can take the day off. I'll just reschedule Kenneth Victor."

"He'll be a total jerk-ass about being put off."

"I don't care." She snorted. "Mathias is running a check on your new neighbor. He's got a friend who's going to get us a copy of his employment file with the Boston PD."

"Are you serious?"

She laughed. "Yeah. You're my friend and I'm going to make sure that you are safe with that guy. Also, starting next week you are going to sign up for a self-defense class of some kind."

"Sweating is overrated."

"You need to be able to protect yourself." She turned her head on the pillow to look at me. "How about a handgun?"

"Absolutely not."

"Stun gun?"

"No." I sighed.

"Mace?"

"I'd just end up blinding myself."

"Large stick?"

I laughed out loud. "Shut up."

"Well, let's hope that the cops processing your bedroom don't list your sex toys among the contents in the closet."

That was discomfiting. "Fuck, I'll have to buy new stuff."

"Excellent. I love going to the sex toy store."

"You got a man."

"So?" She laughed. "He likes the toys, too."

When I arrived home the next morning, a work crew was already replacing my apartment door and another was installing a security door. Since Shawn's apartment door was open, I walked to it and peeked inside.

"Shawn?"

"In the kitchen."

I dropped my purse on a table beside the door and went to the kitchen. He was standing at the stove, a spatula in one hand staring intently at the pancake he was making. Loose fit jeans, a worn Boston PD T-shirt, and no shoes . . . the man looked good enough to eat, forget the pancakes.

"How long did the cops stay after I left?"

He laughed. "Martin sent me off to my apartment when he left. Once the forensic people were done, I locked up for the night. I guess about an hour. The security company got here about an hour and a half ago." He motioned toward the pan. "Want some?"

"No, I was force-fed already." I slid up onto a stool at his breakfast bar and tucked my hands between my knees. "Thanks for last night. I don't know what would have happened if you hadn't been here."

"Don't dwell on it. You'll have nightmares." He added the pancake to the stack he'd already made and flipped off the stove. "Did you get any sleep last night?"

"Yes, well, at least four hours."

"You have the day off?"

"Yeah, they figured I'd need the time to take care of the security stuff and Detective Martin called me this morning. He wants to see me."

"Probably just a follow-up."

"Yeah, he said as much." I wanted to ask him to come with me but I didn't want to sound like a big black hole of need. So, I accepted the bottle of water he silently offered. "Last night was the first time I'd ever even come close to a criminal."

"I feel responsible. I should have went ahead and had security installed while you were gone."

"You couldn't have known."

"And I should have checked your door myself."

I laughed. "I do tend to define quite clearly where my guests are allowed to go in my home and where they aren't. I get that from my grandmother. She could herd people through her house without them even realizing it."

"How about I ride down the station with you?"

I should have said "no." Grown, modern women don't need a man to guide and protect them. Instead, I nodded and smiled. "Thanks."

"I've got good news and I've got bad news."

I glanced briefly at Shawn, who was leaning against the wall to my left. Detective Martin had showed us into a small private interrogation room. A camera was tucked discreetly into one corner.

"Okay, let's go with the good news."

"We caught the intruder. He left a few prints on your closet door and he popped in the system. His name is Peter Stevenson. He's got a pretty extensive criminal background and was paroled recently." He inclined his head. "Is the name familiar?"

"No, not at all." If that was the good news, I wasn't sure I wanted to hear the bad news. But, ignoring something horrible doesn't make it go away. "And the bad news?"

"He was hired to do the job."

My stomach dropped into my feet and Shawn immediately came to sit beside me. He tucked my left hand into both of his and they both sat there while I took several deep breaths.

"By whom?"

"He doesn't know. They met in a chat room about three weeks ago. Once the deal was brokered, Stevenson received five thousand dollars in cash, a key to your apartment, and a vial of semen. He was instructed to put the semen on your bed and mess up your apartment."

"I came home early."

"Yes, Mr. Stevenson was very clear on the fact that he'd watched your routine carefully before you went on vacation and believed that he could get in and out without anyone seeing him." Detective Martin checked his records. "So, after he got off work, he went to your apartment to do the job."

"And I came home earlier than he expected." I rubbed my face with both hands. Before I'd gone on vacation, it had been my habit to have an early dinner with Connor nearly every night after work. "So, he was hired to scare me?"

"Yes."

"Any luck on tracing the people in that chat room?" Shawn asked.

"We're waiting on a search warrant for the company's records. It should come in today. But anyone who watches TV would know to use a public hot spot or a computer at the public library to avoid the activity being traced back to them."

"Why didn't he wait until I'd gone to sleep to leave?"

Detective Martin sat back in his chair. "I think he found being there a little too tempting, to be honest. Ms. Andrews, Peter Stevenson was in jail this last time for a sex crime."

I curled my fingers against Shawn's palm and bit down on my bottom lip. "He'll go back to jail, right?"

"Yes, he's violated the terms of his parole. Assault, home invasion, and conspiracy charges will also be filed against him."

"He won't get a deal for talking about the man who hired him?" I asked. I watched TV, too.

"Perhaps, but because he violated his parole he's going to have to complete the twenty-five-year sentence he received for rape and attempted murder. Even if he gets a deal on your case, he won't be out of jail until he's a very old man."

*Rape and attempted murder.* The words were like a knife in my chest and I took a deep breath. The fact that he would go back to jail was cold comfort, but it was something I could hold on to. "And the person who hired him?"

"We'll do all we can to find him."

The detective left us shortly after that. I sat in that little room for a few minutes, silent and thinking about the people in my life. Who would want to scare me like that?

"Come on, we'll grab some sandwiches and go back to see what the security people are doing."

I nodded and let Shawn guide me out of the police station and to his car. I was relieved, now, that I'd conceded when he'd asked to drive. The thought of maneuvering through traffic in my current state of mind wasn't a very nice one.

# 4

The fifth time I got up out of bed to check the doors, I realized I wasn't going to get much sleep. The events of the last twenty-four hours were crowded in my mind and they pushed sleep far from my reach. I'd taken all of my work clothes to a dry cleaner and spent most of the evening washing the casual stuff.

I was pacing back and forth down the hallway when I heard a knock on the front door. It could only be Shawn because no one had buzzed to get in the building itself. I peeked through the peephole and then unlocked it quickly.

"Hey."

He looked me over. "You've been pacing for an hour."

I blushed. "Sorry, I forgot how thin the walls are." I stepped back to let him in. "I just can't sleep."

"I figured." He held up his pillow. "Thought I could sleep on your couch."

I smiled. "You're very sweet."

Shawn laughed. "I'm very tired."

Blushing, I tucked my hands behind my back. "Sorry. Your grandmother slept like an old log and was mostly deaf. I had a huge Halloween party last year and she slept through every gin-soaked second of it." I hurriedly flipped the lock and put the chain in place.

Having him on my couch dressed in a pair of pajama pants did not seem like a good idea if I planned on sleeping any at all, but I dutifully got him a light blanket and then toddled off to my room to lie down.

I threw myself down on the bed and stared at the ceiling for five long silent minutes before he appeared in the doorway of my bedroom.

"Did you need something?"

He laughed. "Do you?"

"No."

"Then why were you tapping your headboard?"

I sat up and blushed. "God, I'm sorry. I'm just antsy and nervous."

Shawn came in and sat down on the edge of my bed. "You've had a stressful couple of days. You got an ex-boyfriend with issues, your apartment was broken into, and you were assaulted. It's fine if you are all bent out of shape."

"A new guy moved into my building and dashed my expansion plans."

He laughed. "Really?"

"Yeah, I'd hoped to buy the apartment from your grandmother's estate." I sighed. "But I was trying to be respectful and not ask until an appropriate time had expired."

"Thank you. We had twenty offers for the place the day the obituary went into the papers."

"Gross."

"The real estate market is tough, which is why in the end the family voted to give it to me."

"It's a good building and a decent neighborhood."

"Yeah, and I got a fine-ass neighbor."

I gasped. "Me?"

"No, Mrs. Drake across the street."

Laughter spewed before I could suppress it. Gillian Drake was eighty years old going on two hundred. "I bet she was fine in her day."

He laughed. "Probably right. But, yeah, you. I nearly swallowed my tongue when I saw you the other night. I'm surprised that Grant fellow isn't crawling around behind you begging for you to take him back."

"He's British. They are sort of above that kind of pleading." I grabbed a pillow and hugged it tight. "You're the first man who's ever even been on this bed."

He raised an eyebrow. "Pardon me?"

"I always went to Connor. My place has always been sort of off limits to men."

"Want me to go back into the living room?"

"No."

That being said, I wasn't sure what I wanted him to do. In the few days that I'd known him, I hadn't allowed myself to really think about him sexually. He was finely put together and had a great face. I liked his voice and the gentle way he had guided me through all of the police stuff I'd done during the day.

"I've always slept alone." I rubbed the blanket underneath us with one hand. "They took my bedspread. I'm glad; I doubt I could ever look at it again."

"Have you thought about who could have hired him?"

"No. I mean, I don't have anyone in my life that bothers me or who has tried to hurt me. Connor may be pissed about the breakup, but he isn't the type to hire someone to do his dirty work. The last guy I dated before him was a doctor. Around month four, I decided that being his arm ornament for the better part of my life just didn't seem all that interesting, so I dumped him."

"You aren't one of those women who'll just stay with a man because she doesn't want to be alone, are you?"

I laughed. "No. I decided a long time ago that I don't need help being miserable and if I hate being with someone it would just be easier to be alone."

"It's a rational conclusion. But what about being lonely?"

"There are worse things than being lonely."

"What about other men at work?"

"There are twenty men employed at the gallery." The number came easily because I'd spent most of the evening thinking about each of them. "Not counting contracted artists. When I oversaw the sales floor, I supervised five of them. There is one male senior buyer in the administrative area and the rest are security guards."

"Any of them with criminal records?"

"No, all members of staff are thoroughly vetted, interviewed, and tested for drugs. Everyone is also reviewed on a yearly basis for financial problems and/or legal problems."

"What about hiring and firing?"

"Jane and Mercy do that."

"An artist who wanted a show in the gallery?"

"There are hundreds of artists in the Boston area alone that would love a show in the gallery. The administrative staff spend every day going through proposals, viewing pieces, and making selections for the general gallery. An artist is *invited* to do a show with us, and I've never known of one to ask outright for one. Sometimes agents contact us and let us know that an artist is interested in working with us. If they fit with our schedule and needs, we strike a deal."

"So you couldn't have made any enemies that way?"

"I don't see how."

"Having a stranger moving around in your life like he belongs is a difficult thing to assimilate, much less deal with. You're allowed to be upset or scared."

"I'm more angry," I admitted softly. "I mean, honestly, he couldn't even do his own dirty work!"

"That he hired someone to do it is an indication that he might doubt his own ability to pull the situation off or he wants to be able to play your hero." He reached out and tucked a strand of hair behind my ear. "I'm not saying this to scare you."

"I know."

"You just need to pay attention to the men who express interest in you. Evaluate their motives and tread carefully."

"Like you?" I asked.

He chuckled. "You're an attractive woman, Casey. I'd be an idiot not to be a little interested in you. But I'm also not the kind of man who uses a woman. You've got too many men like that in your life."

"You're a nice man, you know."

"Most men consider that the kiss of death."

I leaned over and kissed his cheek gently. "Don't. I like nice men. A girl gets tired of jerks."

"You're playing with fire," he whispered as I kissed his other cheek. "I have excellent intentions concerning you, but I'm still just a man." He lifted his hand as if to touch me and then dropped it with a sigh.

His response was endearing and sexy. I brushed my lips across his before I could help myself. Shawn sucked in a breath and then slid both hands into my hair. He pulled me into his lap in one breathless second. Wrapping my arms around his neck, I opened my mouth to the soft press of his tongue and groaned softly. The man tasted as good as he looked. I was in so much trouble.

Shawn lifted his head and looked over my face. "You've had a rough time of it. It's natural to seek another for comfort."

"Do you think I'm seeking comfort?" I asked softly. I moved astride his thighs and slid closer.

"No."

"If I wanted him, I could call. He would trot over and pick

me up." I moved my hands over the smooth muscles of his chest and curled closer to him. "That may sound arrogant or even cruel."

"You made it clear that he wasn't all that concerned with your emotional well-being."

"True."

His hands slid down my back and cupped my ass. I nearly sighed with relief. "I should put your fine ass down and go back to my apartment."

"Sometimes you have to take a risk."

"And sometimes risks hurt." His lips moved across my jaw and then down my neck. "I could be just as bad as what you left behind."

I laughed. "The fact that I'm not naked and under you tells me that couldn't be true."

"I've pretty much left women alone since I divorced."

"Sensible. We are some pretty difficult creatures." I ran my hands over his head. "Give me a good reason to send you back out into the living room."

He stood suddenly and I wrapped my legs around his waist as he turned and laid me down on the bed. "If I were really all that sensible, I would have let you pace all night."

I moved underneath the weight of him and sighed. "I'm not even going to pretend to be the voice of reason in this situation." I spread my legs wide and gasped at the press of his hard cock against my pussy. "I'm pretty much done talking."

Shawn laughed softly and sat up; he ran careful hands down my thighs to my waist to tug at my shorts. I lifted my hips and then pulled my legs forward. As I jerked my T-shirt off my head, he stood from the bed and disposed of his pants. His cock jutted impressively from his body, but it was his eyes that held my attention as he slid back onto the bed.

I gasped, amazed by the softness of his skin as he moved

over me and settled between my legs. My nipples hardened against his chest and I arched under the weight of him. His mouth covered mine, and I shuddered when his tongue slid into my mouth. Suddenly, it didn't matter that he was a near stranger. His big hands slid down my legs and underneath me to cup my ass. I pulled my mouth from his and gasped softly as he rubbed his cock against my clit.

"Shawn!" I gasped softly and clutched at his shoulders.

"Shhh." He brushed a soft kiss over my lips and then slid down my body with practiced ease.

He slid his tongue between my labia and pressed gently against my entrance and I curled my fingers into the blanket beneath us. Gasping for air, I lifted my hips slightly against his mouth and then collapsed on the bed in wonder. His tongue slid over my clit and I jerked hard against him.

His hands clamped on my hips and held me still. After several agonizing laps of his tongue, he sucked my clit between his lips and I shattered. My vision darkened and I went slack under his hands.

I covered my face with my hands and shook for several seconds. "Wow."

Shawn placed a soft kiss on my inner thigh and slid upward slowly. Kisses that felt like whispers drifted over my stomach, breasts, and upward to my mouth. I moaned against the press of his lips and tongue.

"I'm rushing this," he whispered softly. "I don't mean to."

"You can make it up to me later." I slid my hands down his stomach and wrapped one around his cock. "Fuck me."

He moved against my palm as I explored the length of him. "Condom."

I stilled briefly. "Crap, I might have some in the bathroom." I pointed toward the door.

Shawn chuckled softly and snagged both of my hands. "I can go back to my apartment if there isn't one."

"Fuck." I watched disgruntled as he left the bed and disappeared into the bathroom across the hall from my bedroom. He came back a few minutes later with a small box.

"We're in luck." He tossed the box on the bed after pulling one free. "Not that I wasn't game for a naked run across the hall."

I laughed softly and reached out for him. "Come here."

He rolled the condom on with a practiced ease and moved up between my legs. I spread my thighs farther apart and pressed my feet against the mattress.

I hissed softly as he pressed the head of his cock against me and then pushed inside. "Yes."

Shawn pushed deep inside and ran his hand down the length of my thigh. He lifted me off the bed slightly as he thrust into me. I felt full and overwhelmed at the same time. My clit pulsed hard between my labia and each push of his cock sent a shaft of pleasure up my spine. Wrapping my legs around his hips, I pulled him as close as I could.

I raked my nails down his back and he arched in my arms. His body slapped hard against mine and orgasm started to build deep inside. Then he slowed down and rolled us over.

Arching back, I slid fully down onto his cock and stilled. I pushed my hair back and started to move slowly. His hands moved over my thighs and upward to my breasts. Fingers tugged at my nipples and pinched them just enough to hurt. Heat spread down my stomach and orgasm rushed so suddenly that I cried out.

I moved hard against him and gasped when he pulled me abruptly firm against his chest and forced me still. His hips thrust up against mine several times and then he relaxed slowly beneath me.

We laid there breathing hard and slick with sweat for a few minutes before I carefully slid off him and sprawled beside him on the bed.

"That was . . ." I waved my hand. "Fantastic."

"Yeah, it sure was." He rolled to his side and put his hand on my stomach. "This wasn't what I planned when I came over here."

"I know." I smiled. "I won't hold it against you if you promise to do it again."

"Deal." He leaned in and kissed my mouth softly. "Do you want me to go?"

At first, I said nothing, but then I realized that I'd made it clear earlier that my bed was a no-man's-land of a sort. "No, I think I'd like it if you stayed."

If he was surprised, it didn't show. I wonder if I looked as surprised as I felt. I hadn't slept beside a man in years. He left the bed and disappeared into the bathroom. The rush of water running filled the silence of the apartment. After a few minutes, I slid off the bed and walked naked to the bathroom. He was at the sink.

I pulled a couple of towels from the cabinet and put them on the counter. As I passed by him a second time, he reached out and grabbed me. "Hey."

"You and those green eyes." He touched my cheek and shook his head. "Very sexy."

Shawn pulled me close and kissed my mouth softly. It had been a long time since I'd been treated so gently and carefully by a man. I moaned softly against his mouth and parted my lips to the press of his tongue. His hands slid down my back and I pressed closer.

He lifted his head and sighed. "Shower?"

"Yeah." I smiled softly and slid my hand down his chest. "You should start wearing a full sweatsuit when you jog."

"Why?"

"The women in the neighborhood aren't used to the kind of stimulation that you provide." I tucked my face against the side of his neck and kissed him. "I like that I have to look up to you."

"We're a good fit."

Yeah, we were. I turned and went to the shower to turn it on. On a personal level, I was pretty sure I'd jumped out of the frying pan and into a fire. Shawn didn't strike me as a man easy to put off or control. While it had never been my intention, I'd done most of the maneuvering and manipulating in my relationship with Connor. And maybe that was why it was so easy to let him go. It had become clear several months ago that he wasn't going to let me push him into something more permanent or serious.

"You're frowning."

I glanced back at him as I slid into the shower and adjusted the temperature of the water. "Just thinking."

He moved into the stall and pulled the door shut. "Well, no more thinking, if that is going to be the result."

I rested against his chest when he pulled me to him. His cock hardened against my ass as we stood there under the water. Being with him was too easy and felt so natural that it was alien.

"I thought he was going to rape me."

"I know." Shawn pressed a soft kiss on my shoulder and held me tight. "I'm sorry."

"It wasn't your fault."

"I was the one that had a bad feeling. I should have checked your door myself."

"I'm not your responsibility." I turned in his arms and met his gaze.

"I take your safety very seriously." He rubbed my mouth with his thumb. "I'll push at Martin; he's in my unit. I'll do all that I can to make sure your case doesn't get pushed aside as long as there are leads to follow."

"Thank you."

\* \* \*

"I'm sorry that I've kept you up half the night." I slid beside him under the cool cotton sheet.

"Yeah, well, a man has to make sacrifices for the greater good."

I laughed. "Fucking me was for the greater good?"

"No, that was for me." He pulled me into his arms. "I figure making sure you get some rest is for everyone else."

I shivered slightly as he ran a hand down my back. "I'm normally not so needy."

"I can see that."

"Under normal circumstances, I could wear you out in this bed."

"I'll be happy to let you try."

Stupid mistakes. I've made them all of my life and I'd walked into this with my eyes wide open. It didn't feel like a stupid mistake, so maybe I was just jumping to conclusions. In all honesty, I'd never felt so warm and safe in my whole life. I couldn't help but indulge in that feeling.

# 5

---

Yeah, I hated Kenneth Victor a lot. I watched him walk across the main gallery floor toward me and the small special focus gallery. He was dressed in a dark brown suit, and his attitude hit me right in the face from a full hundred feet away.

"Casey."

I stiffened. "Mr. Victor."

His lips thinned. "I thought we agreed the last time I was here that you could call me Kenneth."

He'd said it. I'd grimaced. I doubted that qualified as an agreement. I motioned toward the room behind me. "If you'll come this way, we can view the space you'll be using this summer."

"I only have an hour." He sniffed delicately as he followed along behind me. "I had more time *yesterday* when we were supposed to meet."

"Yes, I had a personal issue that could not be avoided." I wasn't going to discuss it with him.

"That's what Ms. Tilwell said." He tucked his hands behind

him as he looked over the room. Our last special focus show had closed a month ago and we'd yet to pick an artist for the first half of summer, so the light and nicely lit room was empty. "This is too small."

I swallowed back a sigh and walked toward the French doors. "It's the special focus space. If it won't accommodate the work you plan for the show, we can find another space in the gallery. Unfortunately that will mean pushing your show back to the late fall and into a regular spot."

"No. You'll simply have to have the special focus show somewhere else in the gallery."

Turning to look at him, I smiled tightly. "Impossible. The special focus show is designed to be an intimate but formal event and it takes place in this room. This is not up for debate or negotiation."

His face flushed red. "Are you telling me no?"

This was exactly why I hated working with him. Figuring that he was just a few seconds from having a complete meltdown, I glanced toward the security camera, crossed my arms, and hoped that the ever-present observation that I'd always complained about was in place.

"I'm telling you the limits of the event you've been *invited* to participate in. Since the contracts are not signed, neither of us is obligated to continue."

"First you brush me off and reschedule me like I'm nothing and now you're telling me that I cannot have the space I need for my show."

"I'm telling you the limits of the show space and what can be done."

I forced myself to remain still when he took a step toward me. If past experience held true, I probably had another thirty seconds alone with him. The security staff has always been quick to respond in the past. The last time I'd had to signal for help, I'd been on the sales team.

"This is unacceptable. I demand to see Brooks immediately." He reached out to grab my arm just as Connor came through the doorway.

"Ms. Andrews, is there a problem?"

I met Connor's gaze. "Mr. Victor would like to be escorted upstairs to the conference room."

Victor dropped his hand to his side and glared at me. "You'll regret crossing me, Casey. You'll be lucky to have a job by the end of the day."

Connor cleared his throat. "Mr. Victor, the guard at the door will escort you upstairs to the conference room."

I relaxed slightly as he turned and stalked toward the door. The security guard pulled the doors shut with a brief nod in Connor's direction.

"Thanks."

He sucked in a breath. "What did he say to you?"

"Nothing directly threatening except for that last part." I tucked my shaking hands behind my back and tried to smile. "I guess I'm just a little sensitive . . . he's a domineering man."

"Then why isn't Jack shoving him out the front door?"

"Jack?" I frowned.

"The guard." He motioned toward the door. "You really should keep up with the personnel reports I send out."

"Yeah." I turned and walked to the French doors. The warm afternoon sun felt good on my face. "A Kenneth Victor show is guaranteed money. If it weren't for that fact the gallery wouldn't put up with him at all."

"Okay."

"And he wants to see James." I checked my watch and sighed. "That's not going to be pretty. You know how he hates to be disturbed during the lunch hour."

"So, I told him that it was impossible. He demanded to see you and threatened to have me fired."

James Brooks sat back in his chair and glanced around his rarely used office at the gallery. "Are you worried?"

"No."

He chuckled. "Good."

I crossed my legs and sighed. "Normally I'm much better at managing him."

"Artists can be difficult to work with when they feel they aren't being appreciated." He sighed. "How are you?"

"I'm fine."

"You're pale and you look exhausted; that's hardly fine." His blue eyes hardened and I shifted in the chair. "Mathias updated me on the status of your case with the police. I've asked him to conduct an investigation of his own concerning who might have hired that criminal to break into your apartment."

"I'm sure the police . . ." I paused when he leaned forward in his chair. "Thank you."

He sighed and stood from the chair, came around the desk, and sat down beside me. "Casey, I'm not trying to intimidate you. I realize that it might come off that way."

I met his gaze. "I'm not afraid of you, Mr. Brooks."

"No, and I've always liked that about you." He picked up one of my hands and rubbed it gently. Until then I hadn't realized I was so cold. "You're a member of my staff, a part of my extended family. I'm going to use every resource I have to make sure that we do what we can to protect you. I understand that you have a new neighbor."

"A cop."

"Yes, I've read the report that Mathias turned in on him. He seems on the level, but he's a stranger in your life and I'd like you to be careful."

"He couldn't be responsible for this . . . he didn't even know I existed until a few days ago."

"That's when you met him. You've lived next door to his

grandmother for years, so we can't be sure how long he's known of you."

True and disconcerting. I curled my fingers against his palm. "I don't need a whole bunch of alpha males circling around me like I'm the last woman on earth."

He stilled and then burst out laughing. "No, I don't imagine that you do." Releasing my hand, James stood and went back to the desk. "Indulge our primitive protectiveness at least for the time being."

"I'll try to be gracious about it."

"Thank you. As for Victor, I'll handle him."

I stood. "He's not going to be pleasant."

He laughed. "I assure you that I won't have a problem handling him. If it comes down to it, I'll give the Foundation what he would have made and move on. While I'd much prefer to wrangle other people out of their money, I'm perfectly comfortable with sacrificing my own."

I knew that already. It was no secret that fifty percent of his annual income went to a wide variety of charities and that he did not draw a salary from the foundation. "Thank you."

"I have one more question."

I stopped behind the chair I'd been sitting in and dropped my hands to its back. "Okay."

"You and Connor Grant were personally involved?"

"Yes."

"I understand that relationship has ended."

I flushed. My sex life appeared to be an open book. "Yes, before I went on vacation."

"I've spoken with him already. Since I've already learned an expensive lesson on sexual harassment I made it clear that he is to keep things professional. If you feel that he steps over the line at any time and makes something personal when it should not be, I expect Mercy to be notified immediately."

"I don't expect anything like that."

"Regardless, you are entitled to work here without having to deal with constant drama."

"I apologize for getting involved with him to begin with. It's very foolish to become so personal with an individual you work . . ." I sighed. "It was a mistake."

"We all make them." He leaned back in his chair and shrugged. "I'd prefer that there not be romantic entanglements among the staff at the gallery. But, when you mix so many passionate and creative people together in the same place, sparks will fly. I accept that, but everyone must also accept boundaries."

"Yes."

"Connor knows his."

"Thank you." I blushed. Having a conversation about Connor with James Brooks had been number one on my list of things I never wanted to do, ever.

"Good, now that we've settled that, I'll deal with Victor."

I left his office ahead of him and went to my desk. The bull pen was like a tomb, everyone silent and watching the conference room. The glass wall that separated it from the rest of the room was sparklingly clear. Kenneth Victor was sitting at the table with his glare focused right on me. He'd been waiting for nearly two hours.

James patted Jack, the security guard, affectionately on the back as he entered. The click of the door shutting behind the three of them was like nails on a chalkboard. The moment I'd set eyes on Kenneth all of the anxiety and stress of the morning had returned. I honestly didn't fear for my job; I'd done nothing wrong. The rules for the focus show were set in stone because James Brooks wanted it that way and he wasn't the kind of man who appreciated his rules being broken.

Kenneth opened his mouth the moment James sat down, which was a mistake. Anyone that had spent five minutes with

James Brooks would know that trying to take a dominant position in a conversation with him would not go well.

"We're going to have to find another artist for the show."

I glanced at Jane, who was standing in front of my desk. "Nah, Victor isn't the kind of man to pass up such an opportunity. He'll play nice for the moment."

Well, as nice as a man like Kenneth Victor can play.

Harvey was in rare form when I went to pick him up. I'd had to pay more for his extra long stay but knowing he was safe and cared for made it worth it. He bounced in his carrier the whole way home, so by the time I'd parked and freed him from his prison he was a bundle of energy and affection.

We took a short walk, picked up the pizza I'd ordered, and returned home just in time to meet up with Shawn. Not thinking about him all day had taken a lot of effort on my part. I figured I was in a little trouble when it came to him.

"Hey." He plucked the pizza from my hands and glanced down at Harvey. "Cute."

I laughed. We both knew the last thing Harvey was, was cute. "Yeah, but he's got a great personality." I picked him up as Shawn input the code and opened the door. "Have a good day?"

"Got the bad guy, came home to a sexy woman. Good so far."

"Want to share my pizza?"

"Yeah, let me shower and change."

I unleashed Harvey and let him dart inside the apartment as I turned to take the pizza. "Sounds good."

He leaned in and brushed his lips over mine. "I won't be long."

I lingered in my doorway as he crossed the hall and pulled out his keys. "Tell me I can trust you."

Shawn turned his black eyes serious and concerned. "I won't hurt you."

*On purpose*, I thought and nodded. "Okay."

Shutting the door, I took the pizza into the kitchen, put food and water out for Harvey, and went to change my own clothes. I figured I was too far gone on the Shawn front to lecture myself about starting another relationship so close to the end of another. I didn't want to let myself think that hard about it. Seeking shelter in the arms of another may not be the best choice to make, but it felt good.

By the time I changed, opened two beers, and heated the pizza in the oven, he was knocking on the door. Harvey was living up to his name and making up for lost time by the time we got settled on the couch.

"He's feisty for a dog that just got snipped."

I laughed and snapped my fingers as Harvey latched greedy little jaws on the rug in front of the TV. "Drop it or you'll spend the night in the kennel." Dejected, he released the rug and dropped down on it. "He spent the last week in a cage recovering. The staff at the vet clinic said he did very well."

"Being a dog must suck."

"Well, not so much. I mean they don't have to work, pay bills, or answer the phone."

"How was work?"

"It was par for the course." I leaned back against the end of the couch and shrugged. "I got an artist who could teach diva to Streisand and he tried to get me fired because I told him no when he requested a large space for his show."

"I take it you weren't fired."

"No, but I'm sure he'll find some way to dig at me later in the game. It's part of his deal. . . . He's one of those people who thinks everyone should be honored to meet him or know him." I grabbed my beer from the coffee table in front of us and relaxed. "And you?"

"Well, I've been working a case for a while. Today, someone came in and confessed." He shook his head. "It was the mother of the missing girl. We honestly never suspected her, so the confession was hard to listen to. I see families in situations like that one and I thank God that I was so lucky in the parents department."

"Does it make you wish you weren't a cop?"

"No. Just makes me wish we lived in a better world." He sighed. "And I thought about you."

"Oh yeah?" I took a sip of beer and grinned. "Pleasant thoughts?"

"Yes and no."

"No?" I frowned.

He laughed out loud. "No, not like that. Last night was great and you were awesome. I just feel like I might have taken advantage of you."

If I were going to be honest, I would have told him that if anyone had taken advantage of the situation last night it was me. A small part of me did worry that I used him for comfort without any real thought as to what he might have felt or wanted, but I couldn't force myself to say it. Even thinking it had my stomach churning a little.

"I don't feel that way. It was great—don't overanalyze." I jumped at the thud of Harvey hitting the wall and sighed. "I swear he's going to get brain damage." I looked over at him; he was sprawled on his belly with his legs spread in four directions.

"It may be too late."

I put my beer down and glared briefly at him as I went to retrieve Harvey. "Don't be mean."

"Ugly and stupid are a bad combination."

I tried not to laugh, but I did as I scooped the dog up. Harvey made a soft little growl and snuggled close to my chest as I patted him. "That's okay, baby, you can chew on his house shoes later."

When I sat down on the couch, Shawn stared thoughtfully and then laughed. "I take it back; he's not stupid at all."

"Why?" I looked down at the dog, who snuggled closer and made a sound like a little sigh. "He's playing me."

Shawn burst out laughing. "Yeah, he is."

"The little asshole." I rubbed Harvey's head and shook my head. "I almost had carpet installed a few months back because I was afraid all of that skidding around and hitting the wall was bad for him." I picked up my beer and settled back against the pillows. "I guess I'm a sucker."

"Well, being a sucker for an ugly dog isn't a bad thing." He shifted on the couch so that he could face me. "This artist that was a snob with you today . . . tell me about him."

"I can't discuss contract details . . ." I warned and then took a drink of beer. "He's a fairly well-known artist, mostly sculpture work. He seems to enjoy mangling steel and iron into things that almost resemble something but don't quite make it. This will be his third show with the gallery, but his first special event."

"Has he always given you a hard time?"

"He gives everyone he can a hard time. He didn't come from money, but he likes to pretend otherwise and from what I can gather he thinks treating everyone around him shabbily will give them the impression that he's always been wealthy." It was an ignorant belief on his part, but I truly believed he thought that way. "When he first started out, he wasn't demanding or rude with people. Success made him cruel."

"So you've known this guy for a long time?"

I frowned, because it hadn't occurred to me that I had. "He had his first show in a small gallery I worked at. I didn't have direct contact with him that I can remember. Then three years later, he was the next best thing and we had two large shows for him at Holman. He requested that I work with him on both of them and then this third one as well."

"Odd."

"Not really. There are several artists that request specific staff for their shows. They can be picky, unreasonable, and often irrational, so when they connect with someone it's just easier to ask for that person every time they deal with us."

"And this guy . . ."

"Kenneth Victor." I wondered silently why I had been reluctant to give Shawn the name. I'd avoided it since we'd begun that conversation. It was certainly no secret around town that Victor had received the coveted invitation to do a special focus show. "He's a successful artist."

"He's also cruel and has demonstrated an interest in you."

Put that way, it was sort of disconcerting. "Okay, I'll talk to security about him." I shifted Harvey, who had fallen asleep, and he growled as I put him down on the couch between us. "The fact is that they are probably already looking at him. He was in quite a temper today after I told him no."

"Just be careful."

"I will." I stood, gathered up my empty plate and half-empty beer. "What are the chances that the guy that broke in made it up?"

"They've recovered some of the cash and the key he was given."

That sucked. Denial has always been one of my favorite coping methods and I'd planned on using it. "I don't know how anyone could have gotten a key to my apartment."

He held out a hand and pulled me down into his lap when I took it. "There are people in your life that you trust without even thinking about it. You put your purse on the back of a chair in a restaurant or check your coat at the door of a bar. You leave your keys on your desk or on the counter at the coffee place down the street . . . even for a few minutes."

It was true, which made me want to board up the door to my apartment and stay in it forever. "Yeah."

"How many repairmen have come in and out of this place in the last year?"

"I had a wall repaired, the plumbing . . ." I waved my hand around the room. "The wiring in the hall, a light switch in the kitchen. You name it I've probably had someone in here to fix it."

"It takes one person who's easy to buy off. That one person who can move anonymously in your life and take what they've been paid to take."

It made sense. "What a fucked-up world we live in."

"The world is also full of good people."

"Yeah, how long before the bad outnumber the good?" I snuggled close and pressed my face against the side of his neck. "We're both crazy."

He laughed and ran his hand down my back. "Yeah, I've thought that myself."

"We should probably leave each other alone."

"Yeah." He nodded; but his hand fisted in the material of my T-shirt. "Now really isn't the time to indulge in a physical attraction."

"You've got a militant ex-wife."

"You've got an arrogant ex-boyfriend who carries a gun."

He moved to the edge of the couch and stood with me cradled against his chest. I'd never enjoyed a man's strength more. Shawn made me feel small and very female. "I've probably got a stalker."

"And I probably have a crush on my next-door neighbor."

I kissed his cheek and laughed. "Cool." He walked down the hall and into my bedroom, pausing briefly to push the door closed with a foot. I kicked off my house shoes and swung my feet a little as he walked toward the bed. "I like this carrying-around thing."

"The ex-wife thought I was trying to dominate her when I

tried it with her." He put me down on the bed and pulled his shirt over his head.

I rolled to my knees, took my shirt off, and fired it in the same general direction he'd thrown his. Moving to the edge of the bed, I ran my hands over his stomach and then upward so I could press close to him. "I like a man to act like one."

My nipples hardened painfully as he cupped my ass and pulled me closer. His tongue thrust into my mouth and I accepted the invasion with a needy sigh. Shawn lifted his head with a sigh of his own. "You're wearing too much."

I laughed softly and curled my fingers into the front of his jeans. "You, too."

He stepped back from the bed, took off his shoes, and un-buttoned his jeans. For a few seconds, I just watched and then I remembered that I was still wearing shorts. Slipping off the bed, I pushed my shorts and panties down and kicked them aside.

It hardly made sense that I could be so involved with Shawn in just a short amount of time. Yet, as he pulled me onto the bed with him and took my mouth, it felt like I'd known him for years.

Maybe I was insane.

Shawn used one leg to push my thighs apart as he moved on top of me. His cock, already hard, brushed tantalizingly against my leg. I opened my mouth to the thrust of his tongue and moaned against the invasion. The taste of him was so sexy that I relaxed and spread my legs wide for him.

He lifted his mouth from mine and took a deep breath. "I love how you feel. So soft and perfect."

I moaned a little when he lifted away from me and retrieved his jeans. He pulled several foil packets from a pocket and tossed all but one on the bed with me. Watching him roll the condom over his cock, I licked my lips with anticipation.

He looked powerful and sexy. Muscles moved under his skin as he put one knee on the bed and moved over me. I ran my hands over his head as his mouth latched on to one rigid nipple. His teeth grazed my flesh and I arched under him in complete submission. Lips pulled gently at my nipple as one hand slid between my legs, demanding and receiving immediate access.

Shawn rubbed his thumb over my hard clit casually as he pressed two fingers into my clenching pussy. I was soaking wet and the intrusion was enough to edge me toward orgasm. "Fuck me."

He lifted his head from my breast and chuckled. "I will."

I lifted my hips helplessly and sucked in a breath when he pulled his fingers from me and slid downward. The heat of his mouth made my vision darken. His tongue slid over my silken flesh and then he pressed into me.

"Oh, my God." I moved under his mouth and lifted my hips against his thrusting tongue. "Shawn, please."

He lifted away from me and ran his hands down my legs. "Get on your knees."

I eagerly rolled to my knees and buried my face briefly in the blanket on my bed as he pressed the head of his cock against the entrance of my pussy. He pressed in with one steady stroke, his hands gripping my hips.

I rocked back against him and moaned at how deep he slid into me. "Fuck." He started to slide in and out of me, the rhythm so intoxicating that I met him thrust for thrust. I closed my eyes against the pressure and surrendered to the pleasure of him. "Harder."

He complied immediately. His hips rolled against my ass and he began to move faster with more force. "Talk to me, baby. Tell me how you want it."

"Harder." I gasped and cried out with the shock of orgasm.

Pleasure burst over my clit and I clenched around his penetrating cock with all the strength I had.

Shawn pulled from me abruptly and scraped his nails gently down my back. "Lie down for me."

I rolled over and spread my legs with blatant disregard for modesty. "I want more."

"I'll give you everything I have." He gripped my hips, lifted me off the bed, and pushed his cock back into me.

Pushing up against him, I wrapped my legs around his hips and shuddered against the intoxicating rotation of his hips.

"Play with your clit."

I shuddered against the demand but slid two fingers against my clit as he instructed. He watched with half-closed eyes for nearly a minute, the incessant pressure of his cock making it hard for me to concentrate. Then he lowered me to the bed and began to push full and deep into me with hard, quick strokes.

His sweat-dampened body moved against mine; the pleasure of it was so raw that a sob burst from my mouth and tears stung against my eyelids. I clutched at him as he jerked in my arms. Shawn buried his face in the side of my neck and let his body rest on mine. We lay there, both shaking with satisfaction.

# 6

"The Holman Gallery is one of only a handful of galleries in the United States ever allowed to show the Howard K. Turner collection. The ten paintings, all from the late 1800s, depict numerous scenes that mark the sacrifices of our country's military." I hadn't done a school tour in over a year, but it felt nice to be surrounded by twenty little kids with their eyes wide as they walked through the main gallery. "In the next few weeks this collection will be packed and returned to its home museum. It's been with us just over six months."

A little hand near the back of the group shot up in the air and waved at me until I focused on him. "How much is it worth?"

"Just one of these paintings could sell for two million dollars." One of the teachers in the back of the group gasped and I offered her a smile. "Now, if you guys are ready, we'll head into the learning center where you guys will be working with Lisa Millhouse. Lisa is one of the featured artists at Holman and is famous all over the world for her sculptures. She's here today just for you guys."

After herding the class into the large room that housed the

craft and hands-on area of the gallery, I trudged back upstairs and sat down at my desk. An hour on my feet in cute shoes had not been kind. I slipped off the offending platform sandals and leaned back in my chair.

"Did you have fun?"

I opened my eyes and shrugged. "Not so bad."

Jane chuckled. "Better than Kenneth Victor."

"Any day." I sat up and wiggled my toes. "I think the feeling in my toes might return soon."

"Have the cops made any progress?"

"They recovered some of the money and the key." I glanced around the bull pen; it was mostly empty because of lunch. "I think I'll take a walk and pick up a sandwich. You want one?"

"No, but thanks." She checked her watch and then glanced toward Mercy's office. "I think I'll go down and watch Lisa with the kiddies for a while."

I shoved my protesting feet back into my sandals and grabbed my purse as she walked away. I'd sort of hoped she would volunteer to come with me. Being honest enough to admit to myself that I was scared is one thing. I couldn't imagine admitting it to Jane or anyone else, for that matter. By the time I reached the front doors of the gallery, anxiety was clutching at me. I pushed through the doors and took a deep breath. It was important not to let whoever was trying to scare me win. I couldn't spend the rest of my life hovering at doorways and never venturing outside.

On the other hand, I wasn't exactly thrilled to be exposing myself to dangerous situations. As long as I had no idea who had hired that man to break into my apartment, there was a reason to worry about my immediate safety. Of course, the world isn't a safe place. The murder rate for the average American city proved that in spades. But it was more than that normal casual fear that I've always carried about strangers.

When I reached the deli, I'd worked myself in a bit of a snit.

Anger was easier to deal with than fear. Given a choice, I think almost anyone would prefer to be angry. I ordered a sandwich and picked out a bottled soft drink. It had been my plan to eat in, but one look at the crowded and closely spaced tables changed my mind. I wasn't interested in being that close to strangers.

"Your neighbor is clean as a whistle." Mathias Montgomery pushed a folder across the table to me. He and Connor had cornered me the moment I'd returned from lunch. "His employment record with Boston PD could read like a checklist for cops. Citations for bravery, going above and beyond the call of duty, and regular promotions."

I touched the top of the file but didn't open it. "He's been kind and very helpful with getting the security system installed."

"Good." Mathias sat back in his chair and after a brief glance in Connor's direction continued. "I've looked at several men in your past and none of them have a criminal record or even a hint of behavior that could come close to stalking."

"A few men?" I blushed scarlet.

He flipped open his organizer. "Yes, we have Mark Fitzgerald. He was your supervisor at the Jewel Gallery downtown before you came to Holman."

"Mr. Fitzgerald and I were never intimately involved." I glared at him.

"I know." He didn't look up from his list. "Milton Storey, your boss here before he was forced to retire, also not an intimate partner but a man in your life. He's a domineering and petty man but doesn't fit the profile for a stalker."

True enough, Milton Storey was as subtle as a sledgehammer. "Anyone else?"

"Yes, a doctor named Peter Foley. He no longer lives in Boston and is happily married."

I smiled. Peter and I had dated when I'd first come to Boston, right out of college. "Nice. I bet he married a schoolteacher."

"Yes, she teaches elementary school English." He flipped the page. "Jason Caulder. An architect, still lives in Boston, and is single. After I was finished questioning him, he asked me to tell you that he's available if you'd like to hook up."

"Gross." I crossed my arms over my chest in defense. "I won't need his number."

Mathias laughed softly and flipped to another page. "Dale Cain."

I stiffened and forced myself to relax. Dale and I had dated almost two years and we'd split shortly after I'd taken the job at Holman. I hadn't seen him in nearly three years.

"He has a criminal record and a sealed juvenile record. It appears he likes to hit women."

Yeah, but I knew that already. I looked away from Mathias and locked gazes with Connor by accident. "No, he never hit me. He tried once, but a friend of ours interfered. I left him shortly after the incident." I looked back toward Mathias. "Where is he?"

"He's in jail waiting trial on attempted homicide charges. The only reason he doesn't pop is that he doesn't have the resources to pay someone to stalk you for him. Also, none of the women he's dated before or after you indicated that he stalked them or tried to force them to remain with him." He flipped the page. "Then we have Connor, who passed a lie-detector test this morning."

I gasped and glared at him. "What?"

Mathias looked up and stared at me hard. "No one gets a pass around here, Casey. Somebody in your life or even on the outskirts of your life gave a sexual predator a key to your apartment. If your neighbor hadn't been there, you could have been raped and murdered."

"But he was there," I responded carefully. "I don't like having my private life dissected like this."

"The cops are working their investigation and I am working mine. I'm sorry you find this invasive but your safety is our job."

"Your job is to monitor and protect this collection."

"And upper management is the cleanest method into this gallery after hours," Connor murmured. His entry into the conversation put a fine edge on my nerves. "You, Jane, and Mercy can enter this gallery at will and that makes you an attractive target. You far more than the other two because you live alone."

"The police seem to think that this has little or nothing to do with the gallery."

"I have my orders from James Brooks," Mathias responded gently. "I'm sorry, Casey, but I'm not going to back off."

I already knew that. The determination on his face had been obvious the moment I entered the conference room. I sat back in the chair and rocked a little. "Fine."

"I have some questions."

Yeah, I figured he might. "In that case, I would prefer if we continued in private."

He nodded abruptly and Connor stood. I can tell neither one of them liked it, but Mathias said nothing until Connor was gone. He cleared his throat. "You can trust him, you know."

"Trusting him has already hurt me once," I responded softly. "That road is closed, and I'm entitled to as much privacy as I can be given."

"I agree." He grabbed the water pitcher in front of him and filled a glass. "Would you like some?"

I shook my head. "No."

"I've only investigated the men that Jane knew of. She didn't like giving me the names and only did it under duress."

I almost laughed; as I could only imagine what kind of duress she'd *suffered* under before she gave up the information he wanted. "Are you asking me for a list of my sexual partners?"

"Not exactly. I'm asking you to think about all of the men you've encountered since you came to Boston."

"Encountered? Met? Saw? Boston is a large city, ya know. I bump into and meet people every day that I've never seen before and may never see again." He was trying to give me an illusion that it would be easy to figure out who my stalker was. "He could be anyone; I may have never even spoken to him. I could have cut him off in traffic or he might have delivered a pizza to me a couple of months ago."

"Or he could be in your life and you may trust him. One night he might knock on your front door and you'll let him in."

If it was his intention to scare the hell out of me, it worked. It wasn't like I hadn't considered it but having it said out loud was like being punched. "Am I supposed to fear everyone I know?"

"No, but you should choose your companions wisely."

He knew.

"Who do you have following me?"

"I did it myself last night. I checked out your building, watched you with your dog, and saw you with Shawn Tranner. I left shortly after I confirmed he was with you. The last few nights it has been Connor monitoring your travel home."

"Did you see anything?"

"I didn't notice anyone else following you or see anyone lingering near the building. But if they know who you're sharing that building with, they'll skirt it from now on. He'd be an idiot to try to break into a building a cop lives in."

"The other men that work here?"

"Have all been questioned."

What a total nightmare, and it was coming at me from all sides. There wasn't just one stranger poking into my life—there were the cops, the security people at the gallery, and then there was the real unknown . . . someone who had exposed me to a horrible man. I pushed back from the table. "Can I go now?"

"How long have you been involved with the cop?"

I stilled and cleared my throat. "I figured you wouldn't ask."

"How long?"

"It's new."

"Before or after the vacation?"

"After." I frowned at him. "Why?"

"A new man in your life might have triggered this guy."

I didn't think that was it; but then again it wasn't my job to think the worst of everyone on earth.

I propped my briefcase against the elevator wall and pushed the button to the third floor of the parking garage. It had been one long insane day. I glanced briefly toward Connor, who had walked me out of the gallery.

"Pissed?"

"About what?" he asked coolly.

"About being dismissed from the meeting?"

"No." He turned and reached out for me.

Gasping, I barely had time to think before we were face-to-face. He pulled me close. "Were you fucking that guy while we were together?"

His grip wasn't painful, but it did serve to remind me that I had little defense against a man of his size. "We were never together. I was just a good time for you."

"Are you his good time now?"

I flushed with anger and embarrassment. "Let me go."

"It didn't take you long to replace me." He released me and moved away as the elevator slid to a stop.

I grabbed the handle of the bag and hefted it from the floor. "You weren't anything that had to be replaced; I just moved on." He started to follow me out of the elevator. "No, just go away. I'll be fine."

I glanced back as I headed toward my car. He was standing just outside of the elevator watching me. A part of me wanted what we had back, but that part was small and stupid. He wasn't the man for me and he had no room in his life for my dreams. Connor Grant was familiar, well-traveled territory and a part of that offered comfort.

I popped the trunk and shoved the briefcase in between two boxes of clothes I'd been carrying around for six months to donate to charity. Packing things up for charity was the easy part; parting with my clothes was what hurt. I closed the trunk and looked toward Connor again. He straightened away from the wall, pushed the button to open the elevator doors, and with a brief nod in my direction disappeared into the elevator.

"Thank you for coming in, Ms. Andrews."

Detective Martin looked just as tired and overworked as he had the first night I'd met him. "I thought it would be weeks or months before I saw you again." *If ever.*

He offered a small tight smile. "Actually, your case has garnered some attention from the top and it's been given priority. We were unable to trace the money and there were too many prints on it for it to be a viable piece of forensic evidence. The DNA results should be back in a couple of weeks, but I have a feeling the lab will receive pressure to process it quickly."

I flushed. "I didn't ask for special treatment, Detective Martin."

He cleared his throat. "I know. I'm just tired, Ms. Andrews. I spent the afternoon downtown with my Captain talking to the mayor."

"The mayor?"

"James Brooks is very connected."

*Oh, Christ.* I bit down on my bottom lip. "I'm sorry if he's made your life more difficult."

"Actually, thanks to him my desk is clear except for your case." He laughed. "So it wasn't all bad." He shuffled papers around on the table in front of him and focused on a sheet of notebook paper. "The security firm that your gallery is contracted with sent me a thorough and detailed report of their own activity. With friends and coworkers like yours, I'm surprised that anyone in your life would try to make trouble."

"I was briefed this afternoon on their progress."

"Good." He pushed that piece of paper aside and flipped open a leather notebook. "We were able to confirm that an online conversation took place through an instant-messenging service. We'll have a transcript by the end of the week. We'd like to tap your home phone."

"I haven't gotten any phone calls."

"Yet."

"And if he never appears?" I couldn't imagine how long I could live so exposed and bare before the world. Beyond the security people at work and the cop sitting in front of me, there was another person in my life . . . the reason behind the whole mess.

"Experience tells us that the suspect will make himself known to you in some way. He's already reached out to you once through a third party." He glanced toward the door and checked his watch. "We'd like you to talk to a consultant."

"A consultant?"

He stood from his chair and shoved his hands deep into his pockets. "The mayor has requested that the local FBI office send a profiler in. He's been here an hour going over the evidence and would like to speak with you."

"Okay." I curled my hands around my purse in my lap as he gathered up his stuff and left the room.

The door opened and a man entered. He looked like he could have been plucked out of an action movie. The quintessential FBI guy complete with a neat, inexpensive suit and a gun holster. He put an empty yellow legal pad on the table in front of us. It was an interesting contrast to Detective Martin's mess.

"My name is Edward." He inclined his head. "You've been assaulted, questioned, invaded, and made to feel a victim throughout this entire matter."

"Yes."

"I'm sorry to say that there is nothing I can say or do that will change that." He pulled a pen from his pocket. "Normally I profile a criminal based on his own criminal acts. Currently I only have the break-in he arranged to work on. What I'd like to do is talk to you, Casey, and learn as much as I can about you. Perhaps there is something we can center on that attracted him to you."

"Aren't guys like this just crazy?"

"Stalkers fall into three categories. An obsessive stalker has had a relationship with his victim and is desperate to keep that relationship. The second type is often a stranger to the victim. He's delusional and could believe the victim is his soul mate. The third category is most often related to celebrities."

"And this man?"

"The fact that he hired someone else to break into your apartment makes me believe that you would have known him if you'd seen him. Currently, he's satisfied by maneuvering the people around you. The police activity is exciting for him. He's arrogant about his place in the world and does not fear that he'll be caught."

"Does he want to kill me?" The question burst from my mouth before I even realized that I was thinking it.

"At this point we can't be sure where his thinking is. You should realize that you've done nothing to bring this on yourself. Stalking behavior, no matter its beginnings, is a mental illness. Through all of the reports I've read, this person is not an intimate acquaintance of yours. You didn't break this man's heart or mistreat him in any important way. His relationship with you is likely entirely in his mind."

That was hardly a relief. It didn't matter *why* the man was in my life; it only mattered that he was in my life and wished me harm. "He doesn't love me, not even in an obsessive sort of way."

"Why do you say that?"

I glared at him for a few seconds. "Are you a psychologist?"

"I do hold a degree in psychology." He offered me a small smile. "But I'm not here to take you apart and figure out how you tick."

"You'd be the only one." I waved my hand toward the mirrored window, where I imagined Detective Martin was watching. "This man doesn't love me or even think he loves because he put a dangerous man in my apartment. This man, whoever he is, didn't care if I was hurt or killed."

"So you think he wants revenge?"

"Or something." I sucked in a deep breath. "I think I'd like to go home now."

Shawn was waiting for me as I exited the interrogation room. I looked at him with gratitude and irritation. "How long have you been here?"

"I came down as soon as I realized you'd been brought down." He put a hand at the small of my back and prodded me toward a bank of elevators. "Mrs. Delaney told me they took you away in a squad car."

"Yeah, from my walk. She has Harvey."

"I put him in my apartment and got him some water before I came down."

Once in the elevator, I turned into him and rested my head on his shoulder. "This whole thing sucks. I wish I'd stayed on vacation."

"I know." He patted my back in what I can only think he thought would be comforting.

"I'm not a dog."

He laughed softly and dropped his hand. "Sorry. I'm just not used to women who actually seek out a man's support."

His ex-wife must have been a real piece of work, but that was a conversation for another time and place. I moved away from him and leaned against the wall. "Home, food, and a bed sound great right now."

"Sounds like an excellent plan to me."

I got the food and then the ride home. Connor was waiting on the front steps of the brownstone when we arrived. I sat back in the seat and glanced at Shawn.

"He probably got wind that you were taken downtown. Montgomery's security firm is very well connected, much to the dismay of the chief of police. There is very little that goes on in this city that he doesn't get informed of, especially when it concerns the gallery or the people who work for it."

There was a time when I would have found that comforting. Yet, as Connor stood there and shoved his hands into his pockets I was more than a little peeved that my life was an open book. I sighed and looked briefly at Shawn before lowering my gaze to my feet. "I should speak with him, I guess."

"Yes. Despite your past personal relationship, the man is a part of the security detail at the gallery and has every right to be concerned about your welfare."

I nodded and sat back in the seat as Shawn exited the vehicle. A few seconds later, he opened the passenger door and offered me his hand. He really was a gentle and thoughtful man. It was the little details that made him so vastly different from the men I'd known in the past. I shouldered my purse and handed the food off to Shawn, who nodded briefly toward Connor as he went up the few short stairs to our front door.

Pulling on my gloves, I looked around the near-empty street. "Hey."

He got up from the stairs and came to stand in front of me. "You met with someone from the FBI?"

"A criminal profiler of some sort. I guess the mayor is bending over backward to make James Brooks happy. The conversation was brief. I just couldn't stand to talk about it all." I looked down at my gloved hands and cleared my throat. "Why are you here?"

"I owe you an apology. I was rough and completely out of line with you in the parking garage."

"It's the most emotion you've ever shown me outside of the bedroom." I shrugged. "It was interesting to see you act like a human being."

"Very cold."

True, but it'd become increasingly difficult to be nice. Realizing how horrible that was, I looked away from him. "I should go in."

"This guy." Connor waved toward the front door. "He's got a good record on the job and his ex-wife, despite being bitter about the divorce, says he's a good man."

"For the love of God, you questioned his ex-wife?" I glared at him, the fingers of my left hand curling into a fist. "What the fuck is wrong with you?"

"It's my job." He shrugged and didn't look remotely guilty over it. "At any rate, he checks out."

"Mathias informed me of his employment record earlier today."

"I realize that." He cleared his throat. "Look, Casey, you've been a big part of my daily life for a while and I miss you. It's crystal clear to me that you've moved on and I'm honestly okay with it but I would really like it if we could at least be comfortable around each other again."

I wanted that but I couldn't look at him without thinking about how much time I'd invested in him and how truly foolish I felt about it. "You didn't make any promises to me."

"I'm not a good man."

He'd said that to me so many months before . . . when he'd offered me his hand and I'd taken it. "I made assumptions on your behalf based on what I'd wanted." I cleared my throat and looked away from him. "No harm, no foul."

"Yeah, right. Women don't play that way."

I pulled at my gloves and huffed in a breath. "I gotta go."

He nodded and stepped back from the stairs so I could pass. It occurred then that he'd been blocking my way in. I glared at him at him briefly at that realization and hurried up the stairs. When I opened the door, Harvey was sitting patiently in the open doorway of Shawn's apartment. He bounced a little and shot toward me immediately.

"Hey, baby boy." I scooped him up off the floor and rubbed my face against his. "Did you miss me?"

He cuddled contentedly against me as I let the door shut. When I looked toward the apartment again, Shawn was standing there with no shirt on. I let my gaze drift over his muscled chest all the way down to the loose-fitting jeans. The man looked good enough to eat, forget the food.

"He's probably hungry."

"Yeah." With my free hand, I pulled my keys free from my coat pocket and went toward my door.

I leaned against the counter and watched Harvey eat. It would have been easy to be envious of the simple pleasure he derived from just being a dog. Shawn entered with two wineglasses and handed me one silently.

Drinking deeply from the glass, I considered my day and the men in my life. "I like being with you."

He leaned against the counter beside me and nodded. "Yeah, I'm pretty awesome."

For a few seconds, I was stunned, and then I laughed softly. "It's really quite relieving to be around a man with such a healthy ego." I turned and looked him over with a raised eye-brow. "Hungry?"

"Yeah, but I can take care of that after we eat dinner."

So naughty.

I followed him into the living room where he'd put the Italian food we'd bought. Curled up on one end of my couch, I feasted on pasta and watched him while he took in the evening news. It was interesting to be with someone during such an everyday activity. Not only did I like being with him—it was just easy. Easy to want him, talk to him, and even imagine being with him long term. We had a passionate physical connection but I knew little about what he wanted for the future or if he was even serious about me.

He picked up the T.V. remote and flipped it off. "Okay, you're giving me that look."

"What look?" I poked my fork into my bowl of pasta and stabbed a piece of chicken.

"Like you are trying to figure something out."

"Oh." Well, that was true enough. He turned to face me on the couch, and rested his back against the opposite end from me. "We have really great sex."

"Yeah." Shawn nodded and sipped from his wineglass. "We sure do."

"And I'm just wondering what you are expecting from me."

He drained the glass in one swallow and cleared his throat. "Okay, so a serious conversation."

"Crazy, I know." I grinned as he put the glass down and relaxed against the couch. "We just jumped into the deep end of the bed without really talking about it."

"You're going through a difficult thing right now and I haven't wanted to add to your burden."

"Okay." I nodded and set aside my food. "I get that."

He pulled me to him and spread his legs so that I could lay

between them. I rested my head on his chest and closed my eyes briefly. Maybe I didn't want to have this conversation after all. I wasn't ready for another disappointment.

Shawn pushed his fingers through my hair gently and down my neck. "You are *exactly* what I've been looking for. Smart, beautiful, passionate, and searching for a partner. It's written all over you. Casey, you're a woman looking to settle down. I have to tell you that I find it insanely attractive."

The same thing that had Connor Grant running for the hills had Shawn Tranner snuggling in for the duration. "Really?" I lifted my head and met his gaze. God, his eyes were beautiful.

"Yeah, really." He brushed his thumb across my mouth. "The first time I saw you . . . all I could think was that I wanted to be your man. It's been a long damn time since I've felt that way about a woman."

He pulled me gently and I slid upward until I could cover my mouth with his. His tongue pushed against my lips immediately and I opened to his invasion with a sigh of relief. Big hands slid down my back and cupped my ass with the kind of familiarity and skill that thrilled.

His cock hardened against me and I gave in to the urge I'd had since the first time we'd gone to bed together. Sliding downward, I placed a series of soft kisses on his chest while my fingers tackled the button and zipper of his jeans.

I pushed the jeans out of my way and, with careful hands, I freed his cock from the restraining material of his boxers. Giving a man a blow job had never been on my list of favorite things to do but as I moved my hands over this cock, the silken feel of his dark brown flesh was captivating. I loved the way my pale fingers looked against him.

"Woman, are you trying to kill me?"

I laughed softly and lowered my mouth onto the head of his cock. His abrupt, ragged intake of breath told me exactly how much he liked the heat of my mouth on him. I slid my tongue over the head of his cock, taking in the taste of his pre-cum with a great deal of pleasure. His fingers tangled in my hair. "Casey." My name was breathy and nearly tortured as it slipped from his lips.

I sucked briefly at the head and then I lowered onto him until the tip of his cock brushed against the back of my throat. His hips flexed against me, pushing into and pulling from my mouth with gentle and restricted movements. I whipped my tongue around him repeatedly as I let him fuck my mouth with short, quick strokes.

His hand fisted in my hair and he grew rigid. "You're going to make me come."

That was exactly what I wanted. I increased my pace and groaned against his cock as he came. I swallowed and used my tongue to clean the head of him until he shuddered against me and pulled me upward. He held me to his chest and took several deep breaths. His hands fisted in the material of my shirt as he pulled me tighter against him.

Shawn pressed a soft kiss on my forehead. "Want to play a game?"

I grinned. "Yeah."

"Go into the bedroom, take off all of your clothes, get on the bed, and cover your eyes."

"I have a sleeping mask."

"Yes, that'll do."

I nodded and slipped away.

A few minutes later, I pressed my fingers against the sleeping mask and lay back on the bed. I'd stripped the bed down to just the fine cotton fitted sheet that covered the queen mattress and now I lay spread-eagled in the brazen display he'd requested. I heard the bedroom door click shut and I tensed briefly. It was odd how vulnerable I felt. I was naked and unable to see. It was the ultimate display of trust and I was stunned that I gave over to him without even really thinking about it.

Straining, I listened as he discarded his clothes. The bed shifted as he joined me, and firm and familiar hands drifted over my legs as he urged me to spread them farther apart.

"You're already wet."

"Yes." I gasped as he ran a single fingertip down my slit.

"Did you enjoy sucking my cock?"

Boy, had I. I nodded abruptly. "Yes."

"Have I told you how much I enjoy licking your cunt?"

"No." I pressed against the bed as he pressed his finger into me. His blunt and harsh language was such a turn-on that I could barely think straight.

"I love it. I could eat you for hours."

I wasn't sure I would survive it, but I was game to try.

"Grab ahold of the headboard and don't let go until I say."

I wrapped my fingers around the iron bars of the headboard and bit down on my bottom lip as he moved on the bed. Several still seconds passed and then I felt the heat of his breath on the overheated flesh of my sex.

The tip of his tongue rubbed over me and I gripped the headboard harder. My whole world centered on the feel of his tongue as he rolled it carefully over my clit repeatedly. He sucked my clit into his mouth and worked it with his teeth gently until I wanted to scream with the pleasure of it.

He pushed two fingers into me and hit my G-spot with astounding accuracy. I came in a rush of hard, nearly unbearable pleasure that left me gasping for air. Shawn pulled his fingers away and licked me from entrance to clit until I was shaking.

"Please."

He moved upward, his body flush against mine. His lips brushed softly against mine, and I moaned, as I tasted myself. "I've never wanted anyone the way I want you."

The raw emotion in his voice robbed me of a response, and I was suddenly relieved to have the mask to hide behind. I tightened my hands on the bars and lifted my knees until I could cradle him between my legs. Feet flat on the mattress, I lifted my hips as he pushed his cock into me with one steady and sure thrust.

"You can trust me."

I knew that. I think I'd known since I'd set eyes on him. Just looking at him had flipped some invisible switch on inside me.

"I do trust you."

"Put your hands on me, baby."

I complied immediately, running my hands down his back and over his ass as he started to move. His pace was slow and almost gentle despite the overall feeling of outright invasion. No man had ever made me feel so much at once.

He pulled the mask carefully from my face and tossed it aside. Our gazes locked in the near darkness of the room, and it took all I had not to close my eyes against the intimacy of the moment. I cupped the back of his head and brought him down for a kiss. Our mouths clung together, tongues sliding against each other as we both gave into the plain need for each other.

I was in so much trouble.

"No scars . . ." I ran my hands down his chest and then rested against the cool tile of the shower stall. "Ever been shot at?"

"Yeah." He lowered his head and pressed a soft kiss against the side of my neck. "Took two bullets in the back during an armed robbery about three years ago, but I was wearing a vest."

"Lucky you."

"Safety." Shawn put one hand, palm flat on the wall above my head and used his free hand to cup one breast. His thumb rubbed across my nipple in an almost casual way. "I've always done everything I could to avoid breaking my mother's heart."

I hoped he would be as careful with my heart, but I left it unsaid. Pressing a soft, open-mouthed kiss on his collarbone, I moved away from the wall and grabbed my shampoo. "We need to get some sleep."

"Yeah." He sighed. "I've got court most of the day tomorrow and then I have to run some errands. Speaking of my parents, I have to make a run out to Salem this weekend. Do you want to go?"

"Salem?" I glanced at him as I lathered my hair. "What's in Salem?"

"My parents."

Oh. Shit. The man was actually offering to take me to meet his parents. I pressed my lips together briefly as I considered the ramifications of that. "Wow."

He laughed. "Don't freak out. They won't start planning a wedding or anything."

"Will it bother them that I'm white?" I bit down on my bottom lip, stunned that I'd even asked that question.

"I doubt it." He tapped my nose. "My mother is Greek."

And those beautiful black eyes of his suddenly made so much sense. It hadn't occurred to me that he was bi-racial. I moved under the water and ran my fingers through my hair to get rid of the soap. "Let me think about it."

"Don't stress over it. At the most, my mother might try to force-feed you." He pulled me close and ran his hands down my back. "She'll think you're way too skinny."

Since I was carrying at least twenty pounds of extra weight already, I could only laugh. "Oh really?"

"Yeah."

"Do you think that, too?"

"I think . . . that you are perfect just the way you are." He dropped a quick kiss on my mouth and grinned.

# 7

---

"So, tell me about this neighbor of yours."

I glanced up from my salad and snagged my soda from the table. Lunch with Jane and Mercy had seemed like a good idea until this very moment. I looked around the restaurant but escape seemed impossible. "He moved in a few weeks before I went on vacation. He's a cop and divorced two years ago. The ex-wife is a real piece of work, but he doesn't seem to be overly bitter about marriage as a result."

"He's hot," Jane responded.

I blushed and then sighed. "Yeah, okay, he's attractive."

Mercy laughed softly. "I saw the man, Casey. He's more than just attractive. He's 'find a flat surface and hold on for dear life' hot."

Yeah, he was *that* hot. I laughed softly. "I don't know how I could have lived next door to him for so long without noticing how great he is."

"You were distracted." Jane shrugged. "Speaking of that distraction, how are things with Connor?"

Much better, at least I hoped they were. "It's good. He seems to realize that I was right about what was best for both of us. Men like him don't like being dismissed; they prefer to do the leaving."

"I'm glad you didn't get all twisted and broken over it," Jane pushed her plate away. "He never gave me a chance to get invested emotionally. Connor Grant is excellent at keeping everyone at an arm's length."

I cleared my throat. "There is a guy from the FBI involved in the investigation of my break-in. It seems like an overdramatic response to a situation that has sort of fizzled."

"James is concerned." Mercy pursed her lips as if she had more to say and then cleared her throat. "To be frank, so am I."

My fingers curled into an involuntary fist at the soft and nearly painful tone of her voice. Mercy had been raped by someone she trusted several years before and there were times when it positively haunted her every word. She didn't wallow in self-pity and it was amazing to see how well-adjusted she was. It was amazing what a great therapist and a good man's love can do for a woman.

"The guy who broke into my apartment is back in jail because he violated parole and they've had no luck tracing the man who hired him." I couldn't claim it had been a mistake, but I really wanted to believe that it was completely over. No matter how naïve that might be. "Maybe the guy has lost interest."

Jane snorted. "Don't play that game, Casey. A man that would hire someone to break into a woman's apartment and scare the crap of her would not just lose interest and go away. Not on his own."

"I'm doing all that I can to be safe." I pushed my plate away and sat back in my chair. "Security follows me home, you know."

"I do know." Jane's eyes glittered with determination. "I demanded it and they all knew better than to argue with me about it."

*Hint.* I guess I wasn't allowed to argue about it, either. The fact was, that despite the initial invasion of privacy, it was comforting to know they were there. "Between the security-guard escort and living in such close proximity to a cop . . ."

"I think you should enroll in self-defense classes," Mercy suggested.

"I was thinking she needed to get a gun," Jane interjected and grinned when we both turned to look at her. "Come on, Casey, a gun is a true equalizer in most situations. Stun guns and knives require that you be too close to your attacker. You can shoot a man across the room and most don't do well with a hole or two in them."

I doubted that I could even point a gun at someone, much less actually fire it at another human being. "I don't think so."

An evening of mind-blowing sex versus an afternoon in the company of the biggest pain in the ass in North America. It wasn't even a contest. I tapped my pen on the conference table and stared at Kenneth Victor with the most patient expression that I could muster. Much to my chagrin, it appeared that he was still unwilling to accept the space limitations of the special focus show. He was probably irritated about more than just the space, but that was the topic he'd chosen to focus all of his anger on.

"As was explained to you earlier in the week, the space of the show cannot be altered. It is not a personal attack on you or an attempt to censor your work—to imply that is insulting and inappropriate." I pushed the contract back across the table. "Mr. Brooks had considered this matter solved and while I'm not unwilling to call him for *another* meeting with you, I can't imagine what you hope to gain from it."

He glared at me, his gaze moving from my tapping pen to my face. "I won't tolerate this disrespect from you. In the past, this gallery knew how to treat an artist of my caliber. It's obvious that the change in management has been detrimental."

I flushed with anger; the fact that Mercy Rothell-Montgomery had become the director of the gallery after Milton Storey had been pushed out had been something of a scandal in Boston society. Milton was married to old money. The subsequent sexual-harassment lawsuit filed against him and the gallery had done nothing to dampen the rumors.

Unable to take one more minute of his irrational and childish behavior, I reached across the table and took the contract. "Good day, Mr. Victor." The contract in hand, I stood and straightened my suit jacket. "I'll let Mr. Brooks know that you've decided not to participate."

When I was halfway to the door, he grabbed me. "You bitch."

Stunned, I jerked at my arm and swallowed hard, realizing that the closed blinds had blocked us off from the rest of the administrative staff. I wasn't alone in the building with him, but his touch was completely unnerving. "Let me go."

"Do you think you can treat me this way? I'm one of the best-selling artists this place has ever had the *privilege* of showing." He shook me and I shoved at him.

"Let me go." I slapped at his hand and then drug my nails across his fingers to get him to release me.

He slapped me with the back of his hand. Face stinging, I jerked hard and doubled up my fist.

"What the hell is going on here?" Jane slammed the conference door. "Let her go, Kenneth."

He released me and held out his hands as if to signal compliance. Rubbing my arm, I bent down and picked up the contract I'd dropped. "Mr. Victor was just leaving."

"I haven't signed the contract."

Jane came to me and took the contract from my hand. "There is no need." She ripped the contract in half. "Casey, should I call the police?"

"No." I shook my head and rubbed at my cheek. Heat was spreading and my jaw was aching. "Just get him out of here."

Jane walked to the phone and dialed security.

\* \* \*

"You should file charges."

I glared at Connor and shook my head. "No."

"Casey, the man hit you!"

I pulled the cold pack free from my cheek and took a deep breath. "Yeah, I was there."

"We will handle this matter in the way that makes Ms. Andrews most comfortable." James sat back in the chair. "However, Kenneth Victor will never set foot in this gallery again."

"Understood." Connor looked toward me once and stood. "I'll inform the rest of the team."

I sat back on the couch as he left the room and glanced briefly at Mercy before I closed my eyes. "My self-esteem aside, should I file charges against him?"

Mercy sighed and came to me. She sat down on the couch beside me and picked up one of my hands. She rubbed the top of my hand gently, as if to soothe me. "This is my fault. His interest in you has always been more than was appropriate and I put you in a situation where you were exposed to a man with known behavior problems."

"He's just a jerk." I curled my fingers into hers and smiled. My skin tingled a little at the stretching. "Don't stress out; it's not good for the baby."

She plucked the gel pack from my hand and pressed it against my cheek. "He got you right on the cheekbone; it's going to bruise."

Which meant keeping it from Shawn was going to be impossible. I dropped back against the couch and groaned in absolute displeasure. As cool and even-tempered as the man was, I figured that a bruised face was going to bring all of that alpha-male crap boiling to the surface. The door to James's office opened and in he walked.

"Shawn?" He looked positively furious.

James stood. "Come along, Mercy. I believe we need to give these two some privacy."

I took the cold pack from her and glared at them as they left. Shawn hadn't said a single word and I figured that wasn't a good thing. "Look, I'm a grown-ass woman. I need anyone coming to my rescue."

Which was bullshit, he'd already come to my rescue in many ways.

He sighed and walked to the couch. "Connor Grant reported the assault to Paul Martin."

I frowned. "The detective working my break-in?"

"Yeah." Shawn sat down and without another word picked me up and onto his lap. "I'm doing my best not to go find this guy and beat the fuck out of him, so give me some credit. I came here for you. This is the second time in a week that you've had some guy manhandle you."

I curled into him like a total pansy and blinked back tears. Crying was just not something I was prepared to do. So, I took deep, even breaths and clung to him while I regained my emotional composure.

"Does Detective Martin think that Kenneth Victor is responsible for that man breaking into my apartment?"

"It's his job to find out." He ran his hand down my back and pulled me closer. "I couldn't help but come with him when I heard what had happened. I realize that you don't want a man wreaking havoc in your life, so I really am doing my best to keep a level head. I realize that you're a strong, capable woman, but that doesn't mean that I'm not going to *come to your rescue* whenever it is necessary."

I laughed softly. "I get it."

"I hope so," he murmured ruefully. "I barely do."

Lifting my face from his neck, I looked over his face. I traced his bottom lip with one finger. "I've made your life messy."

"Yeah." He laughed. "I had no idea how much I enjoyed a mess until I met you." With gentle fingers, he brushed my hair back from my face and tilted my chin. "This is going to leave a nasty bruise. How about you give me this asshole's address?"

"No."

"I promise I won't kill him, much."

"Much?" Laughing, I rested against him and tucked my face into the side of his neck. "He's not worth the bother."

"But you are." He pressed a soft kiss to my forehead. "I'd like you to file a complaint against him and request a temporary restraining order."

"Because he lost his temper with me?"

"Because he'll do it again with some other woman and there needs to be a record of his behavior. Don't feel sorry for him, because he doesn't deserve that much consideration from you."

He was right. I sighed. "Can I do it with Detective Martin?"

"Yeah, he said he would come up when he finished with security. After you give him a statement, I'll take you home."

"Okay."

Home. It was odd how good that sounded.

"Based on the report I received from Montgomery Security and today's incident, I'd like to refocus the investigation squarely on Kenneth Victor."

"I don't know how they could be connected." I pressed my hands against the table. "I mean, I barely know the man and I've never done anything to warrant his attention."

"Beyond the fact that you exist?" Connor asked from across the table.

I glared at him. "He's just a pain-in-the-ass artist who lost his temper." I flinched when Shawn covered my hand with his. I turned my hand over and threaded my fingers with his. "I don't see it."

Detective Martin cleared his throat. "You've had dealings

with the man on and off since you came to Boston. He has a history of disturbing behavior with women, though nothing as violent as what happened today. He also has a sealed juvenile record."

"Disturbing how?"

"He was thrown out of an apartment building after he harassed one of his female neighbors so much that she threatened to sue the owner of the building. There have been two restraining orders filed in the past, something I've only discovered this morning, thanks to Mr. Montgomery."

I glanced toward Mathias, who had been silent since the meeting had begun. He looked absolutely furious. "I refused the guard Connor sent up to monitor my meeting with Kenneth. This is my fault."

"I'm not in the right frame of mind to discuss your undermining my authority in this building, especially since it resulted in you getting physically assaulted." I swallowed and felt the blood drain from my face. He swore and pushed back from the table slightly. "Don't look at me like you think I might hit you, too. You did a supremely foolish thing. The man could have seriously hurt you."

"I believe she's aware of that, Montgomery." Shawn shifted in his chair. "The fact is that the two of you are responsible for the women in this building and that should mean ignoring their demands and wants when it's to their own detriment." He glanced briefly at Connor, who looked just as angry as Mathias. "I'd like to take her home, so let's let Detective Martin finish up here."

I was going to absolutely drown in testosterone. I tightened my fingers in his hand to get his attention and sighed when he relaxed in his chair. "This situation was my fault, period. I refused the security guard entry and there isn't a man in this room capable of forcing me to accept a situation I don't want, no matter the right or wrong of it." Connor opened his mouth to speak and I shook my head. "No, I'm done with this part of the conversation and I'd like to move on before I'm forced to punch all three of you in the face with Detective Martin as a witness. The man looks like he's worked two weeks straight, and obviously doesn't deserve the paperwork that would go along with such a situation."

The man in question laughed softly. "Agreed, Ms. Andrews. Now, as I was saying about Kenneth Victor. Thanks to the break-in attempt, I do have the presumed DNA of the man who hired your intruder."

The sperm the guy had brought with him. I scrunched up my nose in response and nodded. "Okay."

"In the morning, I'd like you to come down and file a formal complaint against him for assault and battery. If I can find the right judge, we might be able to compel a DNA sample from Victor, which will answer a few questions for us. I'm not a man who believes in coincidence. This is the second time this Victor guy has been a threat to you in the last week, and that's just within the confines of this gallery."

"He didn't even touch me the first time we argued."

"Yes, but you were unnerved enough to signal for security."

True. Fuck, Kenneth Victor made a lot of sense. I'd always figured he was something of a coward, which would explain why he'd hired someone to do the dirty part of the job. "What could he possibly have gained by having someone break in on me? He wasn't around to *rescue* me or anything."

"But you were scheduled to meet with him the next day," Mathias murmured. "If things had gone according to his plan, you would have come home to a ransacked apartment, not a rapist trapped in your closet because you came home too early. You would have come into work the next day irritated, vulnerable, and probably seeking a little comfort."

Now that was disgusting. Still, it just didn't seem to fit.

"Kenneth Victor has no impulse control and a quick temper. He also is certainly physically capable of doing what that criminal was hired to do."

Detective Martin flushed slightly. "We have the transcripts of the chat, Ms. Andrews. It's true he was only hired to break into the apartment, mess the place up, and deposit the sperm on your bed . . . but he did indicate that he'd been in jail for rape and attempted murder. So, whoever hired him knowingly put a violent sexual predator in your apartment."

I wanted to throw up. Stomach lurching, I bit down on my bottom lip and swallowed so hard that it hurt. "I'll be down to the station first thing in the morning." Shawn stood and helped me from my chair. Trying to smile, I folded my arms over my breasts and rubbed my arms. "I'm ready to go home."

The ride home was done in silence, which I appreciated sincerely. I figured I had a lecture coming on the security-guard front, because while Shawn did appear to blame Connor for not overriding my decision, it was more my fault than anyone else's. Once inside my apartment, I shed my work clothes, pulled on my PJs, and snuggled up with my favorite blanket while Shawn took Harvey for a quick walk.

The deactivating beep from the security system, followed by the click of the dog's nails on the floor, told me when they came back. Harvey hurried into the room, hopped up on the bed, and plopped down on his belly beside me. Shawn entered a few seconds later with a glass of wine and a few takeout menus. He handed me the glass and sat down at the foot of the bed.

"You're pissed?"

He laughed softly, but there was a hard edge to it. "I'm absolutely furious, Casey. I'd like to go find him and beat him until I feel better. I'd also like to turn you over my knee, but that would be archaic and I'd never treat a woman like that. So, I'm going to order dinner and then I'm going to spend the evening trying to remember that you are, indeed, the grown-ass woman you claimed to be and that you don't need anyone making decisions for you."

"I didn't take him seriously as a threat."

"We all realize that." He dropped the menus on the blanket between us and waved his hand over them. "Preference?"

"Do you think Connor is going to be in trouble?"

"I think Connor Grant can handle himself," Shawn muttered.

I glanced at the menus. "Get something that delivers."

"I won't leave you alone again." He rubbed Harvey's head. The dog groaned and rolled onto his belly. "Unless it's to walk this guy."

They had totally bonded. I frowned at that. "You aren't going to break my dog's heart, are you?"

He stilled and met my gaze. Serious and intent, he looked me over. "You're both safe with me."

Harvey groaned again and I laughed before I could help myself. "I think I'm jealous of him."

"Well, he is a great ugly dog." He snagged the menus and stood. "Drink your wine while I get the food ordered."

# 8

I hurried through the front entrance of the gallery and across the main floor to the stairs that lead up the office area. The bull pen was empty; but I expected that since it was Wednesday and most of the buyers would be out and about late in the afternoon. My desk was nearly empty, so that was a relief. I dropped down in the chair and glanced toward Jane's office. The blinds were open and she was pacing in front of her desk with her phone headset on. The dramatic movement of her hands told me that the call was probably not a business one. She always got very animated when she was on the phone with a member of her family.

"How did things go?"

I jumped and glanced toward Mercy's office. She was leaning on the doorframe, her hands rubbing her extended belly casually. A part of me envied her on a level I could barely express. She had everything I wanted . . . a great marriage, successful career, and a baby boy on the way.

"Good." I tried to smile but in the end looked away from

her. "You know some women really enjoy being the center of attention."

"Yeah, but you aren't one of them." She jerked her head toward her office. "Come in here, I got to sit down."

I laughed softly and stood up. One glance into Jane's office told me she was still on the phone. I pulled off my shoes as I entered Mercy's office and walked barefooted to the loveseat. It was my favorite piece of furniture in her office. "Detective Martin and Shawn both believe that Kenneth Victor could be a viable suspect in my case. The ex-con, Peter Stevenson, has been cooperative but not very helpful. We know that the person who did the hiring used a public terminal in the downtown branch of the library. There is no sign-in process and no identification is required."

"Kenneth has always expressed an interest in you."

"Yes, but in the past it's always been sexual and somewhat normal. He isn't the first man to hit on me and not take 'no' as the final word. I don't want to believe that I inspired him to be crazy."

"It isn't your fault if that arrogant jackass has come unglued." She picked up a water bottle from her desk and rolled it around in her hands. "No phone calls?"

"None."

"It's odd, isn't it?"

"Maybe it wasn't something he was really comfortable doing and regretted afterward. He doesn't seem to fit the image I have of men who stalk women. He's a domineering jerk, but he's never followed me home, demanded anything more than any other artist in the gallery, or called me at home." I paused at the description because there was one man in my life that it did somewhat describe.

Connor had followed me home, made unreasonable demands, and generally inserted himself in my life since our breakup. I pulled my legs up under me and swallowed hard. In the past, he'd been a passionate and sexy lover who had never mistreated me. No, the man had passed a lie-detector test. Mathias had cleared him and I needed to remember that.

"What's wrong?"

"It's just insane that all of this is going on at once. I mean, I have the beginnings of a great relationship going on and I've forced myself to make good decisions for myself recently. I came back from vacation with a great sense of my own worth and what I wanted for my life."

"And you need to hold on to all of that. The police will handle the rest."

"Yeah." And the invasion would continue.

A part of me wanted Kenneth to be the guilty party, because that would mean it was over.

"We've got a problem." Mercy and I both turned to look at Jane, who was standing in the doorway. "You both need to come to the security office."

I stood, slipped my shoes on, and braced myself. How could it get any worse?

Mathias was alone in the central security room when we entered. He motioned that we sit and I sat down, my insides shaking. Was he about to tell me he'd been wrong about Connor all along?

"About an hour ago, a package was delivered to Mr. Brooks, downtown. He opened it and then immediately got in his car and came here. James and I are the only ones who have seen the contents of the package and I've notified Detective Martin that his presence was required here. He is en route." Mathias pushed a folder across the table to me and sat back in his chair. "Casey, I'm very sorry."

With shaking hands, I opened the folder and my world crashed down around me. For a few seconds, I don't even think I understood what I was looking at. The first picture was of me and Shawn . . . in an intensely intimate sexual position. I turned it over abruptly and gasped at the image of Connor Grant and myself. I was going to throw up.

There were over twenty pictures and each one was grossly personal. "There are three years of pictures here."

"I've sent Connor to his apartment with a technician. We are looking for the device that took the pictures."

"The first one is in my bedroom."

"Yes. I've put in a call to Detective Traner as well."

Yet again, the men in my life were moving around and invading without my permission. I was torn between being physically ill and screaming at him. But, this situation wasn't his fault. I had absolutely no one to vent at that moment and it was so infuriating that I could barely breathe for it. Gathering the pictures seemed my only recourse, so I slid them into the folder and closed it carefully.

"I spent the day filing charges against Kenneth Victor for assault." My hands tightened into fists on the folder. "Do you think he sent these pictures to you?"

Mathias pushed a single sheet of paper in a plastic bag. "The pictures were compromised when the package was opened. The letter was on the bottom so the police might be able to pull clear prints off it."

There was a single line of text on the piece of paper and it asked one question.

*Do you really want this whore working for you?*

I stood up abruptly from the table and turned my back on him. Jane and Mercy were sitting in the back of the office, both pale and obviously furious on my behalf. Tears sprung to my eyes, and I blinked rapidly to keep them at bay. I was not going to let this son of a bitch make me cry, no matter what he did.

"The package was addressed to Mr. Brooks?"

"Yes."

I cringed and rubbed my mouth. "Where is he?"

"He is upstairs in his office having a scotch and expressing his displeasure to the chief of police."

*Great.*

I jerked at the sharp knock on the door and blushed scarlet when Connor Grant entered.

He tossed a plastic bag full of camera equipment on the table where Mathias was sitting. "I found two cameras. One in my bedroom vent and another in the living room vent. Both are remote cameras with limited range. Digital, high-end, motion sensitive, video, not still images."

"You mean there is video footage . . ." I closed my eyes briefly and my knees weakened.

Jane was there, wrapping her arms around me in an instant. "It's okay."

"Oh yeah? Is there video footage of you fucking?" I flushed at her small laugh. "Sorry."

"No, it's quite all right." She patted my back. "We keep our home videos under lock and key. Isn't that right, darling?"

Mathias sighed. "Jane."

Jane only laughed and maneuvered me into a chair and brushed my hair back from my face. "Just relax, kiddo, it could be worse."

"How?" I demanded.

"At least you look good."

Yeah, at least. I bit down on my lip to keep from laughing. "This is not funny, Jane."

"Of course it isn't. But it isn't the end of the world either."

No, it wasn't. I glanced toward the file on the folder and saw Connor reaching for it. "What the hell do you think you're doing?" I snagged it off the table and pressed it against my chest. "No."

"I'm as much a victim in this as you, Casey."

"Fuck that." I glared at him.

The phone rang and Mathias picked it up. Seconds later, he

hung it up and stood. "Detective Tranner is here with Detective Martin. Let's adjourn to the large conference room."

Detective Martin was sitting at the large table when we entered and Shawn was pacing. Still clutching the folder, I moved into the room and walked to the end of the table. "Hey."

"The camera from your apartment is being removed by a crime scene tech." Shawn glanced briefly at the plastic evidence bag that Mathias laid on the table and then focused on me. "Come here."

I dropped the folder onto the table and curled into him with no regard to the other occupants of the room. His hand slipped down my neck and fisted in my hair. He was as furious as I was hurt and, oddly enough, that was soothing.

"Ms. Andrews, I'm going to take the pictures and letter into evidence."

I jerked and looked at Detective Martin. "No."

"Ms. Andrews." His expression was pained.

"And how many cops in your precinct will see them?" I reached out and grabbed the folder.

"It's evidence."

"It's me having sex. I've already been fodder for one pervert's masturbation fantasies and I'm done with that. You have the cameras . . . that should be enough."

"Casey."

"No, Shawn."

"He's right. The pictures are evidence."

"Oh, really?" I opened the folder, pulled out a picture of the two of us, and held it up for him. "How does this strike you? You want the cops you work with everyday seeing this?"

He snatched the picture. "Christ."

"Yeah."

"You are so hot."

I stared at him for a second and then I laughed, the tension draining away. "Shawn."

"I'm serious." He chuckled. "Look, these men have seen me bare-assed. I'm not worried and they aren't going to take turns taking the pictures into the bathroom. Look, maybe if they were just you . . . but they aren't."

I looked toward Connor. "What about you?"

"He's in them?" Shawn glared at him.

"Of course he is. There were two cameras in his apartment." I took the picture and put it back in the folder. "Connor?"

"I'm not ashamed of my relationship with you, Casey. As the man said—you are hot."

I tossed the folder toward Detective Martin with a glare. "You are not allowed to call me *hot*."

The detective picked up the folder with a small smile. "You are a beautiful woman, Ms. Andrews, and I will make every effort to preserve your dignity in this matter. Trust me."

Dignity. Christ, I didn't know if I had any left. When James Brooks entered the room, I took one look at him and burst into tears. Shawn turned to me and pulled me close.

"Hey, it's okay."

"No, it's not." I curled my hands into his shirt. "There are too many people in this room who have seen me naked." I lifted my head and looked at Detective Martin. "Is Kenneth Victor responsible for this?"

"I'm going to find out."

"Don't make me a promise you can't keep, Detective. I'm liable to physically injure the next man that lies to me."

"It won't be me."

I nodded and he gathered up the cameras from the table and left. "I want to go home."

"Done," Shawn murmured.

The vent in my bedroom was still open when we arrived. A crime scene investigator was up on a ladder with a tiny little duster that looked like something out of a TV show. I watched her a few minutes from the doorway until I heard Shawn and Harvey return. It was starting to suck that I couldn't walk him anymore. I plucked him up off the floor and rubbed his head. "You wanna spend the night over at Shawn's place?" I glanced up to look at him. "If you don't mind?"

"No. I've checked the place over for cameras. But, I've got a better idea."

"Oh yeah?"

"The family house in Salem is empty until tomorrow, when everyone will start to arrive for the weekend. Why don't you call Jane and let her know you won't be in tomorrow? We can go out to the house, let Harvey run wild in the backyard to his heart's content, and we'll be out of the city."

"What if Detective Martin needs me?"

"I'll call him and let him know."

As worried as I was about the prospect of meeting Shawn's parents, the offer was just too tempting to pass up. "Okay."

# 9

A lit fireplace, soft music, good food, and a sexy man is the perfect situation. Yet, as I snuggled close to Shawn on the couch and focused on the fireplace, I couldn't help but wait for the other shoe to drop. I was no longer the only person in the relationship who had an invasive and certainly horrible person moving around in their lives.

"I'm sorry."

"Sorry?" he questioned softly and ran his hand down my back.

"There is video footage of us having sex . . . out there." I waved my hand in front of us. "It's going to end up on the Internet, I just know it."

"Well, it's a good thing we look damn good having sex."

"Not funny."

He brushed his fingers over my cheek and lifted my chin so he could meet my gaze. "I don't blame you. To be entirely honest, I'm not pleased that someone has pictures of you in such a vulnerable state, but you did nothing to encourage this man nor did you willingly give him access to our relationship. I want to protect you, but I find that in a lot of this I just came along too late."

"Yes, but I'm glad you finally got here." I moved closer and took a deep breath. I loved being in his arms.

"Me, too." He kissed my mouth gently. "This place is going to be full to the brim with family starting tomorrow afternoon."

"Yeah."

"Let me take you to bed." He brushed his lips over mine again and thread his fingers into my hair. "Just you and me this time."

I nodded. It sounded amazing and perfect.

He stood, pulled me from the couch, and brought my palm to his mouth. The kiss was soft and startling. "The first time I saw you, I wanted you. You were standing on the front steps of the building dressed in this prim little pale blue suit."

"Did you want to mess me up?" I laughed softly.

"No, I wanted to take you inside, lay you down on a flat surface, and make a meal of you. I imagined all of this sexy white lace underwear that I would find under that suit."

I grinned. "I do have some . . . garter belts, too."

He groaned softly against my mouth. "I couldn't wait to meet you and get to know you."

"What stopped you?" I wrapped my arms around his neck and sighed when he picked me up. I wrapped my legs around his waist and gasped as I came into full contact with the hard press of his cock.

"It became obvious that you weren't single."

"Oh." I flushed. "Yeah, sorry about that."

He laughed. "Now, where was I?"

"You were wanting to get to know me." I rubbed my mouth across his jaw as he carried me to the stairs. "Is that all you wanted?"

"Not by a long shot," he murmured as he laid me down on the bed. Quick, nimble fingers unfastened my jeans. Shawn leaned forward and placed a soft kiss on my belly.

I lifted my hips as he pulled at my jeans and panties. His sudden intensity was startling and thrilling.

He kissed his my left inner thigh, and then lowered further to the damp flesh of my pussy. "I knew you would taste so good."

Arching up off the bed, I spread my legs wide as his tongue dipped into my entrance with familiarity and skill. I relaxed immediately. A part of me had been worried that it would be hard to let go. This was my man, despite the newness of our relationship, and I was absolutely at ease with him.

"Did you want to fuck me?"

He lifted his head and laughed softly. "Yes, I did. Repeatedly."

He flicked his tongue over my clit several times and then moved upward. The thin material of my T-shirt proved no barrier at all for his seeking mouth. He latched on to one nipple, sucking it hard. The soft fabric of his jeans rubbed against my thighs as he moved over me.

"Lick, suck, fuck," he whispered as he lifted his mouth and pushed my T-shirt up. "I wanted everything with you all at once. I couldn't wait to bury my cock in you."

I moved my legs against his and lifted my hips. "Yes."

"Your great smile and this curvy body were just about the most tempting things I'd ever seen in my life."

He went back to my breasts and licked my nipples in turn until my pussy started to clench. Moisture rushed against my labia and the urge to touch myself became overwhelming. I slid one hand between us, covered my pussy, and dipped my fingers between my labia.

"Naughty girl." Shawn lifted away and I stopped. "No, don't stop. I want to watch."

I rubbed my clit in slow circles as he left the bed to undress. "Like this?"

"Yes." He dropped his shirt on the floor and unbuckled his belt. "Spread your legs. I want to see everything."

Pressing my feet against the mattress, I let my legs fall completely open. The brazen display should have been mortifying, but it wasn't. I pushed two fingers inside and lifted up off the mattress.

"Do you like how that feels?"

I nodded abruptly. "Yes, but your cock would feel better."

He pushed his jeans and boxers to the floor and stepped toward the bed, naked and gloriously hard. "The first night I was in the building, I lay in bed and listened to you masturbate. You came quick and hard. For a moment, I was disappointed and then I realized you weren't done. You made yourself come four times that night."

"Did you come with me?" My gaze dropped to his cock; he was pumping it casually with one hand.

"Yes." He moved closer to the bed.

I quickened the pace of my fingers and lifted my hips in time with the stroking motion of his hand, but it wasn't enough. "Shawn."

He moved to the edge of the bed and I sat up, abandoning my throbbing pussy so that I could suck his cock. I clutched at his hips and curled my tongue around the dripping head of him. He let me stroke and taste him just a few minutes before he pulled free.

"Get on your knees."

I rolled to my knees and spread my legs for him as I heard him tear open a condom package. He didn't make me wait and I groaned with relief as he pushed into me with one hard stroke. "Fuck."

Burying my face against the bed, I rocked back against his

invading cock, meeting him thrust for thrust. His hands moved up and down my back in soft strokes as if to encourage and praise me in the same instant.

"Harder." I sobbed against the bed. "Baby, please."

Shawn gripped my hips with hard hands and slammed into me; our skin made a satisfying smacking sound as we came together. "Rub your clit."

I complied immediately, pushing my hand between my legs to find my clit. A few strokes of my fingers and I came. He stilled briefly as my pussy clenched around him and then he slowly pulled free.

"I want you on your back."

I rested on my stomach briefly and then rolled over as he requested. He covered me immediately, pushing his cock back inside slowly.

"I could make you come all night," he whispered softly against my neck.

"Don't let go." I clutched at his back, my fingers slipping against his sweat-dampened skin.

"I won't." He took my mouth then, thrusting his tongue between my lips in a welcome invasion.

I woke to the shattering of glass. Shawn was already out of the bed, the gun I hadn't realized he'd brought with him drawn. He pulled on his jeans as he left the room. "Be careful."

"Put some clothes on, baby." And he disappeared.

By the time I'd found clothes to put on, he'd returned, guilty culprit in hand. Harvey was snuggled up in the crook of his arm. "Oh, no, did he break something?"

"A vase in the living room."

"Please tell me it was just something your mom bought at Pier 1." I took Harvey and rubbed his head. "You bad dog."

He growled in response.

"Actually, I think it belonged to my grandmother."

Great. I wrinkled up my nose. "I'm going to make a great first impression."

"They are going to love you." He leaned in and kissed my mouth softly. "I'll clean up the offending vase. It had a mirror embedded in it . . . so maybe it just startled him."

"What time is it?"

"Almost seven."

"Hungry?" I leaned into him.

He grinned. "For food."

"Yeah, that, too."

I put Harvey down and pointed at a finger at him. "You behave."

In the kitchen, I found very little in the way of food, but since the house wasn't occupied all the time that made sense. We'd brought stuff for dinner but nothing for breakfast. "We're going to have to go out."

Harvey growled.

"Sounds good to me."

I jerked and turned around with a startled sound. "What the hell are you doing here?"

"You left the city."

The man was at least six feet tall, with short spiky black hair, and his green eyes were wild-looking with anger and something else that I couldn't readily identify. I knew his face, but it took me a few seconds to place him. "Has something happened at the gallery, Jack? I have my cell phone on . . . I mean someone could have called."

"You had my camera removed. It wasn't nice. I thought we had an agreement."

An agreement? I frowned at him. I glanced toward the hallway and wondered where Shawn was. Had this asshole hurt him? "What are you talking about?"

"I let you fuck other men so I could watch," he snapped and moved toward me. "I even sent you someone new to play with after you dumped that fucker Connor Grant."

New to play with? Anger and fear merged. "He wasn't my type." I took a few steps back and cleared my throat. "I didn't remove the camera, the cops did."

"I forgave you for calling the cops the first time, but this is too much." He lifted the gun and leveled it at me. "I even accepted this new guy you started fucking. But you removed the camera!"

He was totally out of his mind.

"Are you going to shoot me?"

"What?" He lowered the weapon. "No, of course not, I love you."

"I wouldn't have known about the cameras if you hadn't sent pictures of me to James Brooks and called me a whore."

"You knew about the cameras." The gun came back up. "You performed for me. Just me. I watched you fuck yourself with your fingers . . . for hours. That was all for me!"

"Don't move." We both jumped at Shawn's arrival. He had his gun out and pointed directly at Jack.

"Thank God."

Jack's gun wavered briefly and he turned it on Shawn. "You ruined everything."

Shawn glanced briefly at me and cleared his throat. "You work at the gallery?"

"Yes."

"I didn't realize that the two of you had an agreement." Shawn met my gaze again and I took it for the signal it was. "If I'd known, I would have left the camera where it was."

Jack seemed to relax. "Right, because it's important that she keep her promises."

Shawn nodded. "I agree."

Jack was insane and I wondered if Shawn's playing into it

was a good idea, but I was in no position to question that. Trusting him was my best option, so I took a step back to give him the room I figured he was going to need.

"Stop moving."

I jerked as the gun was pointed back at me. "Okay."

"And shut the fuck up. We can't trust you."

*We?* I looked at Shawn, who appeared just as shocked as I did; thankfully he recovered more quickly and used the fact that Jack had focused on me to move.

"Get down, Casey!"

I hit the floor without a single thought and covered my head. The sound of a gun going off echoed through my mind and mixed with my own screaming.

"I'd never even said hello to him before."

Shawn pulled me close and kissed my forehead. "We knew all along that it could have been a complete stranger."

A near stranger it turned out. "What did Detective Martin say?"

"He's negotiating charges with the police here in Salem." He pulled me closer and sighed. "I'm sorry."

"For what?"

"For blaming your dog for breaking the vase."

I laughed aloud. "Yeah, he's really upset with you." I glanced down at Harvey, who was lying on his back in Shawn's lap. "He may never recover."

"Jack could have killed you."

"He didn't. As always, you arrived right on time." I stretched up and kissed his mouth. "I could get used to having you around."

"I could get **very** used to being around." He curled his hand against the back of my head. "We could get another ugly dog."

I laughed. "That sounds like the makings of a little family."

"Yeah." He kissed me again. "Sounds nice."

It sure did. "What would we call her?"

"Well, considering Harvey's affection for walls and his last visit to the vet, we'd best call her Mary."

I bit down on my lip. "Virgin Mary?"

"Yeah."

"I'm so glad we found each other."

# Seducing Lisa

# 1

I was tempted to shoot him in his so-fine ass. My finger lingered on the trigger as I watched him on the sidewalk through the scope. The last time he'd shown up uninvited, he'd left cursing and bearing a striking resemblance to one of my better modern art pieces. An Armani suit made one hell of a canvas.

Disgruntled, I put down my paintball gun and glared at James Brooks as he strolled up to my porch as if he owned it. The ding of the doorbell tinkled through the house but I remained in the bedroom window staring at the BMW he'd parked in the driveway. Mercy Rothell-Montgomery was a dead woman, as soon as I got ahold of her.

James came down off the porch and turned to stare up at the window I was in. "Are you going to stay in that window all night? We've got an hour to get back into the city and to the gallery."

"This is not what I agreed to." I was being childish. Still, I hadn't agreed to spend a forty-five-minute drive in the company of James Brooks. I would have never agreed to such a thing.

He shoved his hands into the pockets of his pants and glared at me. The light from the porch highlighted every inch of his near-perfect face. "Lisa, get your ass down here and in the car before you make me mad."

"I could not care *less* if you get mad, James Brooks." Besides, I thought with a laugh, he really was quite beautiful when he was angry. "Go back to the city where you belong. I'll drive myself to the gallery."

"On a Harley?"

"Whatever, it'll suit my artistic image."

"It'll ruin your hair and your dress."

"Like I give a flying fuck about that crap." I retreated so he couldn't see me.

"Flying fuck?" he repeated. "*Lady,* you have precisely sixty seconds to come down here or I'm going to consider you in breach of your contract."

"My contract does not state anywhere in it that I have to put up with your spoiled, pompous ass." At least, I was damn sure it didn't.

"No, but it does state that you are to be in attendance for your own show in suitable attire with your best possible appearance."

"It does not."

"It does so."

I nearly laughed aloud. He sounded so put out and snotty that it bordered on being cute. Not that James Brooks had anything to worry about. The contract I'd signed with his gallery did have a stipulation about my appearance.

"Fine." I slammed my window shut and picked up my stupid tiny purse that was only big enough for the lipstick Mercy had made me buy and the keys to my house. It had taken some creative thinking to even get my ID in the thing.

I found him waiting on the front porch when I opened the door. "Mercy told me that Shamus would be picking me up."

"Mr. Montgomery has had a family emergency in New York. He won't be in attendance tonight."

I frowned; I felt a little pettier for making him wait. I pulled my door shut and met his dark blue gaze without flinching. "I hope it's nothing too bad."

"No, apparently not. But pressing enough that he wanted to be there. Mercy is at the gallery arranging things and being a general pest. I'm sure if it had been a serious situation she would have gone to New York with him."

I slid past him and walked down the stairs of the porch. "Good." I was still going to inflict bodily harm on Mercy, regardless of her husband's abrupt departure to New York.

James moved ahead of me to open the passenger door and waited until I was settled in the seat before shutting the door. In truth, James Brooks was good looking, normally well mannered, and sexy. I knew I brought out the worst in him, and God knows he brought out the worst in me. He stood beside the driver's door for a few minutes. I could only assume he was counting to a hundred to avoid blasting me when he got in the car.

He stood around six-two, had a long lean frame that was muscled without that look of a man who spent too much time in a gym. His face was strong, even aristocratic; he had a firm jaw, a nose that had been broken at least once, and a nice full mouth. His dark blue eyes just added to an already pretty package. I wondered, briefly, when he'd shaved his beard and mustache. The change was attractive.

He opened the door finally and settled into the driver's seat in silence. "I expect you to be civilized this evening."

"I'm always civilized." That was a damn lie, but I hated his tone. Despite my contract with his gallery, I wasn't going to bow and scrape at his feet. "We're going to be late."

James turned and looked at me then. "You could drive a saint to drink."

"You're no saint."

"That's right, I'm not." His gaze narrowed and then drifted downward to my cleavage.

I wanted desperately to pull at the neckline of the dress. Why I had agreed to buy and wear it was beyond me. "Stop looking at my breasts."

"At the moment they are the most agreeable part of you." He lifted his gaze to my face and shook his head. "It's too damn bad you are so sexy. No woman should have a face like an angel and the attitude of a hound from hell."

Insulted and pleased at the same time, I turned my head to stare out of the passenger-side window. I had a decent face, but hardly one worthy of an angel. My jaw was too wide and my mouth too generous. Still his compliment made me a little warm inside. What a frustrating development.

The room was full of people who had come with the sole purpose of meeting me and seeing my work. If I hadn't been so nervous, I might have had room to be excited. Despite my appearance, I knew I didn't fit in and probably never would. Every guest at the opening probably had more money than I could imagine.

"You're brooding."

I glanced to my left and snorted. "I'm wearing the dress, I'm holding the wine, and I'm smiling at these idiots just like I promised I would."

Mercy Rothell-Montgomery laughed and sipped from her wineglass. "You look great in the dress. I saw the environmental terrorism you perpetrated on my ficus tree, and these idiots have already spent half a million dollars."

A half-million dollars. My stomach clenched a little, and I took a deep drink of the wine I'd been determined not to drink. "Christ."

"Yeah, I knew that would get your attention."

I frowned and focused on the remaining liquid in my glass. "You could have warned me that Brooks was going to be picking me up."

"You wouldn't have been at home when he got there if I had." Mercy slid her arm around mine and started to guide me away from my corner. "Sorry about the tree, but I told you I hate wine." I looked down at the dark red liquid and thought about all the times I'd been forced to sit through meals with my ex-husband. "Half a million dollars?"

Mercy nodded. "No matter, you aren't the only person on the premises who hates that tree. Jane has firmer numbers. We can catch up with her later. She's currently charming Nigel Montague with the hopes of securing his Monet for display this fall."

"I hope you told her to watch out for his hands."

"Of course." Mercy chuckled. "Come, people want to talk to you. Everyone who is here is pleased with the collection. The critic from the *Boston Examiner* told me that this is by far your best showing."

"Why display a Monet?" I asked. The last thing I wanted to talk about was a critic. The critics had been decent to me during my first two showings and I didn't doubt they would be equally generous this time. "I mean, what's the point? You can't sell it."

"We get people to come in to look at the Monet, and then we herd them through the rest of the gallery. The more famous the piece or the collection, the higher our traffic is. People with a great deal of money like to buy art." Mercy paused and looked at me. "How are you?"

"I'm good."

"Are you sure?"

"Yeah." I glanced around the room and shrugged. "It isn't like I'm afraid of people, Mercy. I just prefer less-crowded places."

"James is very pleased with the crowd and the sales."

Shrugging, my gaze went involuntarily to the place where James Brooks was currently holding court. I allowed myself a moment of resentment; his ability to be comfortable in nearly any situation was irritating, to say the least. James Brooks had a quality about him that drew both men and women, and I would grudgingly admit it wasn't the size of his bank account. People genuinely seemed to like the man.

"Stop glaring at the owner of this gallery."

I blushed and looked down to my wine. "I don't know if I want to murder him or screw his brains out."

"We are all waiting to find that out ourselves." Mercy prodded me toward James. "Be a lady."

"Fuck you."

Mercy laughed softly. "You aren't my type."

"Don't think I've forgotten about you sending him out to get me." I glared at her briefly, but my heart wasn't in it. I couldn't really make myself be angry with Mercy.

"James, if you'd stand guard and protect Lisa from the vulture with the *Post*, I'll do my level best to remove him before he makes a scene."

James glanced between us and then scanned the room. "I thought I'd made it clear he wasn't allowed back in *my* gallery."

Lordy, he had that *King of the Planet* tone down pat.

Mercy blushed and glanced away. "He made it through security due to his date. I can assure you he was not invited and didn't get in on his press pass."

"You can have security remove him by any means that you feel necessary."

"Of course."

I sighed, watched Mercy retreat, and then shifted my gaze to James's face. That certainly explained why she'd pushed me across the room. "You shouldn't let that man get to you."

"If Wilhelm Frees was actually *getting* to me, I would purchase the newspaper he works for and fire him."

I swallowed back a laugh because I was sure he'd do that very thing. "Now, really, the man didn't say anything that wasn't true."

"He aired my personal business like it was his own," James snapped. "He can just be fortunate that I calmed down before I found him."

I pressed my lips together and looked around the room for something safe to focus on. The newspaper story in question had run a few months back. It had painted James Brooks as the consummate bachelor who shed a twenty-year marriage so he could sow his oats. I knew James had been divorced for nearly five years and from all reports, the relationship had ended on good terms.

In the time since his divorce, he'd cut a path through the eligible and beautiful women of Boston half a mile wide. His ex-wife, Cecilia Banks, was also in attendance. I looked briefly in her direction. Her escort was half her age and just as pretty as she was. I wondered if it bothered James.

"No. It doesn't bother me."

I flushed dull red, realizing that I'd actually said it aloud. "I'm sorry."

"No, it's fine." He cleared his throat. "It's good to see her happy."

"Not jealous?"

"It's hard to be jealous over something you lost so long ago. Our marriage was over for years before lawyers got involved."

I knew exactly what he meant. My marriage had been over for years before I found the means to leave. "She's a beautiful woman."

"Yes." He nodded. "Inside and out. I've never known a more generous person in my life." James cleared his throat and swirled the water around the wine glass he held. "The collection is selling well."

"Yes, Mercy told me."

"You look ready to bolt."

I shrugged. The crowd was making me itch. Had I really become such a hermit? "I'm fine. I survived the first two shows; surely I can survive this one." I frowned. "Where did you get the water?"

"There is a waiter circling who is catering to nondrinkers and designated drivers." He reached out and I gave him the wineglass.

I tucked my hands behind my back gratefully and looked around for the waiter with the water. "I wish I'd known that earlier."

"I'll get you a glass." He put the wineglass on the tray of a waiter who paused briefly at his side and then blended into the crowd.

Everyone at the Holman Gallery made it their business to put people at ease. Yet, no matter how smooth the event was going or how quickly the staff responded to my needs, I couldn't make myself feel comfortable around the people attending my show.

They, or people just like them, had made me a very wealthy woman, but no matter how much they spent on my work I'd never be a part of their world. At the tender age of twenty-two, I'd married into their world of privilege and wealth. Greg Carlson had promised me the world and I'd bought it all. His praise, his feigned affection, and even his apologies every time he hit me.

"Here."

I jerked and looked back toward James. He held out a wineglass filled with mineral water and I took it hesitantly. "Thanks."

"These people . . . they're just that . . . people."

"They're wealthy people who are used to getting what they want. Not a one of them has ever had to worry about where their next meal will come from or if they'll have a roof over their head next week."

"And you have to suffer poverty to be a person?"

"No, but having to work for something can make it more valuable to them." I took a sip of the water and met his gaze. "Don't you think?"

"I grew up with a silver spoon in my mouth."

"Your family is known for its charity and generosity."

"My mother founded the Holman Foundation," James responded softly. "I took it over after her death because her dreams were important to me."

"What about your goals and dreams?"

"Leaving my father's law firm and taking over the foundation made her loss almost bearable. My mother was the heart of my family and none of us were the same after she was taken from us." He put a hand on the small of my back and guided me toward a food table. "How are things going with the broker I set you up with?"

"We get along fine as long as he remembers to speak English." The man had a habit of using abbreviations and practically Greek financial terms that made me feel stupid. Or at least, he had until I told him I would take all of my money out of his hands if he didn't start to make sense to me.

"He's very good at what he does and one of the most honest men I've ever encountered."

"I trust your judgment."

"It's just too bad that you don't actually trust me." He removed his hand from my back as we paused just short of the cluster of people around the food. "This should be ending within the next hour; let me when you are ready to go."

"Thank you." I stared down into my water as he left me. Did I trust him? It had been a long time since I'd let myself trust a man, and I knew what kind of trust he wanted.

James Brooks had been pursuing me since the day we'd set eyes on each other. He did it for me three ways from Sunday, but he wasn't the kind of man I could afford to get involved with. I'd promised myself the day I'd left Greg that I wouldn't ever tangle up with another spoiled, rich boy. Of course, there was no part of James that said "boy" to me. No part at all.

The male form was no secret to me, and I'd imagined the man naked thousands of times. In fact, I glanced toward one of my sculptures—everyone in Boston was getting a look at one of my preferred fantasies. I'd carved him in rosewood. His profile was distinct, and I was surprised that he hadn't seen himself in it.

"It's an incredible likeness. There probably isn't a woman in the room that doesn't see it."

I jerked and turned to look at Cecilia Banks. "Pardon me?"

She motioned to the rosewood sculpture. "I'd considered buying it, but I'm glad to see that I'm too late."

It had sold more than an hour ago. "Why is that?"

"No woman needs to be reminded of the most important thing she ever lost, repeatedly." She flushed and glanced down to the near-empty wineglass in her hand. "I've had too much to drink, I think."

"Wine can loosen tongues."

"Yes." She nodded. "He's interested in you; it's as obvious as the sculpture."

"I have no time for rich playboys and womanizers," I snapped and then sighed when my face heated.

"He's neither actually. Certainly rich, but he never once violated our wedding vows." She reached out and touched my arm as if to get my undivided attention. "The society pages like to play up his liaisons because he's rich and entirely too handsome for his own good. They speculated for months about what ended our marriage, in the papers and in quiet conversations around fancy dinner tables in this town."

"And it wasn't him."

"No." She pulled her hand from my arm. "At least, he wasn't the one that made the mistake." Cecilia pushed ash-blond hair over her shoulder and looked around for her date. "I'm only telling you this because he talks about you a lot. You would be cheating yourself out of an amazing man if you dismissed him because of your prejudice."

"I'm not . . ." I stopped and bit down on my lip. Didn't I judge everyone in this room with the same thin criteria? "This is really none of your business."

She laughed. "Oh, I know. I'm sure he'd be livid if he knew I was over here airing his private business to you. You have to get in pretty deep to be privy to his private world."

"I've noticed that about him."

"I think that's something the two of you share."

# 2

---

"What did you and Cecilia discuss?"

"I fail to see how that concerns you." I crossed my legs at the knee and stared out into the traffic that buzzed around us.

"My ex-wife can be intimidating."

"She was charming and entertaining." I almost snorted. It would be a cold day in hell before a rich socialite like Cecilia Banks intimidated me. Been there, done that, was *not* going to repeat the experience. "I'm amazed you managed to marry her in the first place."

"I thought I was the luckiest man on earth," he murmured. "Getting married at seventeen wasn't exactly on my list of things to do, but when she told me she was pregnant with Ryan I couldn't turn my back on them."

"Ryan's in his sophomore year of college?"

"Yes, acting like a grown man and dating a woman eight years older than him." He laughed softly. "I can't even lecture him about it."

"You do date a wide variety of people, yourself."

"Yes." He turned onto the interstate and merged easily with

traffic. "Something he pointed out when I told him he couldn't see her anymore."

I couldn't help but laugh. That conversation must have been one of the most frustrating moments in his life. James had never struck me as the kind of man who liked to be argued with.

"He's a grown-up."

"Funny, I can still remember bringing him home from the hospital. Ugly, all arms and legs, and lungs. He kept us confused and exhausted for nearly a year."

"They do that, I suppose."

"Did you ever think about kids?"

"Yeah, until I married." I frowned and turned away from him. "After it became clear that I didn't want to have children with Greg, I put those goals aside permanently."

"You're still young enough to have children."

"Children deserve a home with two parents if at all possible. Since I can't imagine ever sharing my life with a man . . ." I rubbed my face. "Can we change the subject?"

"Sure, what do you want to talk about?"

Nothing, but we had at least another twenty minutes on the road. "I have no clue."

"We can talk about the sculptures."

I stiffened and jerked my gaze to him. He appeared calm, which put me on edge. Playing stupid was my first thought. "Which sculptures?"

"The ones I purchased." He looked at me briefly and then returned his gaze to the road. "I thought Mercy would have told you."

"You purchased some of my work?" Okay, I had to *not* be angry about that. It would be irrational to be upset with him for purchasing my work.

"Just the one little collection."

"Why?"

"For the same reason your work has been featured in my

gallery three times." He glanced toward me and sighed. "You really are a talented woman and I found a piece in this show that I wanted."

I relaxed in the seat. At least he wasn't bitching about half of Boston seeing him naked. Well, he probably would if he ever realized.

"Okay, fine."

"You're angry."

"I am not."

"Then what are you?"

"Puzzled." I sighed and crossed my arms as I considered what to say. "Why didn't you discuss it with me first?"

"Because I don't discuss my financial decisions with anyone."

"It's my work."

"When you put it on the sales floor, you lose control over what happens to it."

That irked. It irked so much that a part of me didn't want to sell another piece of my work as long as I lived. I'd been thinking about it since the evening of my first show when strangers had viewed, touched, and eventually purchased my sculptures.

I'd been obsessed with it at first and had tried to keep track of every piece. Now, almost two years later I made a serious effort to let it all go and not think about it. Except, now, James Brooks would have something of me in his apartment and I had no recourse.

"Which one?"

"The miniature collection."

"All six pieces?"

"They belong together."

I nodded and agreed. The six animal figures were different in every way, including the material that I had used. Everything from clay to limestone, yet, they did belong together.

"I created them about six months ago; they are all primitive and extinct."

"Yes, I know. I make it habit to study my purchases carefully. Does it bother you?"

"No."

He laughed softly. "You liar."

During the two years I'd known James Brooks, he'd made a play for me so often and so adeptly that they had almost become part of our communication process. So, when he walked me to my door, said good night, and left without another word I wondered where the hell the real James Brooks had gone.

I leaned against my front door, jerked off my high-heeled shoes, and tossed them with a flick of my wrist. Activating the security took a few seconds, and then I started up the stairs. I dropped the overpriced dress in a heap and walked to my bedroom in a pair of panties.

There had been one man since my divorce had finalized. A man in a bar in Chicago. It had been hot and dirty, the good kind of dirty that made my blood heat a little at the memory.

That one-night stand hadn't put a dent in the animal that my libido had become. There had been plenty of opportunities, but I've had a hard time letting go of myself enough to be intimate with anyone. The stranger sex hadn't felt dangerous. In fact, since I hadn't told him my real name, it'd been almost therapeutic.

As a younger woman, sleeping with a stranger would have been an impossible situation for me to even consider. I connected the physical union of bodies with emotional intimacy. My ex-husband had cured me of that. It probably hadn't been the first time he hit me or the last, but somewhere in between.

I sprawled out on the bed and rubbed my stomach. Restless, and hating it, I laid there staring at the ceiling trying to remember when my world had tilted so far from the norm that I'd come close to taking my own life. I rarely allow myself to think about that day, but when it does come to me, I can't let it go.

How close had I come to ending it all because I couldn't bear another day with him? Now, thinking back on it, remembering how desperate I'd been makes me sick. But, those desperate moments had passed that day just as they had all the days before. But, instead of putting away his gun and getting on with the chores he'd left me to do, I'd packed my bags and left.

Nothing about leaving had been easy. The divorce would have been messy even if he hadn't contested it. I'd never once filed charges against him, so his physical abuse had been impossible to prove in court. No one could imagine that a man like Greg Carlson, who came from such a prominent family, could be capable of beating a woman.

He'd fought the divorce to the bitter end, refusing to believe that anyone but him could decide that our marriage was over. Three years later I am clear and free of him. He hadn't shown up in a while, though there isn't a day that goes by that I didn't expect him.

"I hate you." I glared at my television, visions of murdering the fitness diva dancing merrily through my head.

Her name was probably Candy or something equally annoying. I cannot abide people named after food; it's just not right. I kicked my workout ball across the room, turned off the offensive show, and went into the kitchen. Starting the day with exercise should be a criminal offense, but the drive to stay fit and ready went deep. After I left my marriage, I'd been obsessed with physical strength and conditioning.

He'd used his strength against me and I wanted to be able to defend myself. Yet, no matter how many classes I took or how many self-defense dummies I pummeled, the fear lingered. Expensive security systems, a safe room, and a plethora of firearms later and sometimes I still wake up screaming in the middle of the night.

The jarring clang on the phone shook me loose from thoughts I'd had no business indulging. I snatched it up and leaned against the doorframe between the kitchen and living room. "What?"

"You know if you are an example of how friendly and charming Southern women are . . . I'm never going there."

I pursed my lips and glared at the floor. James Brooks. As if last night hadn't been enough time in his exalted presence. "No decent Southern woman would have your spoiled, arrogant ass."

He laughed softly. "I need you to come into town."

"No."

"If you don't, I'll come out there."

"The next time you set foot on my property uninvited, I'm going to do more than shoot paint at you." My fingers curled around the telephone receiver and I fought a grin. "An ass full of buckshot could do wonders for you."

"Are you threatening me?"

"No, I'm forewarning you of my intentions."

"I see." He cleared his throat. "Then perhaps I should forewarn you of mine."

My stomach tightened at his cool tone. "Go right ahead."

"The next time you aim a weapon at me or one of my employees, I will sever every contract the gallery has with you and we'll leave you out there in the middle of nowhere to wallow in self-pity for the rest of your potentially miserable life."

"Just who do you think you are?" I demanded, stunned.

"A man that has indulged your selfish and militant behavior for the last time. You've been warned."

"Fuck you." I turned off the phone and tossed it on the kitchen table.

Arguing wasn't a good way to start the day either. I wasn't miserable and I rarely let myself indulge in self-pity. It was a waste of time and I knew better than anyone how pointless that could be.

I pulled my goggles off and put aside the staple gun I'd been using to secure the canvas to the wooden frame. The large gleaming white surface in front of me seemed to be begging for something. It had been years since I'd really been interested in painting. I normally preferred the physical satisfaction of sculpture.

After a cursory inspection of the paint, I'd decided that I would need to order more before I really got started. Snagging the list I'd made, I checked my watch and shoved my feet into a pair of shoes near the door. It had been nearly two hours since my phone call with James Brooks and I fully expected him to make an appearance sooner rather than later.

I checked the security panel as I entered the house. The front gate would sound off when he entered, so I would at least be prepared for his arrival. Liberating my laptop from my desk in the den, I took it outside and started browsing online stores for paint. I'd gotten half the things on my list when the security system dinged. He had arrived.

I put my feet up in the chair in front of me and kept browsing the Web site I'd found. The doorbell rang once and then again; I heard footsteps on the gravel path that led out to the barn. Disconcerted, I stood and abandoned my purchases. Having him or anyone else for that matter in my barn set my teeth on edge. I rarely worked with models, but when I did letting them into my sanctuary was always the worst part.

The side door was open by the time I got around the side of the house. I stomped off toward the barn. The man had gone too far. A passing glare at his car had confirmed the identity of my *guest*. I squinted in the barely lit barn and hit the light switch. He was a few feet away staring at the large canvas I'd made.

"What do you think you're doing?"

James turned and looked at me. "I was looking for you. You haven't worked in paint since you were at the academy."

I stiffened.

He laughed. "Surprised? I actually do pay attention to the artists that come through the academy. In fact, when I tasked Mercy with finding you, I assumed she'd find you holed up with a room full of paintings."

"I suppose the near-pornographic sculpture was a surprise."

"A pleasant one." He pushed his hands into the pockets of his slacks. "Look, I was harsh with you on the phone."

"And I was harsh back." I pointed out into the yard. "You're in my private space."

He raised one eyebrow but nodded.

I took one deep breath as he passed me. "What do you want?"

James pulled an envelope out of his coat pocket and handed it to me. "It's the transaction details on the wire transfer the foundation did this morning. Your percentage for the show last night."

I took it and pushed it into the pocket of my jean shorts. "Thanks." It was odd seeing him in my yard with his entirely too expensive suit neatly pressed. "Have a nice drive back."

Turning on my heel, I started back toward the patio.

"That simple, you think?"

I stopped and turned slowly to glare at him. "Simple?"

"You think that I drove all the way out here to give you that receipt and that I'm going to leave without finishing our conversation?"

Heat swept across my face. "What conversation?"

"The one you cut short with the words 'fuck you.' " He came to stand in front of me. "I'm still trying to decide if that was an offer or just genuine frustration on your part."

I clamped my jaw tight to keep my mouth from dropping open and swallowed hard. "Of course it wasn't an offer. I don't even like you."

"So you say, and what's even more interesting is that you don't even pretend you do. Most people at least pretend."

"Your money might buy the insincere platitudes of hundreds of people in this city, but it would be good for you to remember that I'm not one of them." I took a deep breath. "I didn't ask to be *discovered*, Brooks. I didn't ask you to sic Mercy on me and make me a fucking success. If I want to wallow in my own misery until the end of time it is none of your business."

"I have never met anyone as ungrateful and ill-mannered as you. Hell, I'm not even sure I like you either."

He looked so exasperated, I had to bite down on my lip to keep from laughing. It was the second time in two days we'd both been reduced to frustrated silence. Since I had nothing intelligent to say, I turned and stalked toward my house. I figured he'd follow along, but a few seconds before I hit the front porch I heard the car start.

Once inside I threw myself down on the couch and stared at the ceiling. Angry and maybe a little more entertained than I should have been, I sat there tapping my foot against the floor trying to decide if I had won or lost that argument.

# 3

---

A phone call from my agent had me up at the ass crack of dawn on a Thursday morning. One simple question out of her mouth brought me fully awake and instantly furious. James Brooks had struck again. When her number had registered on the caller I.D., for a few seconds I'd worried that he had followed through with his threat and dumped my work. What she had to say was in some ways worse.

A popular auction house in town had an event coming up for charity and James Brooks had donated the suit I'd covered in paint. The auction house had called her to confirm the authenticity of the garment being sold. The entire city had known about my paint gun since some kid had invaded my property with a group of friends armed with camera phones. There were blog posts about me as a result.

My appointment with him wasn't until two in the afternoon, so I treated myself to a morning in a spa. By the time I arrived at the Holman Foundation, I'd been buffed, scrubbed, and painted to nearly pink perfection. Housed on the tenth floor of a high-rise downtown, the Holman Foundation was probably one of the most successfully run charity organizations in the state. Created and used for encouraging the arts in the public schools and at the Holman Academy, it remains one of my favorite things on earth. The foundation had taken me from poverty and near starvation. They had taught me, nurtured me, and eventually released me into the world an educated woman. What I'd done with it really wasn't their fault.

His secretary rose to greet me as soon as I entered. She was one of those exceedingly graceful creatures who made you want to apologize for spoiling her environment by being just human. "Helene."

"Lisa!" She smiled and held out her hands. "I was surprised when you called. You haven't come down here willingly in . . . well, never." She frowned. "Nothing's wrong, is it?"

"No, things are good." I accepted the brush of her lips on my cheek and stepped back. "Just a change in strategy."

She laughed and glanced toward his office door. Her white-blond hair slid over her shoulders elegantly. I figured some part of me had spent the better part of four hours in a spa this morning so I wouldn't look like a troglodyte in her presence. Though I seriously doubted she did it on purpose, the woman did make everyone else look a bit primitive in comparison.

"He asked me to see you in immediately."

I let her guide me to the door and open it. He held up a hand, motioned me in, and pointed to the headset he was wearing. He ended the phone call after a few seconds and pulled the headset away. The click of it dropping on the smooth finish of the ebony desk filled the silence as the door behind me closed. Now that I was here, I regretted coming. I sat down in one of the plush chairs in front of his desk and stared at him.

"Lisa." He inclined his head and looked me over. "Did you do something different with your hair?"

I touched my hair briefly, vaguely remembering that the

stylist had put highlights in my otherwise dirty-blond hair. "Yes, just something bright for summer."

"It looks good." He picked up a pen and tapped the surface of the desk for a few seconds. "When Helene told me you'd requested to see me today, I was surprised."

I stood, suddenly nervous, and smoothed the wrinkles out of my slacks. "I'd like to discuss the Armani."

"What about it?"

"My agent called me. Kendrick's Auction House is asking her to confirm that I'm the *artist* for a suit you've given them to auction."

"You play, you pay." He raised one black eyebrow. "I considered selling it on the Internet, but I figured that that it would garner more interest locally. Especially since you were caught on film last summer running those kids off."

Okay, fine, there was talk all over Boston about the hillbilly porn artist with the paint gun. "They can all kiss my ass."

"Yes, I believe all of Boston has gotten that message." He laughed softly. "And they love you in spite of it. The success of last night's show is certainly proof of that."

I liked his laugh. To be honest, I pretty much liked everything about him. But I made a serious effort to keep that under wraps. The man hardly needed any encouragement from me. "I'll give you ten thousand dollars not to give that suit to a charity for auction."

"No deal."

I stared at him. "I'll donate ten thousand dollars to the charity of your choice in your name."

"No."

"Well, what the hell do I have to do?"

Mistake. I knew the moment it came out of my mouth.

James leaned back in his chair and looked me over. "An apology."

"For what?" I pointed a finger at him. "I gave you fair warning. You had a full minute to get off my sidewalk and get your snobby ass back in your car. You're just lucky that a BMW is too pretty to shoot at or I'd have given it a new paint job, too." He stood up abruptly from his chair and came around the desk. Stilling the urge to back up, I dropped my hands to my sides and resisted the urge to tighten them into fists.

"I couldn't care less about that suit." He paused inches from me and met my gaze unflinchingly. "I want you to apologize for lumping me into the same category that you put your ex-husband in. I want you to apologize for treating me like shit because of your ex-husband. And finally, I'd like you to apologize for not trusting me."

Stunned, I stared at him. "First, I've never once thought that you were like Greg. Second, if I've treated you in a way you don't appreciate it isn't because of him, it's because of you. You are arrogant and spoiled. As for trusting you, I don't trust anyone." I poked my finger into his chest before I could think better of it and sucked in a deep breath. "I didn't invite you into my life, Mr. Brooks, and you'd best remember that. You ignored me when I was at the academy and as far as I'm concerned you can continue to ignore me in the future."

He grabbed my arm when I turned to leave. "I never ignored you. When you were a student, you were brilliant and a child. I saw you as one. When you volunteered at the academy, you were all grown up, but I was going through a messy divorce and you were married. I've always known who you were, yet the few times we interacted you seemed uncomfortable with me. I'm the one that awarded you the arts scholarship that got you out of that run-down shack in Greeneville, Tennessee. I read your essay about how much you loved art and how you had no dreams for your future. You were barely fifteen years old and already you felt your life was over."

"Your mother—."

"My mother let me choose scholarship applicants for nearly

twenty years. She never had time to read the essays and review the portfolios personally." He released me and took a step back.

I looked away from him, overwhelmed by his confession and uncomfortable with the knowledge of how long he'd been in my life. "I'm not a charity case."

"No, and you've more than made up for the scholarship you won. The money you've provided the foundation through the gallery has nearly doubled the scholarship fund in the past two years." He shoved his hands into the pockets of his slacks. "So, now what?"

"I can't think around you."

"That sounds promising."

I glared at him. "A smart man wouldn't view rejection as a challenge."

"You've never told me 'no.' You just blow up and have a fit whenever I try to get close." He moved toward me and I stiffened. "If you want me to leave you alone, tell me 'no.' "

"Why on earth would I want to spend time with the biggest man-whore in Boston?" I demanded and took a step back.

"Man-whore?" he repeated softly as he wasn't quite sure what to make of the insult.

"You haven't dated the same woman twice in a year." I held out my hand when he moved closer. "You're invading my personal space."

"And you still haven't told me 'no.' " He reached out, grabbed my arm, and pulled me to him in one quick motion. "Say 'no.' "

"Fuck you," I snapped just before he covered my mouth with his.

Big, strong hands slid down my back and I relaxed against him. The soft moan that escaped my lips as his tongue slipped into my mouth caught me so off guard that I jerked away from him, glaring. "Does this strong, alpha-male crap work with all of those ditzy twenty-two-year-olds you date?"

"Mostly I just have to say hi."

He used my shock against me, because seconds later I was back in his arms and his mouth was on mine. I clutched at his shoulders, confused by what I should do and what I desperately wanted to do. So, I did nothing but moan a little and open my mouth to the sweep of his tongue. I felt thoroughly invaded and it was awesome.

His hands slid downward to the small of my back and pressed so that I was flush against him. His cock was obviously hard and temptingly pressed against my belly. This was the wrong time and definitely the wrong man. His taste was intoxicating and I knew that it would be easy to get lost in him.

James lifted his mouth from mine and sighed. "I like your mouth when you aren't talking."

"Arrogant bastard."

"See." He chuckled. "Don't be vicious, Lisa. Not every man that wants you is out to make your life a living hell."

"You don't want me; you just see me as a challenge."

"I stopped playing those games a long time ago." He rubbed his thumb across my lips. "I just want you. I want your time."

"You want to fuck me," I snapped.

"Repeatedly." A smile slipped across his lips. "I've wanted you so long that I don't remember what it was like not to want you."

It was hard to respond to that. I backed up a few steps and took a deep breath when he let me go. "I'm not the right woman for you."

"Oh, yeah?"

I laughed at his tone and shook my head. "I'm nothing like your ex-wife."

"I would agree." He shoved his hands into his slacks and shrugged. "What makes you think that I would want another woman in my life like her?"

"She's beautiful."

"Yes."

"Cultured, old Boston family."

"Yes, old money as well. Her family has always treated me well, despite how we came together and married. But no one is perfect and our marriage had its problems."

"Problems that lead to a divorce?"

"To be frank, it was the strain of practicing law and running the foundation that lead to the demise of our marriage. My wife got lonely."

"Being alone a lot is hard to deal with." I knew what being alone was, and, for the last several years, I'd convinced myself that it was exactly what I wanted. Companionship, friends or lovers, just came at too high a price.

"She dealt with it by fucking someone else," James responded evenly.

"Ouch." I dropped my gaze to the floor between us and bit down on my bottom lip. It had never crossed my mind Cecilia Banks might have cheated on him. The woman I'd seen and spoken with didn't seem the kind to violate the vows she made.

"Yeah, I was angry for a while but then I realized we were both better off apart. We'd been making each other miserable for years and didn't even know it." He shrugged and looked out the large window behind his desk.

Another surprise. I wonder if anyone else knew what had finally ended his marriage. I knew I'd caught him in a weak moment. Our confrontation had led to quite a few confessions from both of us.

I walked across the room and stopped beside him. "I'm not someone you want to be involved with. I'm moody, inconsiderate, and arrogant ninety-five percent of the time."

"And the other five percent?" he asked softly.

"I'm asleep."

"And what would it hurt to try?"

"A lot. Our business dealings . . ."

"Are business. I've never let my personal life interfere with the Holman Foundation and you will not be an exception to that rule."

"It's an honorable thing that you do here," I admitted. "I've always thought so."

"Thank you."

The need to escape was building up inside. I couldn't stay but didn't want to leave. The last thing I need in my life is someone as complicated and demanding as James Brooks was. He represented the life I'd risked everything to escape and I had no interest in stepping back into that world. My ex-husband had come from an old Boston family, steeped in wealth and privilege. In that respect, he and James were no different.

"I should go."

"Lisa."

I shook my head and walked toward the door. "I'm sorry."

"For what?" he demanded roughly.

Turning to look at him, I swallowed hard. "For not trusting you."

Ignoring the look of shock and hurt on his face, I jerked open the door and made my escape.

By the time I reached the parking garage and had settled in my truck, I felt like absolute shit. It was irritating. James Brooks *was* probably the biggest womanizer in Boston and I was sitting in a stinky parking garage angry with myself for hurting his feelings.

# 4

---

The best part of my farm is the barn. The first thing I'd done was renovate it to use as a workshop. I kept one stall and had it converted into a shower. The rest of the large structure was the home of various projects and storage space for supplies. I shoved off my house shoes and curled my toes briefly against the cool tile that covered the entire lower level.

It was a perfect place for me to create and it had been the reason I'd bought the property to begin with. In Greg's home, as it had never felt like mine, there had been no room for my work or my dreams. In one of my more honest moments, I'd realized that living his life had been easier than pursuing my dream as an artist. Unfulfilling but easy.

I walked over to the empty canvas. Just standing in front of it brought the smell of paint rushing into my nose. I hadn't painted in years, even after my divorce had become final and I was free of him. The box of paints and the new brushes were on the floor beside the canvas. With a sigh, I sat down and pulled the box to me. It was time to work past it, time to deal with the loss.

I opened the brushes first, checking each one for flaws before setting them on the floor in a row. By the time the door to the barn creaked open, I'd sorted the paint and was staring at the blank canvas again. Glancing briefly toward him, I pursed my lips and returned my gaze to the empty space.

"I haven't painted for nearly eight years."

James sat down beside me and ran his fingers over the row of brushes. "Why is that?"

"I'd been married a year; things were going well, I thought. We'd even talked about starting a family." It was hard to think about, much less say. "Greg had decided that I should quit volunteering at Holman Academy. He thought it was a waste of time. So, I did it. I mean, he was my husband and it was my duty as his wife to see that he was happy, right?" I shrugged, as I didn't expect him to answer. "But I painted at home and he seemed okay with it. We had a party; and there was this couple there. Elegant and sophisticated, to be honest they were so striking and seemed so in love that I could hardly believe it when I'd heard they were divorcing."

I glanced his way once but he didn't respond. "The man made a few comments in passing about a painting on the wall in the dining room. Greg pretended to like hearing that my work was beautiful and that I was so talented."

"But he wasn't happy."

"Not at all." A shudder slid down my back and I swallowed hard. "After all the guests were gone, he turned on me like a rabid animal. I'd upstaged him in front of important people, he said. One minute he was screaming at me for being so selfish and the next thing I knew he was hitting me."

"God."

I jerked. "I'm sorry. You don't want to hear this."

He grabbed my arm when I started to stand. "No, tell me the rest."

I relaxed on the floor and carefully started picking up the brushes. "He was furious with me for days and I retreated to my little studio. It was all I had that made me feel safe, so I tried to ignore what had happened and tried to do everything I could to make him happy when I had to be in the same room with him."

"But it wasn't enough."

"No, a week after that party he took every single painting in the house that was mine and all the work in my studio . . . and he burned it. He made me watch while he ripped them apart and tossed them on the fire in his office."

"And you haven't painted since."

"I couldn't bring myself to give him more ammunition against me. He did more to me in destroying those paintings than he ever had with his fist and he knew it. When there was nothing left, he just stared at me and smiled."

"What did you do?"

"The next day while he was gone to work I emptied out the studio. I threw away everything and I pretended that none of it mattered any more."

"It was me." James sighed. "The one and only fucking time I see the two of you and I cause . . ."

"NO." I put the brushes aside and grabbed one of his hands. "It was him and if it hadn't been the paintings it would have been something else. Greg Carlson is not a normal man and he never was."

He nodded and turned my hand over in his. I jerked a little as his fingers brushed over my palm gently. "I've been surrounded by artists all of my life. My mother's cause became mine when she became ill and it's something that my father didn't understand."

"Maybe one day he will."

James shook his head. "No. I doubt it. He understands tangible things and taught me to stand up and pay attention to my responsibilities. He's just profoundly disappointed that I paid attention to my mother's dreams for me instead of his."

"You went to law school for him."

"I went to law school to keep my son." He released my hand and stood. A few steps away from me, he cleared his throat. "I grew up without wanting for a damn thing. My parents loved me, didn't leave me to servants to be raised, and genuinely wanted me. When Cecilia ended up pregnant, we were both barely sixteen. My father agreed to the marriage and that we could keep the child as long as I went to college and then law school."

"You made the best choice you could."

He nodded. "Yeah. Her parents were no more thrilled with the situation than mine were. However, at the end of it we all made the best of the situation. I wouldn't trade Ryan for anything in the world and I've always tried to teach by example."

"So you left your father's law firm and took over the foundation."

"Yes."

"And the divorce?"

"Most of the time I think Ryan understands that his mother and I just stopped wanting to be together. As far as I know, he doesn't know she was unfaithful."

"He's a grown-up."

"Yes, twenty going on thirty. But that still doesn't give him access to my private life." He walked to stand in front of the canvas. "So what are you going to do with this?

"I don't know yet." I stood and stretched. "I just had the urge to paint so I bought the supplies and built a frame."

"You built it yourself?"

I laughed at his raised eyebrow. "Well, yes, it's part of the process for me." Watching him move around my space suddenly wasn't so bad. "You know most men who spend this much time in my studio are naked by now." His stunned expression was amusing and the tinge of red that swept across his cheeks endearing. "Not that I'm asking you to take your clothes off."

"No, I didn't think so." He cleared his throat and shoved his hands into his pockets. "I've never wanted to push you."

"I know." I gathered up the paint and started to put it away. "The fact is that you think I'm wasting my life out here."

"I do not."

His snappy tone of voice almost made me laugh. "You assume that I've made myself a hermit out of some need to protect myself. The fact is, James, I like being alone and I like being out here. Some women need a man and a ton of social obligations to feel worthy of life. I don't."

"I don't think you are a hermit." He waved his hand around the barn. "I do think you hide out here."

"Some people are just happier this way." I pressed my lips together to keep from saying more.

"Yeah, but you aren't one of them. I saw you before your marriage, Lisa. You ate life and you lived hard. Your art was full of joy and spoke of a love of the world."

"And now?"

"Your work is violent and so edgy that it cuts at the people who are fortunate enough to see it. The fact is you are an amazingly gifted artist and no matter what medium you work in or what emotion you feed, that talent shines through and demands to be recognized."

"Thank you." I picked up the box and shoved it onto a shelf with shaking hands. "I hope that people are moved by the work that I do; it means that my time has been well spent." I rubbed my damp palms on my shorts and looked at him. "I'm starving. Would you like a sandwich?"

"You've never invited me into your house before."

"You'd better haul ass before I change my mind." It was a bad idea to have the man in my house. I knew it and he probably knew it, too.

So, a few minutes later when he was at my kitchen table while I slapped peanut butter on bread I was totally at a loss as to what I was going to do with him. There are very few men in my life, and the ones that I allow aren't romantic entanglements.

"Don't be so serious."

I glanced toward him and tried to smile. "It is not every day that I have a man in my kitchen."

The wood creaked as he left the chair. I refocused my attention on the sandwich. I felt the heat of his body before he touched me. The tips of his fingers moved across my shoulders and then down my arms. So gentle, it was almost as if it didn't happen. I sucked in my breath and closed my eyes.

"Am I making you nervous?"

"No," I whispered and the bit down on my bottom lip. "I'm not afraid of you."

Warm air lingered over my neck and then the softest kiss I've ever known brushed against my shoulder. I forced myself to relax against him as he moved closer. "Good."

I put down the knife and cleared my throat. "James."

"Now, that's nice."

A small laugh slipped past my lips. "I think you are playing with me."

"I think I've been pretty consistent with you. This isn't a game for me." Hands, firm and reassuring, slid to my hips and across my stomach. I felt him take a deep breath as he pulled me flush against his chest. "I can't even pretend that I don't want you."

I let my head fall back against his shoulder in what could only be called surrender as he pressed his cock firmly against my ass. "This isn't good."

"I think it could be so good."

His body was hard and enticing against mine. Fingertips grazed the undersides of my breasts and I arched slightly in his arms as moisture rushed between my legs. "We're bad for each other."

Teeth grazed the skin of my neck. "Tell me no."

Yeah, that was going to happen. He cupped my breasts and rubbed his thumbs over my nipples. The thin material of my T-shirt offered little resistance against his rough and knowing fingers. James turned me carefully in his arms and covered my mouth with his own. He thrust his tongue between my lips and all I could do was cling to him.

A shudder ran down my back as he pressed me against the counter. I wanted him. I'd always wanted him. Pulling my mouth from his, I took a deep breath. "I thought you were hungry."

"Oh, I am."

I blushed and pushed at his chest halfheartedly. "Don't. I'm not one of those empty-headed socialites you date."

"No, you're not," he murmured and placed a light kiss on my forehead. "And there haven't been that many empty-headed socialites."

"Whatever."

"I thought you didn't care." He lifted my chin so he could meet my gaze. "I won't hurt you."

"On purpose."

"God, you are hard on a man." James pressed a soft kiss against the side of my neck and ran his hands down my back to cup my ass.

I moaned softly as he lifted me up off the floor. Wrapping my arms and legs around him, I closed my eyes and let myself go. He pressed me against the counter, his cock hard against me, and covered my mouth with his. I shuddered against him as he thrust his tongue between my lips. Heat rushed over my body in a heady wave of awareness and arousal.

This was what I'd spent more than a year fighting, and as his mouth left mine, drifted across the line of my jaw, and down my neck, I couldn't help but call myself ten kinds of a fool. "Please don't let me regret this later."

Gentle fingers pushed my hair back from my face and our eyes connected. "There won't be any room for regrets."

He released me carefully and let me stand on my own feet. I'd never seen him look more intent or focused. It should have scared the hell out of me, but it didn't.

"My bedroom is down the hall."

"Not upstairs?" he asked, amusement slipping into his voice.

"No." I brushed my mouth against his. "Why?"

"The Armani? You always seem to be upstairs in that window with your paint gun."

I laughed and looped my arms around his neck. "Shut up about that suit and be a man about it."

I'm not sure if I meant to challenge him; but the way his eyes darkened was exciting as hell. He grabbed me with quick, firm hands and tossed me over his shoulder. I should've been outraged, but all I could do was laugh.

Less than a minute later, he dropped me on the bed and looked me over with a calculating gaze. "I'm not an easy man to deal with."

I sat up and pulled my T-shirt over my head. "Who wants easy?"

He pulled his shirt from his pants and shook his head. "You are in so much trouble, lady."

I ran my fingers over my nipples, flushing slightly at the way his gaze dropped to my breasts. To say that I was adept at self-pleasure would have been an understatement. The habit of touching myself, seeking my own arousal, was so ingrained that it was embarrassing. I dropped my hands and watched him undress.

James Brooks had a casual grace about him that belied the predatory and dangerous edge that had always been so obvious about him. My gaze dropped to his cock. Thick and long, I couldn't wait to have him inside me.

I pushed my shorts and panties down and scooted out of them. This had been coming for a long time and now that I was finally about to have the man . . . the one man I'd been determined to never have . . . I didn't want a damn thing in his way.

He ran his hands over my legs and spread them. I sucked in a deep breath as he bent and kissed the inside of my thigh. Curling my fingers into the quilt beneath me, I laid back and resisted the urge to move. Fingers drifted gently over my exposed sex and spread my labia. Cool air on my clit a scant few seconds before his tongue.

James pressed one large hand against my stomach to keep me still and pushed the tip of his tongue into me. My insides clenched against the invasion and I spread my legs farther apart and tried to lift my hips against his questing mouth.

"Yes. Yes." But the shallow penetration wasn't nearly enough to sate the ache that was building.

He moved upward suddenly, his smooth, muscled body moving over me in a fluid movement that brought me back into the moment in an instant. He slipped his hands into mine and lifted my arms above my head. Pressing them against the mattress, he rocked against me. His cock slid between my slick labia with delicious friction. Stark pleasure slid over my body, reminding me of a sensual past I'd tried so hard to forget.

"You made me wait so long for you."

I laughed softly and relaxed beneath him. "Do you think I'm going to change my mind?"

"Yes."

I rubbed my feet along the sides of his legs and shook my head. "Not going to happen."

He brushed his lips over mine and I shuddered against the invasion of his tongue. He tasted like me and the knowledge was intoxicating. James Brooks in my bed, his mouth on mine, was so fine. His hands tightened on my wrists as he lifted his head.

"I want you every way possible."

"You can have me," I whispered. "Any way you want."

He rubbed his lips against mine in a soft kiss, released my hands, and sighed. "You are so sexy."

"And mean." I nibbled at his bottom lip.

"Yeah, really mean." He chuckled.

Gasping, I moved underneath him and shuddered when the head of his cock brushed against my clit. I rubbed my legs against his and then wrapped them around his waist. Who knew he would be so gentle with a woman? His mouth, soft but persistent, drifted over mine in exploring kisses that left me wanting to beg him for more.

"Are you trying to drive me insane?"

"And if I am?" he asked softly and then he moved, pressing the tip of his cock into me.

Gasping softly, I arched against the intrusion and closed my eyes. "Stop teasing and fuck me."

He thrust into me in one hard stroke. In that full, sharp instant, everything clicked into place. I shuddered beneath him and clung with desperate hands as he started to move. Pleasure rolled over me in waves with each penetrating stroke; it was amazing and thoroughly intoxicating.

"Like this?" he asked and then ground his hips against mine briefly, before he started to thrust again.

"Yes." I dropped my feet to the bed and lifted up against him. "Yes, James."

He shuddered against me and buried his face in the side of my neck. The vulnerability of the moment was unnerving. I wrapped my arms around him and rocked against the repeated push of his thick cock inside me.

"Harder." I dug my fingers into his shoulder blades and

arched against him. James met my demand in one powerful thrust and I gasped as orgasm rushed against my clit. "Yes."

He jerked against me as he came and moaned softly against my neck. "Damn."

I ran my hands down his back as he rocked his body gently against mine. "One of us is in trouble."

"I think it's me." He pressed a soft kiss against the side of my neck and carefully pulled away. With soft, nearly inaudible groan, he rolled to his back beside me on the bed and rubbed his face. "I forgot the condom."

"Oops." I laughed softly.

"Not funny, woman. I haven't forgotten a condom since I was sixteen. Trust me; I learned that lesson very well." He rubbed his face briskly, his whole body tense.

I bet he had. Being a teenage father probably hadn't been a picnic, no matter how much money both he and the girl had come from. "I've got birth control covered and I'm clean."

"So am I. But still, I apologize." He rolled to his side and ran his finger down the middle of my body. "I've spent years drilling into my son how important it is to protect his partners and I lose my head in a matter of seconds with you. I just honestly didn't expect to ever get this far."

"Protection is a two-way street, Brooks. I forgot, too."

I sucked in a deep breath as his hand slid between my legs and covered my pussy. He pressed two fingers between my labia and rubbed my clit with a lazy rhythm that took my breath in an instant. I closed my eyes and lifted my hips against his hand.

"Look at me, Lisa."

Forcing my eyes open, I met his gaze and shuddered with pleasure as the pace of his fingers increased. I searched his face for some sign of his intent. Those smooth, classically Roman features revealed nothing. His dark blue eyes were lit with desire and seriousness.

"What do you want from me?"

"Everything." He rubbed his mouth over mine in a soft kiss. Lifting his head, he continued to rub my clit in a slow sensuous circle. "I want to be inside you every day."

*Inside me every day.* How great did that sound? "You're crazy."

I bit down on my lip as the pleasure of his fingers on my clit intensified. I was fast approaching another orgasm, and the way it was building, I knew it was going to hurt in all the right ways. "I don't even think you like me."

"You don't want me to like you." He lowered his head and sucked one hardened nipple into his mouth. His tongue flicked over it repeatedly, matching the rhythm of his fingers in such a way that all I could do was lay there and drown in it.

God, it was so true. No part of me wanted this amazingly, sexy man to like me because it would lead to all kinds of crap that I didn't know how to deal with. He lifted his head and I touched his smooth jaw.

"What made you shave your beard?" He'd worn it for years and the difference was intriguing.

"I needed a change."

"Change is a very scary thing." I'd spent the last few years endeavoring to change as little as possible. My life was full of routines and expectations that I demanded be met by everyone around me.

"Does this change between us scare you?" he asked softly, and then slid two blunt fingers into my clenching pussy. "Be honest."

My eyes widened and I lifted my hips up off the bed. "Yes."

"You make me want things that I never thought I'd want again."

I closed my eyes and shuddered at the sensual play of his fingers and words. The situation was going to be impossible to control. This wasn't some stranger in a hotel room that I never had to see again and I was in way over my head.

"Open those pretty eyes, lady."

I laughed softly and forced myself to relax under the pleasure of his fingers as I met his gaze. "I don't know what to do about you."

"Right now or tomorrow?"

"Right now for a start." I brushed a lock of hair from his forehead and bit down on my lips as the rhythm of his fingers increased. My G-spot pulsed with each thrust of his fingers. Heat rushed over my body in a quick wave of sensation as another orgasm started to build. "I can't take much more."

With exaggerated slowness, he pulled his hand free and slid over me, using one leg to push mine apart. "You're going to take all I have to give."

I wanted to deny it, wanted to deny him, but as he thrust his cock into me, I couldn't do anything but nod and moan softly. He pinned my arms over my head with one hand and urged my legs around his waist with the other.

His obvious need to control my body and my pleasure, his dominance didn't even make me pause. I knew this about him. Almost anyone who spent any time with him would even anticipate it. Arching under him, I surrendered to his will and then climaxed so hard my vision darkened briefly.

Hands tightened on my wrists and his body strained against mine. "Stay with me."

"James." I let my legs drop to the mattress and I started to meet each thrust of his body with an upward lift of my hips.

The pleasure of his penetrating cock ebbed over me and I rocked helplessly against him as another orgasm rose to the surface. I pulled at my hands, panic edged in around me, and when I thought I would beg for release his mouth covered mine. My world exploded in a burst of emotional and physical pleasure.

# 5

---

I pulled my legs up into my favorite recliner and curled both hands around the coffee cup I held as if my life depended on it. James Brooks was sprawled, bare-assed, on my bed asleep and I was hiding in my barn staring at a big empty canvas. Why I had made something so big was just beyond me.

The click of the door told me I was no longer alone. I glanced over my shoulder and saw him standing there, barefoot and clad in a pair of jeans. The man would consume my whole life if I allowed it. I wasn't above wondering if it was already too late.

"Not working?"

I shook my head and set aside my coffee. "No. I'm still thinking about it."

He walked to the empty model platform, sat down, crossed his legs at the ankle, and leaned back on his hands. "I'd offer to model for you, but you've already proven that you don't need a model to capture me."

It would have sounded arrogant if it wasn't true. I assessed him. "I didn't realize you noticed."

"I didn't realize you thought I was an idiot." He looked around the studio. "The only reason it stayed on the floor is that I was rather flattered."

Laughing, I stood from the chair and walked to him. "Were you?"

"Yeah, but I bought it."

"You didn't tell me that the other night."

"Buying myself cast in bronze was actually rather weird. It took me a while to even get my head around it, but I couldn't imagine it being on display in someone's house."

"Me either. I don't even know why I put it in the collection." I moved to him, slid astride his lap, and pushed him back on the cushions. "You're not angry?"

"No."

"I don't think you're an idiot. It isn't often that I use someone in art without permission; I don't even know why I did it."

"Don't you?" He sat up and pulled me close. "It was what made me think I had a chance."

"A chance?" I asked softly as I wrapped my arms around his neck. "A chance at what?"

"At a relationship with you." James slid his hands under my ass and pulled me tight to him. "Up until that point, I wasn't sure if you were really attracted to me."

I ran my fingers through his hair and sighed. "It's probably a bad idea for us to get involved. I'm not the kind of woman you need in your life."

"Back to that, are we?" He pressed his lips against my throat and tightened his hold. "And exactly what kind of woman do you think I need?"

I let my head fall back to give him better access and closed my eyes. "Graceful under pressure, demure . . ."

He laughed aloud. "Well, demure you'll never be."

"Fuck you." I yanked on his hair gently.

"What makes you think I want some socialite in my life?"

"You married the epitome of socialite."

"Cecilia is a graceful and demure woman. She is the perfect hostess and near the end of our marriage we were both so damn bored that we could barely stand to look at each other." He stood up and with careful hands laid me out on the platform. "But I'd rather talk about you."

"Okay." I pressed my feet against the cushioned surface and spread my legs. The thin T-shirt and brief cotton shorts I was wearing weren't going to be much of a barrier for him. "So . . . let's discuss me."

"You're beautiful."

"I'm a hermit." I countered.

"You like your privacy and I appreciate that about you."

"People think I'm crazy."

"So?" He laughed as he ran his hands down my legs to snag my shorts. "In polite society, people with the kind of money you have are considered eccentric."

"Some people call me a porn artist."

"*Those* people can kiss my ass." He tossed the shorts over his shoulder. "Take off the shirt."

I pulled my T-shirt over my head and tossed it away. "Bossy."

He ran his hand, palm down, between my breasts all the way down to the apex of my thighs. "You are an amazingly gifted artist."

"Very true."

"With a healthy ego."

True, in some respects. I rubbed my legs together as his fingers ran down them. He stood and shed his jeans.

"You give your time to charity."

I nodded, but really, at that point he could have said I committed serial murder in my spare time and I would have probably agreed. He wrapped one hand around his cock as he came back to me.

I spread my legs. "I'm done discussing my merits. Stop teasing me."

"Are you always so demanding?" he asked as he moved over me. His mouth lingered over mine. "I can't believe I even bothered to ask that question."

I laughed. "Yeah, it was a little silly."

He let his weight rest on me as his lips brushed against mine. His tongue slipped inside and brushed mine and my whole body responded. When his mouth left mine, he moved downward and latched on to one hard nipple. I curled one hand into his hair and twisted in want beneath him.

James slid down further and spread my legs roughly. I gasped as his mouth covered my pussy and groaned when he rubbed his tongue over my throbbing clit. Two fingers pushed into my clenching cunt and I fought back against the almost instant need to come.

"Fuck me, James."

He lifted his head, his eyes dark with some emotion I couldn't identify. "Get on your knees."

I met his demand, my body shaking with anticipation. One large hand pressed against the small of my back and I tilted my hips in response. A shiver of need slid down my back as he pressed the head of his cock against my opening. His fingers dug into my hips as he pushed into me. Rocking back and forth against him, I closed my eyes as he started to greet each backward motion with a hard skin-slapping thrust.

The urge to confess a darker need surfaced; but I couldn't. I curled my hands into fists and let my forehead rest on the cushion as I came; my whole body was rigid with pleasure and when he came warmth drenched my insides in one quick burst of sensation.

Careful, even gentle, hands pulled me close and we both laid down on our sides, still connected in the most intimate way possible. James wrapped one arm around me and pulled me tight to his chest.

"We could use a shower."

He laughed and pressed a kiss against my shoulder blade. "Agreed."

"There's one in that stall." I waved to it but I knew I wasn't going to be moving any time soon.

"I should get started." He ran his hand down my hip to my leg. "I have a dinner party in the city tonight."

"Gotta go pick up your date." I laughed when he stiffened. "I'm not stupid, James, these events are planned months in advance and people expect you to show up with a woman on your arm."

"I was actually thinking about letting Helene off the hook and asking you to come with me."

I wrinkled my nose. "You make your admin assistant date you?"

"Of course not. It's an event for the foundation and she volunteered to attend with me because Cecilia, my normal partner on such occasions, left this morning for a trip to New York."

"Do people stare at the two of you like you've got two heads when you show up together?"

"No. Most of our friends understand that our marriage was a good one and that our divorce, while painful, was necessary. I actually consider her a good friend at this point."

He moved against me, pressing his cock against my G-spot in the most delicious way, and I sucked in a breath. "How do you do that?"

James laughed. "Do what?"

"Find just the right spot." I shuddered when he moved again. "I pay attention, and this may be an overshare, but my ex-wife and I left little unexplored sexually in the twenty years we were married."

"So, I should send her flowers." I buried my face in the cushion and groaned when he did it again. "Lots and lots of flowers."

"Say you'll come with me."

"Oh, I'm going to come." I bit down on my lip to keep from laughing. "But I'm not going to a dinner party."

James pushed me gently onto my stomach as we rolled and used his body to spread my legs further open for him. Pressed between his body and the cushion, I could do nothing but curl my fingers into the fabric and grit my teeth as he started to move. Each excruciating slow brush of his cock against my G-spot sent a cutting, almost painful, surge of pleasure over my clit.

"Come with me, Lisa." He placed soft kisses across my shoulder, his teeth grazing the skin slightly. "A few hours of smiling at people you don't even know or have to remember and I promise you I'll make it worth your while."

"You know I hate . . ." I closed my eyes as he started to move just a little bit faster. "James, please!"

"Please what?" he demanded, his breath brushed against my neck. "Please you? Is that what you want?"

"Yes. Yes."

His teeth clenched briefly on my shoulder and I shuddered in response. James shoved one hand under us both and pushed two fingers between my labia. The double stimulation was all that I needed; I came hard and collapsed beneath him as he thrust once more and groaned my name.

The man had made me stupid. I leaned against the doorway of the kitchen and watched the woman he'd hired to cater the dinner with a critical eye. Why I felt responsible for this aspect of the event was absolutely beyond me. She was doing a good job and the menu had been planned for weeks. So, I'd spent the last hour draped in a silk dress, holding a glass of white wine, and watching her handle James's fine China.

A warm hand slid up my back and a pair of lips brushed across my bare shoulder. "Is Stephanie irritating you?"

I shrugged. "I haven't played hostess in a while. I'm not sure what I should be doing."

He laughed softly and slid one arm around my waist to lead me away from the doorway. "Be beautiful, smile at my guests, and relax."

"Funny how you didn't mention that this was your party when you dragged me out of my house." I glanced to my left as we passed the dinning room. Place settings for twenty . . . the whole thing was insane.

"Yeah, well, I was concentrating on getting you to say yes." He traced the line of my spine upward and took a deep breath. "This is a great dress, by the way."

"One of the many things that Mercy made me purchase the last time I went to New York with her and Jane." I wrinkled my nose at the thought. I hated shopping, but the two of them were practically athletes at it. "Shoes, too."

His gaze dropped to the strappy red sandals that I had tortured my feet into. "If I asked you to keep them on later . . . would you think I was a freak?"

"Yes." I laughed. "But I'll do it anyway." I stiffened at the sound of the doorbell. "And the torture begins."

"Money for the foundation," James murmured. "Smile and be mysterious. People love that about you."

People loved that I sculpted near-porn that they could buy and put in their homes to shock their friends and loved ones. I was also nothing like them. As an artist, that served to make me different and even somewhat attractive. In the past, when I'd attempted to blend in with them it had made life difficult as hell.

Expensive cologne, suits, and dresses whose cost could feed the average family for a month streamed through the door. I swallowed back years of distrust and—yes—disdain and smiled. I was in his penthouse against my better judgment, but I was going to do my best to be a lady. After all, I'd promised the man I would be.

\* \* \*

Crab appetizers, an hour of chitchat, and a lobster dinner later, I was seriously pissed at myself for promising to be a lady. Rufus Fitzgerald, Jr., was the direct cause. The man was a living, breathing poster boy for birth control. Six foot, two hundred pounds, blond hair, and blue eyes. The man looked like he'd been carved out of Swiss cheese. I'd known him for years and I'd hated him for about two seconds longer than I'd known him.

"Divorce looks good on you, Lisa." He flashed big white teeth at me.

My eyes actually burned under the effort of not rolling them. I focused on the contents of my nearly empty wine glass and nearly moaned with relief when an already familiar hand slid into place on my hip.

"Lisa is beautiful no matter her circumstances." James pulled me closer. "Your wife is looking for you, Fitzgerald."

I watched him swish away. "I don't think he's human. He's like a pod person, I swear."

James laughed softly and tugged me toward a group of people. "Do you know Keith and Marcia Woods?"

Of course I did. I smiled. He was new money and she was his trophy wife. All of that aside, they were people who had always been nice to me and they had a reputation for charity work.

"Lisa." Marcia wiggled her fingers.

*Christ.* How on Earth could have I forgotten that the woman was a hugger? I coughed a little at the impact of 110 pounds of barely covered silicone-filled flesh. "Working out, Marcia?"

She laughed. "Once a week with Claude and four times a week with Daphne." Looping an arm around mine, Marcia leaned in. Her scarlet red hair fell all over me. "I've been taking stripping."

I closed my eyes briefly at the thought of Marcia astride a pole. "I see."

"Great for an aerobic workout."

"I just bet." Once glance at James told me he was trying to get a mental picture out of his head as well. "You know, Marcia, I'm teaching a live model class at the academy next week. Would you like to help out?"

"Help out?" She wiggled eyebrows.

I laughed. "Well, it's for a junior high class, so there will be no nudity. Just your pretty face."

"I'd love to."

James led me away a few minutes later, pressing a kiss against my jaw. "Keith is probably already writing a check."

"I'll make sure that my instructional copy is something she can take with her."

"Who said you wouldn't be good at this?"

Who, indeed? It was different, working this party with James. I felt like we had a common goal and that made us a team . . . not something I'd had with Greg. I knew how much the money would mean to the students at the academy, how much that money had meant to me. Mine was an example of the sort of future that an education and a chance could create.

"James, Lisa, I was just trying to explain to Marcus here how the Holman Foundation works."

I swallowed hard. Cassidy Dawson. I knew her from the society papers. She'd been on James's arm several times during the last two years, but I'd never really paid much attention to her before now. The woman was stunning and graceful. Jet-black hair fell down her back, and her jewel-green eyes sparkled with good humor.

James held out his hand. "James Brooks."

"Marcus Cain."

Land developer, lots of money. He also owned several of my pieces. "Lisa Millhouse."

Marcus took the hand I offered after he released James's and inclined his head. "Ms. Millhouse, I'm honored to meet you. I've purchased several of your pieces, though never in person."

His personal buyer had a standing invitation to every private show in Boston and he did very well to match his employer's taste with purchases. I nodded. "Yes, I know. I was sorry to tell you 'no' last year when you tried to commission a piece. Due to my schedule at the academy and my own projects, I haven't taken a commissioned piece in nearly two years."

"It was no problem. I found another artist, though they hardly replaced you." His mouth tightened briefly but he didn't appear to be entirely put out. "Cassidy was trying to make me part with my money."

"Giving someone else hope is the best thing you can do with your money. The scholarship drive that is currently under way for the academy is an excellent way to buy into everyone's future."

"True. Yet, she couldn't name a single nationally renowned artist to come out of the academy that started on a scholarship."

Most couldn't. Greg had certainly taken great pains to keep my poor past a secret and, after I'd divorced him, I'd never corrected anyone when they assumed I grew up in some nice middle-class home. "You're looking at one."

James pulled me in close. "Lisa is just one of the many success stories to come out of the Holman Foundation. Talent and the drive to create beauty know no economic boundaries, Mr. Cain."

"Call me Marcus." He looked at me with a critical eye. "How old were you when you came to the academy?"

"Fifteen, and obviously it gave me opportunities that I would have never had otherwise."

# 6

"Marcus Cain cut the foundation a check for a half-million dollars."

I leaned against the counter and grinned. "A little self-sacrifice on my part went a long way."

"Yes, it did." He dropped his suit jacket on the back of a kitchen chair and came to me. "But you didn't have to tell him a damn thing."

"I know." I put the glass down. "Did it embarrass you?"

He put his hands on either side of me, effectively caging me between the counter and his body. "Not at all. You worked this party like a pro, but I felt like you were miserable. I'm sorry I asked you to do it."

"It wasn't so bad." I touched his face with the tips of my fingers and then chuckled. "I do hope that Marcia Woods wears something that covers what God and her plastic surgeon gave her for that art class."

"You can drape her in something if she doesn't. She can pretend she's in Greece." He leaned in and kissed my mouth. "Thank you."

"Everyone seemed to have a good time."

"And you?"

"It wasn't as bad as I thought it would be."

"Is this the part of my life that made you push me away for nearly two years?" His hands moved over my shoulders and down my back to the tiny zipper that started just short of the small of my back.

"Part of it." I let my head fall back as his lips made a soft, taunting trail down my neck.

"The other part?" He asked softly, the zipper slid down easily under his hands and the dress loosened. "Have I told you how much I love this sexy red dress?"

I laughed. "You did mention liking it."

"The other part?"

The dress slid downward and I shivered slightly as it brushed against the back of my legs to pool at my feet. "My life is complicated."

"So."

"You are like a whole new level of complicated."

"I'm a simple man."

I laughed and then gasped when he ran his hands down my side and then went down on his knees. "Yeah, simple. The everyday man."

He ran his fingers over the lace of my panties. I'd put on the ridiculous lace boy-shorts panties for him and as I watched him lean in and place a soft kiss on my belly I figured he was worth the effort and the discomfort. Another disconcerting thought. A day ago I wouldn't have given a thought to exciting James Brooks. He dipped his tongue into my belly button and my knees weakened.

His hands tightened on my hips and he pressed me against the counter. Thumbs rubbed gently over my skin, pushing at the lace. James sat back on his heels and looked me over, his gaze lingering over my bare breasts before traveling downward.

"So tempting." His hands slid down my legs as he sighed. "Did you wear this bit of lace for me?"

"I put it all on for you." I bit down on my bottom lip as his hands moved back up. My nipples tightened and I curled my fingers against the edge of the counter to keep from touching them.

"You are a lovely contradiction." He stood and his hands moved upward leisurely until he could cup both breasts.

I arched against his hands and moaned softly when his thumbs scraped over the flesh of my nipples. When had I gotten so needy for the touch of another person? His mouth covered mine as he pulled me into his arms. I shook a little as my breasts pressed against his chest.

He caressed my back gently and brushed his lips across mine. "I want to take you to bed."

"What's stopping you?"

"Just the feeling that you think that sex is all I want in all of this."

Actually, it was far from what I thought. I was pretty sure the man meant to take over my life. "Don't you want to know what I want out all of this?"

He met my gaze without hesitation. "More than anything."

I barely knew. "I'm not sure. Two days ago I wanted to shoot you with my paint gun and now all I want to do is wrap myself around you." I ran my fingers through his hair and sighed. "I will say that I know you are holding back on me."

"Holding back?"

"Sexually." I raised one eyebrow when he stiffened. "I'm not afraid of you, James and I'm not going to fall to pieces if you get a little rough with me."

"You think I like it rough?"

"The short answer is yes." I grinned when he flushed. "How long have we known each other?"

"More than a few years, if you count all of that time we spent ignoring each other." He pulled me closer; his hands slid downward to cup my ass.

"Then what makes you think that I don't know you?" We both jerked at the sound of a slamming door.

"Hey, Dad!"

James turned and put himself between the kitchen door and me just as it swung open. "Ryan, you know better than to just show up here . . ."

I almost laughed. Burying my face against his back was my only haven. I could hardly believe I'd been caught practically naked in a kitchen and it wasn't even my own kitchen. I peeked around James to get a look at his one and only child. Ryan was a near replica of his father, and at twenty, he still had an air of innocence.

"Holy shit, Dad." Ryan did a complete about-face and threw up his hands. "Is that Lisa?"

"Shut up, Ryan."

I picked up my dress and pulled it on, both amused and suddenly disappointed. Ryan's abrupt appearance had surely put a damper on the rest of our evening. James turned around and arranged my dress carefully, then turned me and zipped me up.

"First off, young man, when you walk in on something like this the decent thing to do is *leave* the room . . . not stand there in the doorway and inquire as to the woman's identity."

"I didn't realize that Emily Post covered catching one's father with a fine half-naked woman in the kitchen."

I burst out laughing. "Thanks, Ryan."

"Do not encourage him."

"She is *fine*."

James' eyes darkened and I rose up on my toes and kissed his mouth very softly. "Go wait in my office, Son."

Ryan sighed and made a quick exit.

"Is that like being sent to the principal's office?"
James laughed and pulled me close. "I apologize; I didn't realize I'd left the door unlocked."

"I make you lose your head."

"Yes, you do." He traced my jaw with steady fingers. "Don't leave."

"Not a chance. I was thinking about taking a swim in your tub."

I winced at the slamming of his office door as I slid into the hot bath he'd taken the time to draw me. It was perfect except that I figured that Ryan was getting his head handed to him for invading his father's privacy.

What did I want from James Brooks? I was way too old to be thinking about marriage and children. I'd set aside those dreams a long time ago and I doubted seriously he was in the game for anything like that. He'd already gone that route, and had a grown smart-ass son to show for it.

I flipped on the switch above my head that turned on the jets in the tub and sunk down deeper. So, if I had no sweet white-picket-fence dreams to pin my hopes on, just what did I want? The last three years had been no picnic, but I'd learned that I was capable of living on my own and providing for myself.

Though it was a long time coming, I'd proven to myself that I did not need a man to survive. Life is a tricky thing, because on the night that I left Greg Carlson survival had been the only thing on my mind.

The bathroom door opened and James entered with two glasses of wine. He sat down on the edge of the tub and handed one to me. "Sorry about that."

"No problem." I sipped from the glass and rubbed my legs together. Just the sight of the man was getting me worked up. He'd removed his tie and his shirt was open, just a few buttons so it was more of a tease than anything else. "Was there a problem?"

"Beyond the fact that he has no manners?" James trailed his fingers in the steaming waters. "The woman he's dating is pressuring him for something more serious and he's a little freaked out about it."

"Ah, commitment is a dirty word."

"It should be for a man his age," James muttered drily. "She's practically thirty and I see her mind working the numbers."

"You think she's after money?"

"Ryan has a sizable trust fund and has inherited money from both sides of the family. We taught him to be smart with his money, but things happen." He leaned back on one hand and took a drink of his wine. "Why don't you like red wine?"

I glanced down at the contents of my wineglass; he had served white wine exclusively at the event. "It reminds me of my ex-husband. Greg bought the stuff by the case. We had it at most meals and he insisted I drink even when I didn't want it or made it clear I didn't care for it. In fact, he said that in hating red wine I was showing the world exactly how backward and country I truly was." I met his gaze and wasn't surprised at the anger on his face. "It's one of a hundred little hateful things he said to me and one of many that stuck."

He took another drink of his wine and seemed to consider his words carefully. When he finally did speak, his words were cool. "I could ruin him."

"Pardon me?"

"I have the money and resources to make his life absolute hell. Within a few weeks, I could put his entire family on the bottom rung of Boston society."

It's wrong to get all warm and fuzzy over such an evil idea, but I couldn't help but grin. "What a romantic you are."

"I'm serious."

"I know you are." I put my glass down and sat up in the tub so that I could touch his arm. "It's been a long time since I've thought about getting revenge against Greg Carlson."

"It's been a long time since I've thought of anything else," James admitted softly. "I'd like to take the man apart in more than one way."

"I could say he's not worth your time."

"I know he's not," James plucked up my glass and stood. "So, where were we before Ryan came along?"

I inclined my head. "What did you tell him about the woman?"

"I'm meeting him for lunch tomorrow. That conversation requires a great deal more attention that I was inclined to give tonight." He put the glasses down on a counter across from the tub. "You were saying that I was holding back on you."

"Yeah." I lifted my leg out of the water and used my big toe to trace the edge of the tub. "I guess restrained would be a better term."

"I outweigh you by seventy-five pounds."

"You sure do." I looked him over and wet my bottom lip. "You like to hold me down when we fuck. Would you like to tie me up?"

He raised one eyebrow and focused on my foot as it slid back into the water. "I don't have to tie you down to control you."

I laughed softly, amused both by the truth of it and his arrogance. The need to cater to his sexual desires had come out of nowhere but I wasn't unnerved by it. In fact, if anything it made it all easier. He'd made me a liar, because obviously I did trust him. I trusted him with all that I was.

James moved away from the counter, picking up a towel as he came to me. "Are you ready?"

"Ready?"

"For more." He flipped off the jets and offered me a hand.

I took it and stood up from the tub. He wrapped the large towel around and swept me up into his arms. "You're getting wet."

He laughed. "Not worried."

I pressed a kiss against his neck and wrapped one arm around his shoulders as he walked down the hall to the bedroom. The bed was huge. An adult playground elevated on a platform, it was certainly the centerpiece of the room.

He stepped up onto the platform, put one knee on the bed, and laid me out. I ran one hand up his thigh; the smooth material of his slacks gave me little purchase. James spread the towel out beneath me as he slid astride my hips.

Large hands slid up my rib cage and over my breasts. He used his thumb to tease my nipples until they were tight and hard.

"Tell me you're ready for more."

I arched under him, rubbing my legs together as wetness dampened my thighs. "Yes. Whatever you want."

He moved then, his hands resting on either side of my head as he lowered and took my mouth in a hard kiss. I let my hands slide down his chest to the buckle of his belt. Unfastening it took a few frustrating seconds. As I jerked the belt free from his pants, he lifted his head and met my gaze.

I tossed the belt aside and ran one finger down the cover of his zipper. His cock was hard, tenting the material in such a tempting way that I grabbed the tab of the zipper and tugged.

His eyes darkened as I slid my fingers into his boxers and wrapped my hand around his cock. "Tell me why you made me wait."

Swallowing hard, I closed my eyes. "I wasn't ready."

He rocked against my hand. His lips brushed over mine in a soft kiss. "I'm really glad you decided to come out and play."

I moaned against his mouth as he kissed me again. His tongue brushed against my lips and I opened to him immediately. I loved his taste and the way he took me over with just the melding of mouths. The kiss was hard and so invasive that when he pulled his mouth from mine we were both gasping for air. He moved off me and jerked his shirt free. I rolled to my knees, tossing the towel away, so that I could watch him. I rubbed my stomach as he came back to bed and grabbed me. I wrapped my legs around him as he lifted me off the bed. I arched in his arms as he pushed into me. He gripped me tightly, his hands biting into my ass. He encouraged me to slide up and down on his cock. I shuddered each time I came down; the pleasure of it was amazing.

"God, you're beautiful." He laid me out on the bed and pushed hard into me. "No, don't let go. Hold on."

I put my arms around him and tightened my legs around his waist as he started to move. Clutching at his back, I held him close as orgasm started to tease my senses. He pulled out almost completely and then pushed back in with a steady stroke. He did it again and I came in a sweet rush of wet heat.

I'd covered the entire canvas in black paint. The dark gleaming surface had been calling to me since I'd left it to dry. I'd thought that sitting in front of it, with my paints laid out in front of me, had been the frustrating part. Now that I could paint, the urge was gone.

Entering a new level of frustration was not unheard-of for me. Having no inspiration wasn't a surprise . . . creative blocks happen. Damn it. I stood from the floor, abandoning the project with a sigh when the phone started ringing. One glance at the caller I.D. had me wishing I hadn't bothered to get up. The last person I wanted to talk to was my ex-husband, but I'd stopped hiding from him long ago.

I pushed the button and was silent for a few seconds. "What do you want, Greg?"

"You're fucking James Brooks?"

In silence, I walked over to the canvas and stood in front of it. "My relationships are none of your business."

"Don't talk to me like that." His voice was tight and angry. "You think that bastard would give you a second glance if you weren't my ex-wife? You think that crap you make . . . that porn is really art? Brooks made you famous just to get back at me."

I would have laughed but it was hard to get amused in the face of his venom. "You don't know what you're talking about."

"He's always wanted what I have and he wanted you. Now, you're spreading your legs for him like the whore I always knew you were."

"Go to hell, Greg."

"Were you fucking him while we were married?"

I hung up. Discussing it would only validate him and the last thing I wanted was him showing up on my doorstep. History had taught me that arguing over the phone with him always ended with his arrival. I walked to the security panel on the wall and activated the motion sensors on the property line. People made fun of my need for security . . . well, people who had never met Greg made fun of it, but those who *had* understood well why I'd place thousands of dollars of electronics between me and him.

I put the phone down and went back to the canvas. My muse, the naughty wandering bitch that she was, had returned.

Six hours later, the front gate alarm sounded followed by the telltale sound of someone entering a code. I walked over to it and smiled, James followed through with his promise to bring me dinner. Back at my canvas, I waved absently at him when he entered.

"Hey."

I smiled and gathered up my brushes. "I need to wash these and then I'll be ready to eat."

He put the food down on a small empty worktable and came

to the canvas. "This is . . ." He paused and cleared his throat. "I see that I'm not the only one that got a phone call from your ex-husband."

I stiffened and turned away from the sink to face him. "What?"

"He called several times and left messages for me. I called him back this afternoon." He grimaced. "That man is a real asshat, you know."

"Yes, I do know." I turned and shoved my brushes under the still-running water. "I had no idea he would call you."

"Apparently one of my guests last night was indiscreet."

I nodded because that had crossed my mind as well. "It's not something that was supposed to be a secret." Biting down on my lip, I blinked back tears. "I'm sorry he called you."

"Do not apologize for him," James snapped.

I nodded and sucked in a breath. "I hope you told him where to go."

"I made my feelings on the matter perfectly clear."

His hands brushed over my shoulders and he placed a soft kiss on the top of my bare shoulder.

I shaped the tip of each brush and shoved them in a jar, handle down, to dry. "I haven't had a relationship since my divorce."

"As much as you enjoy sex, you can't tell me that I'm the first man you've had since you left Greg Carlson."

"No." I leaned back against him as his hands drifted over my hips. "There was a man . . . but it wasn't anything long term or serious. To be frank, the few times I've allowed men to take me out have led to a phone call like the one you received today. But I figured that Greg wouldn't have the balls to call you."

He turned me carefully and touched my jaw with gentle fingers. "It was certainly a mistake on his part. I've never invited myself into his business or his life, no matter how tempted I might have been to make him pay for what he did to you. But today, he opened a door he shouldn't have."

I pursed my lips. "James."

"Don't. The man tried to tell me where I can put my dick and I take that extremely personally."

I just bet he did. "He's not worth it."

"You get your amusement where you can and I'll do the same." He took one of my hands. "Come eat and you can tell me about that." He pointed toward the canvas with his free hand. "That is one beautiful and violent sea you have there."

A sea that would reveal to a more studious observer hundreds of faces . . . each one a picture of tragedy. I stopped in front of it; suddenly haunted by it. Black, blue, touches of red. On its surface, it looked just like the sea . . . deceptively beautiful.

"It just seemed to fit." I shrugged. "What did you bring me to eat?"

"I stopped at that Greek place on the way out of the city." He picked up the bags and motioned toward the door. "Inside or the garden?"

"Garden. I'll grab some plates."

# 7

"So, tell me what that asshole said."

I sat back in my chair, and looked out over my garden briefly before meeting his gaze. "That you wanted me because I was his ex-wife and that my art was garbage and that you made me famous to get back at him."

"Well, isn't he full of himself?" James pushed aside his food and picking up his beer. "Anything that you have, you've earned."

I knew that and because of my marriage, I knew it on a level that most would never understand. Greg Carlson had stripped me bare of every ounce of self-worth and respect, and getting it all back had taken more work than I'd ever like to admit.

"I've never doubted my talent."

"Good." He set aside the beer. "Are you going to push me out of your life?"

"Don't you mean my bed?"

"Being in your bed is important to me, but if you wanted nothing else from me than friendship I could learn to deal with it. You said you've tried to get involved with men in the past . . .

what you didn't say was that every time Greg Carlson made a phone call or interfered you sent those men packing."

"The first man went packing on his own. Greg might not have your influence but there are plenty of people in Boston who have reason to fear him and his family when it comes to making a living. As for the other two, yes I stopped seeing them because it wasn't worth the hassle of trying."

He was silent for a moment as if he didn't know what to say and then he cleared his throat. "I'd damn well better be worth the *hassle.*"

Yeah, in about a thousand different ways, but I wasn't going to dignify his arrogance with a response. I stood and stretched. Most of my body ached from the effort I'd put into painting. Making war with a canvas and a fistful of brushes could, oddly enough, be tiring.

I looked toward James, he was lounging back in his chair inspecting me as if he was about to launch a full-scale invasion. It was thrilling to have his attention like that but I was exhausted. Damn. "How was lunch with Ryan?"

I returned to my seat when he sighed and rubbed his face.

"Apparently, this woman has been pressuring him to move in with her." He frowned and stood. "That's the road to commitment and an accidental-on-purpose pregnancy, if you ask me."

"And I take it that you shared that with Ryan." I bit down on my bottom lip when he shrugged. "I'm sure calling the woman he loves a gold-digging, manipulating liar went over so well."

"Yeah." He paced away from me. "About as well as you can imagine. I don't care if he's angry with me as long as he's taking me seriously."

"Do you feel that your ex-wife trapped you into marriage?"

James paused, obviously startled, and then shrugged. "I honestly don't think so. She was just as devastated as I was when we first found out. A baby didn't mesh with either of our plans for the future; but it was done and all we could do was make room for a lot of changes."

"How does Ryan feel about all of that?"

"He knows that he wasn't a planned pregnancy and that we love him. I honestly wouldn't change a thing . . . having him in my life changed me in ways I never even thought about. Life would have been so different and empty without him."

"Why is he an only child?"

James flinched, as if he'd been struck, and then turned his back on me. "Cecilia didn't want any more and no amount of discussion ever changed that. She truly loves Ryan, but I don't think she would have ever had children given a choice."

I was finding it increasingly difficult to like his ex-wife. Gracious and charitable woman or not, she wasn't the wife he'd deserved. "I'm sorry."

"Don't be. Ryan is a great kid and I'm honored to be his father."

"I hope you tell him that often enough."

James chuckled. "So much so that he knows he can run roughshod over me any day. He has since he was born. I can hardly believe he's a grown man when I look at him."

"You are young enough . . . there could be more children if you wished it." He shrugged and then shook his head. "You are only thirty-five."

"Thirty-six, actually." He came back to the table and started to collect the remnants of our meal. "I can't stay. I have a very early meeting in the morning."

"Okay." I stood and shoved my hands into the pockets of my shorts. "Thanks for bringing dinner."

He laughed and abandoned his task in favor of walking over to me. "That isn't an excuse to avoid talking to you about this. I honestly have a telephone conference with a museum in Japan at the ass crack of dawn."

"Ass crack?"

"Jane has been working on broadening my vocabulary." He touched my bottom lip with the tips of his fingers and then leaned down to brush his mouth across mine. "Come into the city tomorrow."

"I plan to. I have a class to teach at the gallery and lunch with Jane and Mercy. You can be certain I'll bring up your deplorable language with Jane; she shouldn't teach you such bad habits." I wrapped my arms around his neck with a little sigh and rested fully against him. "Or would you prefer that they not know about us?"

"There's an 'us'?" he asked gently. "I want there to be; but I'm worried that you're going to run for the hills any second."

"I don't run." I tugged at his hair a little. "And there is an *us*; despite my better judgment. So we're both just going to have to adjust and get used to it."

"As for whether or not they know . . . Mercy is very connected and it's likely she knows already. It'll probably hit the social column in the next day or so." He kissed me again. "Does that bother you?"

"Bother me?" I laughed softly. "Shouldn't you be concerned about it? I mean, you are the one hooking up with the hillbilly porn artist with a well-known gun fetish."

"And that makes me one very lucky man." He tightened his hold on me. "That reminds me, I'll pull that suit from the auction."

"No." I shook my head. "Don't . . . in fact, I'll have my agent call them to verify it and even offer to sign it."

"Really?"

"It's for a good cause and I can be a good sport." I rose up on my toes and kissed his mouth.

He sank into the kiss without a single hesitation, his tongue thrusting into my mouth as if he owned me. I moaned against his mouth as his hands gripped my ass and lifted me. James pulled his mouth from mine as he coaxed my legs around his waist.

"I really should go home."

"You really should give me some cock." Just a touch and I'd already forgotten about how much my body ached and how tired I'd been just a few minutes before.

He chuckled. "Are you telling me where to put my dick?"

"I'd be happy to give you a list of places you could put it." I kissed his mouth softly and then his jaw. "But, if you must go, I guess I can dig around in my toy box and find something to play with."

"Christ." His grip on me tightened. "That's a fucking evil thing to say."

"I'm not about playing fair." I gasped as my back met with the screen door that lead to my sun porch.

He let me slide down slightly until he could tuck his erection against my pussy. Heat rushed over my clit and I grew wet just at the press of him against me. After a few agonizing seconds, he lifted me away from the door, pulled it open, and took me inside.

I chuckled as he set me on my feet and jerked my T-shirt over my head with unsteady hands. Tossing it aside, I curled my hand into the front of his slacks and tugged. The back of my legs hit the lounge chair and I sat down while I unfastened his pants.

James's hands drifted over my head, tangling briefly in my hair as he pushed off his shoes and then stepped back briefly to rid himself of his pants and boxers. When he came back to me, I took his already-erect cock into my mouth. He groaned softly, his hands coming to rest on my shoulders.

I let him slide all the way back until the tip of his cock rested against my throat and one hand slipped into my hair, fisting, but offering no pressure or guidance. Using my tongue, I explored his taste and texture as I worked him in and out of my mouth with a steady rhythm that had his hips flexing each time I let him touch the back of my throat.

The need to make him come was overwhelming, and the knowledge that he was surrendering the control over his own pleasure was such a turn-on that I could feel the crotch of my shorts dampening and clinging to my panties.

"Too much." He pushed my hair back from my face and sucked in a breath.

It wasn't nearly enough, I thought. Using one hand to grip his hip, I cupped his balls with the other and he groaned my name. He jerked against me and with careful hands pulled me off him and to my feet.

"I wasn't done with that." I wrapped one hand around his cock and stroked him as he took my mouth in a hard kiss.

"I want to be inside you." He brushed his lips against mine again and then placed soft kisses along my jaw as he jerked my shorts open.

Impatient hands pushed shorts and panties out of the way; I barely had time to kick them away before he was turning me around. I gasped as he pressed me against the glass surface of the single table in the room. My nipples, hard and aching, tightened against the cold table and a full shudder ran down the length of my back.

"Spread your legs."

I met his demand, and curled my hands around the sides of the table as he gripped my hips and pushed into me. My pussy clenched around his invading cock and I rocked back against him in acceptance. "Yes."

"Hold on, baby." His hands tightened on my hips as he started to thrust.

Gripping the table, I moaned softly as my nipples scraped across the smooth glass with each hard push of his body into mine. Pleasure rushed over my clit as he slid two fingers between my labia and started to finger me in time with the penetration of his cock. My body clenched against the double stim-ulation and I came hard.

James collapsed against me briefly as he climaxed. "Fuck, you'll be the death of me."

I let my head rest against the table as I laughed. "What a way to go."

He kissed my shoulder and lifted off me. "I wasn't too rough?"

"No." I sucked in a little breath as he pulled his cock from my body. "You were perfect."

# 8

---

"So, are you actually going to make us ask?" Jane propped up her chin on one hand and waved her fork toward me. "You look like you've been rode hard and put up wet for about a week."

I laughed and glanced toward Mercy, who had put down her cell phone at the beginning of Jane's question. "What's to discuss?"

"You and James Brooks," Mercy murmured. "The man you swore you were not going to hook up with. The man who has chased after your mean ass for nearly two years. I don't know who I should worry about more at this point."

Flushing, I looked away from her. "He's a grown man, Mercy."

"You both are very important to me." She reached across the table and covered one of my hands with hers. "Are you happy about it?"

How could I not be? The man had invaded me in a couple hundred delicious ways and all I could think that I'd wasted two years running scared. "Yes."

"Good." She smiled. "I heard from Julie Fitzsimmons, who heard from Rufus Fitzgerald, that the two of you worked that fund-raiser so well that people didn't even realize they'd agreed to give money until after the ink on the checks had dried."

"We're a good team. He's all business and people find the artist in me attractive." I sat back from the table as the waitress arrived to pull the salad plates. "Thank God, I'm starving for real food."

The woman laughed softly. "It'll be out shortly. Can I refill your drink?"

I nodded and watched her walk away, pleased at the slight reprieve. "James is a private person. I'm sure he wouldn't appreciate my discussing our relationship."

"So, it's a relationship?" Jane raised one eyebrow. "You guys aren't hooking up for wild pig sex four or five times a day?"

*Wild pig sex?* I couldn't help but laugh, Jane was creative if nothing else. "We're taking things slowly and I'm not discussing our wild pig sex."

Jane crossed her arms over her breasts. "I'm trying to live vicariously through you."

Since she'd been hooking up with Mathias Montgomery for going on a year, I couldn't imagine that she needed to live through me. "Yeah, I'll be sure to let Mathias know that you are bored."

"He won't believe your cruel lies." She grinned and sighed when a plate of food was placed in front of her. "Thank God. I could eat a whole cow."

I could totally relate. I picked up my silverware roll as a plate of chicken and pasta was placed in front of me. "Did you hear about Marcia Woods?"

Mercy laughed. "Boy, did I! I also saw the check her husband cut for the Foundation. That was some superior maneuvering on your part."

"She's got a good face, classic but not simple. It'll be good practice for my class." I pursed my lips. "And her hubby's pockets are deep."

"Is James really going to auction that Armani you used for target practice?" Jane asked softly, as if it were almost a secret.

"Yep, I even agreed to sign it." I stabbed a piece of chicken with my fork and shrugged. "I was in a charitable mood."

"Yeah, it's amazing what dick can do for a woman's disposition."

My mouth dropped open as I turned to look at Mercy. Her ladylike appearance was often *so* very deceptive. "That was positively crass."

She grinned. "I'm just trying to make you comfortable."

I laughed softly. Comfortable, indeed. The fact was that I was very comfortable with the both of them. It was an odd thing since neither one were remotely the kind of woman I hung out with before or during my marriage. Jane, a cop's kid and an ex-cop herself, a woman who had put herself through college and fought like hell for everything she had. I both admired and resented her strength. If a man hit her, he'd better hope that he'd managed to find a way off the planet by the time she got up.

Mercy Rothell-Montgomery was old New York money. She probably had relatives that landed on Plymouth Rock. Cultured, beautiful, and so very passionate about life. When I'd first met her, she'd been consumed with fear and full of self-doubt. I was glad to see that she'd learned to trust herself again.

"It certainly did wonders for you."

She blushed and pursed her lips as her cell phone rang. "Speaking of my husband, he's home with Julian all alone. The nanny has the day off." She tucked it to her ear. "Hey, baby."

Julian was her son and Shamus, her husband, was obviously in over his head. He'd called six times in the past hour. I'd known Shamus for years, since college, and it was nice to see him so settled and in love with his family.

"He's not alone," Jane raised an eyebrow. "Mathias is over there."

I tried to picture the two of them at the mercy of a five-month-old baby, and I couldn't help but ask. "Do you suppose we should go rescue them?"

Mercy snorted as she hung up her phone. "If the man can't hang tough for two hours while I have lunch, he requires more help than we can provide." She bit down on her lip. "He's adorable, you know. I had no idea that fatherhood would turn him into such a worrier. Between the two of us, the poor kid is probably going to start begging his nanny to stay the night. Last night we must have checked to make sure he was breathing like six times."

I laughed. "I take it he's starting to sleep through the night?"

"Yeah, it scared the hell out of me." She frowned and checked her watch. "Which the doctor assures us is fine."

"What was wrong?" Jane asked.

"Nothing, he invited James and a *date* over for dinner tonight." She cut her eyes at me. "They honestly think they have secrets from us."

I laughed. "Did James agree?" My cell phone started ringing and I dug it out of my pocket. "Never mind."

Another dinner party. At least it was with people I genuinely liked. A couples event was an all together different animal. He'd left it *entirely* up to me, as I'd sat in front of Mercy and Jane discussing it with him. While not feeling exactly pressured, I hadn't been able to express my honest opinion about it.

"We don't have to stay long."

I chuckled as I pulled on my jacket. "Shamus promised to show me a new project, so it's not exactly going to be total torture."

He turned the car off and looked around the dark street.

"Sometimes it's hard for me to separate my different relationships with them."

"We do have a very tangled social circle." I brushed his hair from his forehead and ran my hand down the side of his neck. "But as important as working relationships are, friends have an immense value."

"Most of the socializing I do is business." He admitted softly. "It has been that way since my divorce."

I leaned in and kissed him. "Is this your way of telling me that you're uncomfortable?"

He laughed. "Not uncomfortable, just sort of out of practice."

I adopted a serious expression. "If it would help, I could act like one of the simpering debutantes you normally date."

His mouth dropped open briefly before he clamped it shut with an audible click of teeth. "Would you cling on my every word and pretend you think I'm amazing?"

"Absolutely."

"Then, we go home . . . you could put on a red wig and I could call you Suzette."

I burst out laughing. "You went too far."

"Stephanie?"

I gave him a hard kiss and grabbed my purse. "Let's go. Maybe the baby will still be awake."

By the time he rang the doorbell, a little bit of nervousness had settled in my stomach. The door was thrown open and Jane appeared, baby Julian balanced on one slim hip. Julian Montgomery was a beautiful mixture of his parents . . . light brown skin and Mercy's bright green eyes. I'd fallen in love with him the day he'd been born. To keep my biological clock from bursting from my chest in a full-on fit, I'd kept from visiting him too often.

"Practicing?"

Jane glared briefly. "He's baby enough for all of us and I can give him back when he's dirty."

I shrugged out of my jacket as James closed the door. "Is Mercy cooking?"

"Yeah, right, you know she grew up with a maid."

"I heard that!" Mercy came into the foyer. "The men are cooking. We decided it was their turn." She looked pointedly at James. "I'm supposed to send you in there."

He laughed. "I grew up with a maid or two, myself."

And he totally abandoned me, his fingers brushing over my shoulder as he slid past me and headed toward the kitchen. I figured he was more interested in finding a beer than actually cooking. Frowning, I followed Mercy and Jane into the great room where a large flat-panel television was the obvious focus.

I sat down and Julian was promptly deposited in my lap. He giggled and curled into me, his soft little face rubbing against my neck. "What a player already."

"It's the tits." Jane sat down across from me. "He loves women with breasts."

"That's not a surprise since Mercy breastfed." I rubbed his back. "Are you telling me that holding this little guy doesn't make you want one of your own?"

She flushed and pursed her lips as if I'd asked her to reveal a state secret. "Yeah, maybe."

Mercy came through the swinging door with three glasses of wine, shaking her head. "My kitchen is going to look like a smart bomb was dropped on it."

I took the glass and set it down on a table. "What are they cooking?"

"Steaks." Jane chuckled. "That's all they are allowed to cook. Believe it or not, they have the gas grill fired up on the back balcony."

I could hardly imagine it.

*   *   *

Dinner hadn't been a total nightmare. As couples, we were all very different. Shamus and Mercy were openly affectionate with one another, but not in a way that made everyone want to go home. Jane and Mathias were a shrewd pair, with a passion for one another that was obvious with every look they gave each other.

I couldn't even begin to guess what the four of them thought of us . . . they'd all had ringside seats to our long battle of wills. James was a reserved man but he had an easy humor and social skills wrought through years of running a charity foundation.

After the meal, Shamus offered to show me his studio space and everyone let us go without much of a fight.

"You've made some great progress with this place."

Shamus nodded. "Yeah, finding a building big enough for all of us plus my work was a challenge, and of course letting go of the storefront was a little painful."

I nodded. Shame was one of the few artists I knew who liked interacting with people, especially those who bought his work. I tried not to think about the people who bought mine . . . because that whole part of the process drove me insane. A part of me would have been content to live in poverty and hoard all of my work.

He walked over to his current work and pulled a sheet free. "I've been driving Mercy insane over this."

I stopped, my heart caught in my throat. His wife was his favorite private subject and it was obvious why. This was a sculpture of her and the baby, in rosewood. Only one breast was bare, an unusual thing for him, as he preferred to sculpt women nude, and Julian was nestled against that bare breast.

"It's beautiful."

I cleared my throat and blinked back tears. It was, in fact, the most amazing thing I'd ever seen him do. The details of their faces were stunning, but it was the love that practically poured out of the wood that would make anyone stop and stare in wonder. I regretted not bringing my wine with me.

He reached out and brushed a tear from my face with his thumb. "I didn't mean to upset you."

I shook my head and rubbed my face. "No, it's okay." I moved closer to the sculpture and traced a single strand of Mercy's hair as it fell gracefully over one shoulder. "You know, every time I see your work I can't imagine how you could make anything more beautiful. Yet, you always manage to surpass your best."

"I was surprised when Mercy told me you'd finally let James catch you."

I chuckled at his tone. "Yeah, I'm sure."

"I don't know whether to lecture him about not hurting you or ask Mathias to give him self-defense lessons."

Overall, I have to say that Mercy expressed that very concern much more nicely. "We're both grown."

"Yeah." He sat down on a stool and motioned me to sit as well. "Still, I know things haven't been exactly easy for you when it comes to men."

True enough. Shame knew more about my marriage than I would have liked, but he'd been the one on hand when I'd finally had a come-apart over it. We'd been lovers in college and our friendship had lingered long after our sexual attraction had burned itself out. It was so odd seeing him married and thoroughly domesticated.

"Greg called me over it already."

"He always does." He grimaced. "And he will as long as you tolerate it."

I laughed. "Divorce papers, four restraining orders, and a fifty-thousand-dollar security system haven't given him a clue, Shame. What exactly do you propose I do?" I rubbed my face.

"Besides, he made the mistake of calling James as well. As you can imagine, that went over so well."

"He's an idiot."

"Yes, he is."

We both turned. James was lounging in the doorway. "Mercy is putting the baby down."

Shamus stood and abandoned me with a little wave of his hand. I turned and focused on the sculpture as James came fully into the room. "It's beautiful, isn't it?"

"Yes." He paused beside me and ran one hand down my back. "You ready to go?"

"Early morning?"

"Yeah, I was hoping you'd stay with me."

I grinned. "I brought a bag."

"Good." He touched my face as he turned me to face him. "I like having you in my bed."

I just liked having him. I could care less where it was. He leaned into me and I met the kiss halfway. I sighed when he lifted away. The door to the studio opened and Jane stuck her head in.

"Good night!"

"Night." I waved at her and she laughed.

"I'll see you tomorrow night."

"Tomorrow night?" I frowned.

"Yeah, it's Casey's party. Liquor, strippers, and lots of trashy lingerie. It promises to be grand."

"Strippers?" James raised one eyebrow.

Jane chuckled. "A fireman and a cop. I know how to throw a party." She gasped when an arm snaked around her middle. "But I don't plan on touching, honest!"

Mathias laughed and tugged. "Come on, leave these two alone."

James laughed as the door swung shut. "Strippers?"

I shrugged. I'd totally forgotten about the party; but it was going to be fun. Casey Andrews was Jane's assistant and was actually one of the most charming women I'd ever met. She'd skipped lunch earlier in the day for a fitting. Her wedding was less than a month away.

"I don't know why she'd hire a cop stripper." I slid off the stool. "Casey's marrying a cop. It isn't like she can't play with handcuffs all the time."

James wrapped an arm around my shoulders. "What kind of stripper would you have hired?"

"Construction worker." I grinned when he snorted. "I love tool belts."

"Come along, Bambi."

"No way, I'm not answering to Bambi." I elbowed him. "Keep trying."

"Candy?"

"Women named after food piss me off."

He laughed. "I'm sure I'll think of something."

# 9

---

I paused in the doorway of his office and looked the room over. His home office wasn't very different from the one at the foundation. Large, dark furniture and nice comfortable-looking chairs. The difference was my work. I pursed my lips as I stared at the sculpture I'd done of him. It had been stupid of me to think he wouldn't notice.

"I'm a poor host."

My gaze snapped back to him. "No. I don't expect you to put everything on hold to entertain me."

He sat back in his chair and closed the laptop in front of him. "Why did you sculpt me?"

"Because you are . . . as Jane has put it more than once, *James Bond* fine." I moved into the room and walked toward the desk. "You would simply not believe how many times I masturbated while I was creating it."

His eyes widened briefly and then he cleared his throat. "Come here."

With a small smile, I pulled at the end of my belt. My robe

parted, the heavy silk no match for gravity. He picked up his laptop and slid it into a drawer of his desk.

"What do you want me to do?" I asked softly.

He patted the ink blotter that covered the middle of the desk. "Sit down."

I laughed softly, slid between his chair and the desk, and hopped up on it. He moved closer and snagged my ankles. I shrugged the robe off as he propped my feet on the arms of his chair.

Leaning back on my hands, I spread my legs, as he seemed to want. It was a brazen and completely unseemly position. My pussy dampened immediately as it was exposed to the cool air. Thank God, I'd taken the time to do some down-below maintenance.

"Did you shave for me?"

"Very arrogant question." I arched a little as he ran his hands up my legs to my knees. I scooted a little closer to the edge.

"Do you like it?"

He slid one hand down my leg and ran the tips of his fingers over my bare labia. "Sexy and so revealing. You're beautiful, Lisa."

"Thank you," I whispered and then sighed when he removed his hand.

"Touch yourself." He leaned back in the chair then, his hands moving to encircle my ankles. "Pinch your nipples."

I sat up and covered both breasts with my hands, using my fingers to tease my nipples, as he demanded. His eyes darkened as he watched and his fingernails dug briefly into my skin.

"Harder."

I flushed at the instruction but did as he bade, pain and pleasure mixed as I pulled my already distended nipples. "Like this?"

"Yes." James shifted in the chair and my gaze dropped to his lap.

His cock was pushing against the material of his slacks.

Moisture dampened my labia as I thought about how it was going to feel when he fucked me. I rocked my hips a little, unable to help myself, and bit down on my bottom lip. His grip on my legs kept me from moving the way I wanted, and I assumed that was his intention.

"I want to watch you play with your pussy."

I leaned back on one hand and then pushed two fingers between my already parted labia to play with my clit. "Like this?"

"Like you do when there is no one around. Make yourself come."

I dipped two fingers into my entrance and then spread the moisture I found there up over my clit. My clit hardened further and started to throb. Each little circle I made with my fingers sent arousal spiraling over my entire body. My internal muscles were clenching around nothing, a circumstance I was all too familiar with.

"I can't tell you how many times I've pictured this." He wet his bottom lip with the tip of his tongue and leaned forward. "All those times you masturbated, did you ever think about me fucking you?"

"Yes." I was beyond a point where I could be coy. I shuddered as I shoved two fingers into my cunt. Wetness seeped out and ran down between my ass cheeks as I started to rock against my hand. "You're all I've fantasized about for the last year."

"Did you imagine me eating your pussy?" His hands moved up my legs to my knees as he moved the chair closer to the desk. "Sucking your nipples?"

I nodded, my teeth clenched against the orgasm I was close to having. I couldn't remember ever wanting to come so badly in my life.

"What else would I do for you?"

"Fuck my pussy."

"And your mouth?"

"Yes."

"You like sucking my cock?" he asked softly.

I bit down on my bottom lip as he spread my legs further, his fingers running along my inner thighs. "Yes. I loved it."

He grabbed my hand and slowly pulled my fingers out. "Enough."

It wasn't nearly enough. Groaning in frustration, I started to protest but before I could, he sucked the fingers I'd been using on myself into his mouth. His tongue swirled gently and knowingly, cleaning off my juices as if it were a task he'd done all of his life.

"What else do I do for you, in here?" He tapped my forehead gently.

"I don't what you mean." I flushed as he pulled me off the desk and onto his lap. Sitting back on his thighs, I let my head fall back as his big hands cupped my breasts. Need still clawed at my insides, but I was willing to take it as slow as he wanted.

"You said I was holding back on you."

I gasped when he gripped my hips and pulled me against his chest. With my pussy nestled against his cock, I could tell exactly how much our play had done to arouse him. "I don't understand."

"You're comparing me to the man you invented in your head . . . the lover you assumed I would be." He cupped my ass with both hands and I had no choice but to put mine on his shoulders to brace myself. "You like to be dominated, but I didn't think you'd be into anything heavy like spankings or punishment. Am I wrong?"

"No." I wrapped my arms around his neck and stilled as he moved his hands up my back, his nails gently scoring my skin. "I don't think I could ever get hot over a man hitting me."

"You like sex to be rough and fast."

"Yes, at times." But there was something about James that made me crave gentleness, as well, something I knew he was very capable of delivering. "But, I love it when you take your time."

"I know." He sighed, picked me up, and put me back on the desk. "I see you aren't going to be up front with me."

I frowned. "I am being perfectly honest with you."

James sat back in the chair and looked me over, his gaze lingering on my hard nipples before traveling downward to my pussy. He reached out and grabbed my hand just before I could slide my fingers back inside. "I'm going to give you some instructions and if you follow them to the letter, I'll let you come."

I grinned. "Okay."

"Go into the bedroom, take everything off the bed except for the sheet, lay down spread-eagled and facedown in the middle of it, and wait for me without touching yourself."

Hesitating, I inspected his face, looking for some indication as to what he had planned. "I won't have to wait long?"

"Not long, I promise."

I scooted off the desk and stretched my arms over my head as I walked toward the door. "Should I leave the lights on?"

"No."

The urge to finish myself off was strong; but I understood that delayed gratification had its own reward. I threw the pillows and covers off, then I crawled onto the bed pleased with the feel of the cool Egyptian cotton and assumed the position he had requested. A full minute passed before I heard the bedroom door click shut. With the light from the hall gone, the room was utterly dark. From the rustle of clothes, I could tell that he was undressing.

His watch clicked against the wood surface of the nightstand and he pulled open a drawer. "Are you ready?"

"Oh, yes."

James chuckled as he joined me on the bed, I nearly sighed with relief when he moved to straddle my thighs. "So eager."

He put one hand on the small of my back. "No moving until I say."

"Okay." A shiver of anticipation zipped down my back as he leaned forward, his cock sliding temptingly between the cheeks of my ass.

His hands came down on either side of my head and he kissed my shoulder. "I have a few more questions."

I curled my fingers into the sheet beneath us to keep from screaming. "Whatever you want."

Laughing, he pressed his cock firmly against me and flexed his hips. "Promise me you'll be honest."

I couldn't imagine what he would ask that I wouldn't answer honestly. I've never been a shy woman when it came to sex, but considering his current activity I knew which question he was about to ask. My pussy clenched at the mere thought of it. "Of course."

"Tell me what I did to you the last time you fantasized about fucking me."

Clearing my throat, I lifted my ass against the rocking motion of his body and he stilled. I relaxed against the bed and he placed a soft kiss on my neck in approval. "It was about a month ago."

"Okay."

"The sculpture of you was the last I finished for the show. It stayed in my barn until the day before the opening. Every time I looked at that damn thing I would get wet." I forced myself to relax my fingers and release the sheet. "You came into the barn while I was working . . ."

"Yes?"

I laughed. His breath had hitched a little bit, and I could tell he was surprised that I began describing it without more prodding on his part. "You walked over to me and grabbed me."

"Did I kiss you?"

"No, I wasn't in the mood for games." He moved again, and his balls brushed against my ass. "You told me to get on my knees and suck your cock."

"Jesus." He pressed his face against the middle of my back briefly.

"So, I went down on my knees, pulled your cock free from your pants, and started to suck you. For a few minutes you were still, and then you started to thrust into my mouth."

"Did you make me come?"

"Yes." I jerked when he lifted away, and then sighed with relief when he ran his hands down my back. Sharing my fantasies with a man was a new and somewhat terrifying experience. "We undressed and you licked my pussy."

"I do like to eat you." He pushed one hand between my legs and cupped my pussy from behind. The tips of his fingers grazed my throbbing clit, and I moaned at the contact. "You taste so good."

"You made me come and then you put your cock in me."

"In your pussy?"

I paused. "At first."

"Then?"

"You asked if you could fuck my ass."

His hand moved away from my pussy and slid back up until he could press two damp fingers against my anus. "And did you let me?"

I pressed my face against the mattress briefly, stunned that I was going to reveal something I'd promised I'd never tell another man, ever. "Yes."

"Did you enjoy it?"

"It was the best orgasm I've had masturbating in a very long time." I waited for his reaction, and relaxed when his fingers pressed gently against me. "You don't think I'm a freak?"

He laughed. "Oh, I know you're a freak. I just like it, *a lot*."

Gently, as if he had all the time in the world, his fingers rubbed and slightly penetrated. "You'll have to be patient with me. It's been a while since I've had a woman that enjoyed anal sex."

I rocked back against his fingers and then stopped when I heard the faint click of something opening. "What's that?"

"Lube."

"So, I wasn't wrong about you."

His fingers left briefly and then returned, gloriously wet, and ready for a more thorough introduction to my ass. One finger pushed inside and he stopped when I clenched down on him. "No, baby, you weren't wrong. I like a woman to be completely open and available to me. Knowing that I can put my cock in your mouth, your pussy, and your ass . . . it's very sexy to me. The fact that you're going to enjoy it makes it all the more appealing."

When I started to relax, he pressed his finger in more deeply and then withdrew it. He reentered with two fingers, and I made a sound that was practically foreign to me. James worked his fingers in my ass until I started to squirm beneath him and then he pulled away and lifted off me.

"Turn over."

I complied immediately and spread my legs for him. "Will you suck my clit?"

"Yes." He reached over, turned on the small lamp on the bedside table, and retrieved a condom that was laying there. "And then I'm going to fuck that pretty ass of yours."

He dropped the condom on the bed beside me and then moved downward. His tongue stabbed between my swollen labia and found my clit the instant his mouth made contact with my aching flesh. The heat of his mouth on me was enough to bring orgasm rushing to the surface and when he pulled my throbbing clit into his mouth with soft lips, I came.

James pushed his fingers back into my ass as the orgasm started to fade. He lifted his head. "Are you ready?"

I nodded, abruptly. "Whatever you want."

He rolled the condom into place and then picked up the bottle of lube again. "How long has it been for you?"

"Several years." I spread my legs wide and tilted my hips as he pressed three lube-covered fingers into me. "Fuck." It was so hot and dirty that I could barely stand it. I lifted up off the bed in helpless demand.

"Relax, baby, I got this. It'll be good."

I nodded and closed my eyes. "I know."

"On your back or knees?" He kissed the inside of my thigh.

"Just like this, I want to see you."

He gripped my hips with firm hands and lifted me slightly off the bed as he pressed the head of his cock against my back entrance. I clenched around him as soon as he gained entry and he paused. After a few agonizing seconds, he started to rock back and forth, each push forward an enticing glimpse of the fullness I had to look forward to.

My insides started to burn and I forced myself to relax against his intrusion. The last thing I wanted was for him to stop. James slid his hands underneath me, lifted, and pushed until he was buried deep. The pleasure of being full and a little pain mixed until I could do nothing but wait for him to continue.

He lowered us both to the bed slowly. "Keep those legs spread for me, baby. I don't want to hurt you."

I nodded and lifted my hands above my head as he preferred. I chuckled softly when one of his hands slid up one arm and clasped both of my wrists. His lips brushed over mine quickly once, then again as he started to move. Eyes, now the darkest of blues, met mine.

"Good?"

The burn of penetration had slowly turned and now each slow, measured stroke of his cock into me brought pleasure and a welcoming heat. "Yes. So good." I pressed my feet against the bed and tilted my hips.

His hand tightened briefly on my wrists and he sucked in a breath as he sank a little deeper. "I'm trying to take it easy."

"I know."

"But you're making it difficult," he ground out through clenched teeth.

"Fuck me, Jamie. Fuck me like you want to."

I lifted my hips and he took my mouth in a hard kiss. His tongue thrust into my mouth as he increased the pace of his body inside mine. When he lifted his head to watch my face, he paused briefly and then slowly withdrew.

"You're going to drive me crazy, I know it." He cleared his throat. "Turn over."

I slid upward away from him and moved onto my knees as fast as I could. Bracing my hands on the headboard of the bed, I spread my legs wide for him and groaned softly when his hands settled on my hips. Seconds later, I felt the push of the flared head of his cock as he reentered my ass. He held me in place for several minutes, his body slapping against mine in a rhythm that had my insides quaking.

Then, as if he understood my insane desire to move, his hands drifted upward to cup my breasts. I pushed back against him as he thrust forward, and his hands tightened on my breasts. Fingers pinched and pulled at my nipples, feeding the dull ache of need that had developed and spread over me in the few seconds it had taken to get on my knees.

One hand abandoned my breast, snaked downward, and cupped my pussy. He pressed two fingers against my throbbing clit and started to rub it in time with the hard thrust of his cock into me. The double stimulation was more than I could take and I came. I clenched down on him, my body quaking from the pleasure of him, and he groaned. His body stiffened against me.

"Lisa."

My name was a soft whisper as it fell from his lips and I shuddered as he gathered me in his arms and held me there. I rested against his thighs and let my head drop back to his shoulder while he ran his hands over my body in a way that was so soothing.

# 10

---

"Look, I don't give a fuck what you've been told. I am not, nor will I ever be, interested in discussing my ex-husband with the press." I disconnected the call with a shaking hand and fought the urge to throw up.

It had taken Greg Carlson just a few minutes to destroy every single ounce of peace I'd managed to earn for myself. When we had divorced, he'd been adamant that the details of our marriage remain private. By the time he was making that particular demand, I'd been more than willing to accept the condition. The year and a half it had taken us to get any kind of agreement had taken its toll.

He'd been so afraid the press would paint him a monster and now there was an article being published in a society rag about the domestic violence I'd suffered in my marriage to him. And to beat it all, he was the fucking source.

I stared at the phone for several seconds, before I punched in his number. It rang once when he picked up. "What the fuck were you thinking?"

"What? Look, you can't call me and talk to me like this."

"Sure I can, Greg. I'm the one with the restraining orders, not you." I closed my eyes and leaned against the kitchen counter for support. "I just received a phone call from *The Society Chronicle* wanting a fucking quote on an article. An article about our marriage."

"Yeah, I meant to tell you. I did an interview."

"You violated our agreement," I snapped through clenched teeth.

"The agreement was that you wouldn't claim that I beat you or any other such nonsense to the press." He responded. "The article is an interview about me, not about you. They asked to talk to me! Not you!"

"Oh really?" I demanded softly. "Then why did she ask about the restraining orders? Why did she ask about your arrest last summer? Why did she ask me how I could have stayed married to a monster like you for so long? Why did she ask me how many times you beat me during our five-year marriage?"

He was silent for a few seconds, his breathing ragged. "What the fuck did you tell her?"

"Nothing, you stupid bastard. I told her nothing and while our divorce proceedings might be sparse on facts I doubt seriously that your arrest report from last summer is." I rubbed my face with one shaking hand and swallowed hard. "I've never talked to the press about the abuse and no one in my life would be so indiscreet. Because, unlike you, they respect my privacy."

"If I found out that you've told them anything. . . ."

"What will you do?" I demanded. "Sue me for the divorce settlement? Go right ahead, because that would make for a great headline." Tears gathered and fell. I brushed them from my face, angry that he'd reduced me to such a state. "She also asked me how I felt about you being in a twelve-step program for alcoholics. She wanted to know if I thought that would make you a better man."

"I'll find out who told that reporter. If it was you or one of your friends . . . you'll all pay."

"I would suggest, Greg, that you look at your own life for a culprit. And it would be good to remember that the last time you came at one of my friends, you were left with an arrest for assault and a cracked jaw." I ended the call with a push of my thumb and closed my eyes.

I'd been home barely an hour, having lingered in bed with James until a meeting had forced him to go to work and now I knew I had to go back into the city to have a discussion with Mercy.

The drive into town had given me time to calm down. I didn't think for a single second that Mercy or Jane had discussed my ex-husband or me with a reporter, but this kind of negative press certainly wouldn't be the kind of thing either of them would appreciate for the gallery. Mercy had worked hard to make the Holman Gallery a place of gentle dreams and amazing art that funded the hopes of children . . . the crown jewel of the entire Holman Foundation.

Casey Andrews met me at the stairs with a smile and came in for a hug. I let her hug me more out of the need for comfort than anything else. She was one of those *hugger* people and most of the time I tolerated her with a great deal of goodwill.

"You look great."

She smiled. "Thanks. You ready to party tonight?"

Somehow, I doubted it, but I didn't want to hurt her feelings. I let her hook an arm through mine and lead me toward the stairs that would take us to the administrative level of the gallery. When I'd called on the way into Boston and demanded a meeting with Mercy, Casey had immediately made room for me on the meeting schedule.

"Would you like some coffee?"

"Yes, that would be great." I sucked in a breath as we came all the way up the stairs. James was standing with Mercy just outside her office door. He was, honestly, the last person who I wanted in this meeting.

I started to turn and run, but just then, they both turned and caught sight of me. Mercy waved me over with a smile. "Hey you, come here. I was just telling James about our little impromptu meeting."

Casey abandoned me with a murmur that she would bring the coffee to me and I trudged over to them.

"Hey."

"Hey, yourself." He frowned as he looked over my face. "You look pissed off."

I swallowed hard. "I was hoping to speak with Mercy alone."

His mouth tightened into a thin line. No man liked to be dismissed and for a man like James Brooks . . . well, hell, I might as well have kicked him in the balls. "I see." He checked his watch. "I'll be upstairs if you need me, Mercy."

Mercy nodded, her expression clearly surprised. "Lisa?"

I watched James walk away in silence. Hurting him hadn't been my intention, but I didn't think I could hold it together while I explained it and I wasn't ready for him to see me looking like the crazy-ass crying woman I was probably going to be. "Can we talk in your office?"

"Sure."

I paused to accept the coffee that Casey had appeared with. "Thank you."

"No problem." She glanced between the two of us. "I'll just be at my desk if you need me, Mercy."

I let Mercy guide me into her office and shut the door. In silence, I sat down on her couch and curled up into one corner while she closed the blinds on the large windows that looked out on the bull pen. Every office in the building was like a fishbowl; I don't know how they managed to stay sane with so little privacy. I had noticed that the blinds had gone up as soon as Mercy had become the director of the place.

She let me sit and drink my coffee for several minutes in silence before she cleared her throat. "Okay, tell me what got you here in my office on an unscheduled visit."

I swallowed hard. "I received a phone call this morning."

"Not a good one."

"No." I set the cup aside when I realized my hand was shaking. "Some society hack writer is doing an article on Greg. He thought it was a personality piece, probably because of his family's money. He always loved to get into those stupid social columns when we were married."

Mercy walked over to the couch and sat down beside me. "This is really bad, right?"

I nodded and sucked in a breath that almost turned into a sob. Christ, the last thing I wanted to do was cry like a little girl. "How did you do it, Mercy?"

"Do what?"

"Handle all of the speculation and the questions when it came out that you'd been raped? They covered that trial in Boston and in New York. All of those pictures of you, coming out of the courthouse . . . the press never let up on you."

"It was news. The wife of Shamus Montgomery a rape victim, and pressing charges nearly three years after a rape." She sat back on the couch. "Actually the worst part with the pictures was when that picture of my face all bruised and swollen ended up in the *Times,* I thought I would literally die. Shame was no help because he was just a walking knot of fury by that point. He would have killed Jeff King that day if he could have gotten to him." She picked up one of my hands and curled her fingers in it. "Your hands are like ice."

"Sorry."

"The events of my rape were no secret to him; but faced

with a picture of me . . . hours after it happened was a little more than he could stand even in the courtroom. But when one made it to the papers . . ." She sighed. "Well, it was not a good day."

I remembered that picture well. Seeing it had been like a fist in my chest. To see a friend so obviously emotionally destroyed, with the evidence of violence all over her face in a myriad of bruises had been almost too much to bear.

"She asked me how many times he beat me before I left him."

"Christ." Mercy cleared her throat. "He talked about abusing you to a reporter?"

"He claims not." I rubbed my mouth in frustration. "But he's an indiscreet bastard; most of our so-called friends knew that he hit me whenever he felt like it. Hit me and I took it."

"Don't go there."

"Go where?" I demanded softly.

"Do not blame yourself for that son of a bitch hitting you. I won't stand for it." Her fingers tightened against my hand.

"It's not the same, Mercy. I could have left him. I stayed here . . . I let him hit me. I'm the one that got up off the floor every time it happened and did nothing to save myself. I am absolutely ashamed." I blinked back tears. "And now, it will be fodder for some of the most vicious gossipmongers in Boston. It was one thing when they thought I was a hillbilly porn artist. Now they can talk about how bad they feel for me. How weak I must be to stay with a man like that . . ."

"Greg Carlson betrayed your marriage." She wrapped an arm around and held me tight. "He is a man with no integrity and no honor. You gave him love, faith, and trust. He gave you years of heartache, disappointment, and a fist."

"You would have left him." I used my free hand to rub at my face. "Hell, Jane would have been digging a hole in the backyard for his body."

Mercy laughed softly. "Yeah, she sure would. In fact, she might dig a hole for his body, anyway . . . and she was never married to him."

"Yeah." I pulled my hand free and gently extricated myself to stand. I needed to move. I walked to a window that offered a view of the front parking lot. James's car was still in its assigned spot. "Greg was good at making me believe . . . for so very long I thought he would stop and that he did love me as he claimed. I didn't grow up with a lot of love, which is a cop-out, I know."

"Wanting to be loved can make you desperate for any bit of affection you can wring out of another person."

"Yes." I nodded and the tears fell full force. A sob rose in my throat and I buried my face in my hands.

Mercy walked to me and led me back to the couch.

I sat down and accepted the box of tissues she held out. "This sucks. I can't believe I'm on your couch crying like a big third-grade girl."

We both jumped at the sound of a knock on the door and Jane stuck her head in. "Hey . . ." She stopped when she caught sight of me. Stiffly, and with an alarmed expression, she came in and closed the door. "What the fuck is going on?"

I bit down on my lip when Mercy sighed. "Your foul language is going to get prissy panties in a knot over here." I pulled another tissue from the box and wiped at my face. "You tell anyone you saw me like this, Jane, and I'll kill you."

Jane crossed her arms over her chest and stared. "What did he do?"

"Who?"

"James. Casey told me you sent him off to his office when it was obvious he expected to sit in on this meeting. So what did he do? Because I'll go up there to his office and tell him how to behave." She tapped her foot for emphasis.

I loved her feistiness. In fact, I figured one day I'd get her in my studio for a sitting . . . maybe canvas. Her vibrancy nearly begged to be captured in oils. "James did nothing."

"You sure?"

"Yeah." He was practically perfect, but I sure as hell wasn't going to say it.

"I'm sorry I interrupted." She walked towards the door. "I thought it was business."

"No, wait." I pulled my legs up on to the couch and shoved my shoes off. "You can stay. I'm going to need your help."

She sat down in a chair across from the couch, crossed her legs, and stared pointedly at me. The meeting suddenly felt more like a council of war than a crying jag for my friends. I stilled myself to repeat it and started to twice only to shrink back against the couch. I'd turned into a total ninny.

"There is going to be an article published . . ." Mercy paused and looked at me.

"*The Society Chronicle.*"

"In the worst tabloid in the city detailing her marriage to Greg Carlson. He gave an interview to a reporter and apparently that darling girl, whom we can find and kick the crap out of, did some actual investigative reporting and discovered that Greg Carlson was a wife beater."

Jane sat up in her chair and then leaned forward, her body a sudden ball of tension and anger. "What?"

"Tomorrow's edition." I whispered.

"Why the hell didn't you tell James?"

"He's going to find out soon enough and I was hoping to find a way to let him know before the article comes out."

Jane shook her head stood. "No, you don't understand. James Brooks owns that piece of society garbage." And walked out of the room before we could say anything else.

Mercy cleared her throat. "Did you know he owned it?"

"No." I shook my head. "You?"

"No, it's not in the Holman Foundation holdings." Mercy stood as the door was thrown open again. "Sir."

James glanced at her briefly before focusing on me. He got a little pale; but, to his credit, I doubted he could have possibly expected to find me in such a state in Mercy's office. I tossed away a saturated tissue and reached for another.

"Mercy, if you would leave us, please?"

"Of course."

He shrugged off his jacket and tossed it over a chair as he came to me. "Jane just burst into my office and told me you were down here crying."

I sniffled. "Total tattletale."

James knelt down in front of me and put one hand on my knee. "Baby, did I hurt you last night? Did I do something . . . ?"

Startled, I put my fingers to his lips. "No, of course not. Last night was perfect. Jane didn't tell you?"

"Honestly, I didn't give her time to." He moved up the couch and pulled me into his arms. "Tell me what's going on."

"There is going to be an article in the *Chronicle* on Wednesday." I took a minute to collect myself. "About me and Greg Carlson. The reporter knows about the abuse, the restraining orders, the stalking charge, and the incident at the farm last summer when he broke in on me and Jane."

One hand tightened into a fist against my back and then it relaxed. "I'll take care of it."

"That simple?"

"No, but it'll be done, anyway."

"I didn't come here so that you could stop it. I didn't even know you owned that gossip rag." I paused and lifted my head from his shoulder. "Why do you own it?"

"Because it makes money." He ran his fingers through my hair, as if to soothe me. "And while I enjoy my work with the Holman Foundation, the position is unpaid."

"Oh." I frowned. "Unpaid?"

"My mother never drew a salary and neither will I." James used the tips of his fingers to touch my cheek and then sighed. "I'll not allow something I own to cause you pain. Not when stopping it would only take a phone call and a few choice words with a man who can't afford to piss me off."

I didn't want him to bully someone on my behalf, but I couldn't imagine how that article could possibly do me any good. Perhaps letting other women read it . . . for them to see that I'd eventually escaped him would be some comfort. But I knew I was entirely too selfish to deny his offer.

"Yes, please call him."

James pressed a soft kiss to my mouth and stood. "I'll do it in my office."

I sat there and watched him leave, my whole body relaxing. A part of me did wonder how many papers he could have sold if he'd allowed the article to go through. I sighed and sat back against the couch. Letting a man take care of something for me was practically alien, but I'd been letting him run the show for a week now. Oddly, it was . . . it was comforting.

The door opened. Mercy, Jane and Casey entered, each one's face showing a mixture of relief and anger. I figured James had made it clear he would make the situation go away.

Mercy sat down beside me and picked up my hand. "It'll be all right."

"Just because that one paper won't print it . . ." I sighed. "It won't stop her from selling the story elsewhere. It's going to come out eventually; it's hardly a secret anymore. Then my world will be open for everyone in Boston to look at, talk about."

"Privacy is a luxury." Jane sat down on the table in front of me. Her gaze met mine. "Yes, there will be talk. Yes, people will speculate. Yes, eventually all of that crap will hit a newspaper. You are a well-known artist both locally and nationally. And due to a step no woman in this room, including yourself, thought you would ever take, you will be news for an entirely different reason."

I glanced upward where I knew James's office to be located and snorted. "Yeah."

"You are good for each other. I haven't seen him happy like this in a long time."

Mercy's words sunk in a little deeper than I would have liked. I wanted to make him happy. I wanted to be everything to him. *Fuck me running*, I'd gone and fallen in love with James Brooks. I stood abruptly and shoved my hands into my jeans. "I need to wash my face. I must look like crap."

Swinging my little purse from two fingers, I leaned back against the wall of the elevator as it zipped upward toward James' apartment. The all-girl, plus two strippers, party had been tame by the standards of most, but it had been fun. I hadn't really felt like going, but it was important to Casey and I wanted to support her in that. Besides, it had given me the opportunity to buy some truly sleazy lingerie . . . for her and for myself.

I entered the apartment using the key James had slipped into my hand earlier in the afternoon. What greeted me made my knees buckle, briefly. The woman's legs were up on his shoulders, her fingers buried in black hair as she clutched at his head. And for several horrifying seconds the man between her legs, having what could only be called a *meal*, looked like James. But I knew his body, and the shoulders weren't broad enough, the hair too long. I closed my eyes briefly and leaned back against the door as it closed. The noise of it shutting was enough, obviously, to catch their attention.

She screamed and Ryan Brooks shot straight up from the floor.

"Jesus, I'm sorry, Lisa."

I looked away from them as they hurriedly righted clothes. "Ryan, your father . . ."

I rubbed my mouth with a shaking hand. The scare had been enough to make me want to throw up. We hadn't made any claims on each other . . . but the thought of him with another woman nearly made me physically ill.

"He's out with some guys." Ryan tucked his shirt in his pants. "I'm so sorry."

"Why the fuck are you apologizing to her?" The woman demanded and shoved at his arm. "This isn't her place; she shouldn't even fucking be here."

Ryan glared at her. "It's my father's home and Lisa is . . ." He looked at me. "I'm a dead man."

I shrugged off my coat. "I won't say a word."

"You don't have to."

Gasping, I turned. James was in the doorway and I realized that Ryan hadn't been looking at me at all. "I didn't even hear the door open."

"I can see that." He glared at the two of them over my shoulder. "But, I can just imagine what you just witnessed."

"Dad . . ."

"Ryan," James interrupted. "See your *friend* to the elevator and then return, immediately."

"He's a grown man," the woman snapped.

"Shut up, Dana." He grabbed her coat off the couch. "Get your purse."

I watched Ryan usher the woman out with a grimace in James's direction. He looked furious.

"Where my son is concerned, Lisa, I would prefer that you not keep secrets from me."

I winced. "My bad."

He chuckled, obviously tired, and walked to the dormant fireplace in the large room that served as both foyer and living room for the apartment. "The only thing I wanted was to come home, crawl into my bed, and hold you. Now, I've got . . ." He stiffened when the door reopened. "You owe Lisa an apology."

"He already apologized."

James raised one eyebrow and stared pointedly at his son. "Ryan."

Ryan shoved his hands into his jeans pockets. "Lisa, I am very sorry that you walked in here and saw that. It was inappropriate on so many levels I don't even know where to start."

I swallowed hard. "For a few seconds," I started and then looked away from the both. "I thought it was . . ."

"Me," James finished in a hard voice. "My son and I are often mistaken for each other, at least from the back."

"Yes." I nodded and looked at Ryan, whose eyes were wide with horror having realized how close he'd come to damaging his father's relationship, before settling my gaze back on James. He looked tense and barely controlled. I figured he was pretty close to blowing his top. "It's your apartment."

"I don't blame you," James murmured gently and turned to glare at Ryan. "As for the woman, I'll not have anyone in my home who would speak to me that way."

"I won't be seeing her again," Ryan whispered. He rubbed his mouth in a way so much like his father that I softened a little. "She said some pretty stupid things at the elevator."

"I realized pretty quickly it was you." I looked between them again. "I'll just leave this to you guys to discuss."

"I am sorry."

"I know." I gave him a little smile and hoped that James wouldn't take too much skin off his ass.

I put my coat away in the closet and then went back to the bedroom. I walked to the bench that sat at the end of the bed and plopped down on it. It had been one hell of a day.

He walked into the room, his fingers pressed against the bridge of his nose. Using a foot to push the door shut, he walked toward his dresser. There he placed his watch, cuff links, BlackBerry, and various objects from his pockets into a clay bowl.

He sighed. "I cannot believe he was *servicing* that woman on my Italian leather sofa. I could cut him out of my will for that alone."

I bit down on my bottom lip. "Like father, like son."

"Not funny." He pulled his shirt from his pants and started to unbutton. "And I wouldn't have a woman like that witch."

"Most would say I'm the meanest creature on the planet." I leaned back across the bench and rested my head on the bed. "We left this place a shambles."

"I have a cleaning service." He came to stand in front of me, his shirt gone, belt undone, and pants unzipped.

I wet my lips at the glimpse of his dark blue silk boxers. Lord, the man knew how to dress. He still looked particularly vexed, which only added to his appeal.

He nudged one of my legs with one knee and I spread them so he could move closer.

I sat up completely, and ran my hands up his thighs. "My only reason for saying that I would not tell you what I saw was that I figured it would put you in a crappy mood."

"His complete and utter lack of respect for my home seems to know no bounds."

"He's young."

"So?"

I slipped my fingers into the opening of his boxers and traced the edge of his cock. It immediately began to harden under the attention. "Lust can be a heady thing . . . make you forget where you are and what the right thing to do is."

"Bullshit," he muttered.

"Oh yeah?" I worked his boxers down and freed his cock. "Remember that first day . . . you were so hot to get in me. So ready to fuck me you totally forgot to get a condom." I wrapped one hand around him and used my thumb to rub the seeping head of his cock. He jerked against my attention.

"Not the same thing. That piece of ass hadn't been playing hard to get for two years."

I laughed; his tone had been full of ire. "Am I the *piece of ass* in our situation?"

"No." He ran his hands into my hair and pulled me up from the bench to cover my mouth with his. The kiss was soft, and when his tongue thrust between my lips, I relaxed against him. He lifted his head as he found the zipper of my dress and tugged it down. "You are . . ." He stopped and cupped the back of my head. "You're my woman."

How positively primitive. "Yours?"

"Yeah, mine." He brushed at the straps of my dress and then pushed it down my body in one swift motion. I stood there in a pair of high-heeled platform Mary Jane–style shoes and dark green transparent silk panties with a matching bra. Both pieces were a few inches of cloth and a bunch of strings.

He took a step back and swallowed hard. "Christ, I wanted to talk to you about that article before . . ."

I trailed my fingers from my navel upward to the valley between my breasts. "Before you fuck me?" One glance at his cock told me he was more than ready. I pouted a little when he tucked himself away and zipped his pants. "Hey, I was going to play with that."

James chuckled, walked to a closet, and pulled out a robe. "Put this on."

I shrugged the robe on and tied it with a frown. "Do we have to do this right now?"

"Yes." He motioned me to come with him out of the room and I reached down to take off my shoes before following. He stopped at the door. "Keep the shoes on."

"You freak." I laughed softly but fastened the one I'd gotten undone and straightened to follow him.

In his home office, I sat down in a chair in front of his desk and crossed my legs. The robe fell open all the way to my waist and I just grinned when his gaze dropped to my lap immediately. He sat down at this desk and flipped open his computer. "I had the editor of the paper send me a copy of the article." He motioned toward the printer just as it activated. "I'm loath to bring this up now, since you are in a good mood but I want to get this settled." James stood, retrieved the article from the printer, and brought the pages to me. "It's not pleasant."

It was more than unpleasant, and it began with the first sentence. "Society wife?" I snorted. "What happened to famous fucking artist?"

James laughed softly and returned to his chair. "It will not be printed. In fact, a letter from Carlson's lawyer arrived about twenty minutes before I called. The editor in chief, Dillon Keener, was working up the courage to call me to talk about it. The reporter is also facing a personal lawsuit. Apparently, Greg Carlson doesn't remember saying half the crap she put in the article."

"She got him drunk," I whispered. I was trying hard not to shake but the quotes in the article were echoing in my ears. I could practically hear him. "He always talks like this when he's drunk." I finished reading it in silence and then put it aside. "Okay."

"This article won't be published and the reporter will likely be sued within an inch of her life by your ex-husband."

"Eventually it will get out."

"Some of it." He shrugged. "But I believe it's time that some of it did come out. It would free you from him."

"I'm under a legal obligation to never speak of the abuse that I suffered at his hands," I whispered.

"And if you did?"

"Our divorce settlement could be reviewed." Forcing myself to relax in the chair was a challenge but I did it. "I'd have to return the settlement money."

"And that's something you could live with?"

"Yes, I'm more than comfortable." I swallowed hard. "But he could probably also sue me for damages."

"I'm sorry I can't protect you from this entirely. I would if I could."

I flushed. "I don't expect you to ride to my rescue."

"I *expect* it." His graze dropped to the article. "It has passed through the hands of many people during the last week. Katrina Howard, the writer, has been working on the piece for a month."

A whole month. A stranger had been moving around in my past gathering information on me and I hadn't even known it. "Why?"

"Why what?"

"Why was she doing an article on me?" I picked it up again and read through to the fourth paragraph. "This is about me, James, not about Greg. The crap on Greg is less than a third of it. She has information about my work, where I grew up . . . and not that I expect to be treated like a victim. But I was a victim of abuse and she's treating me like I asked for it." I tossed the article aside.

"When I spoke with her . . ."

"You spoke with her?" I demanded.

"Yes, I was in on the meeting that we had with my lawyer concerning the matter. She made several comments about your work and Greg's claims that you had bizarre sexual needs . . ." He stood and walked away from me. "She's a prude, Lisa, and something of a religious nut. She normally writes fluffy society pieces; and apparently became interested in you around the same time those bloggers trespassed on your property and caught you on their camera phones with the paint gun."

Great. "So I'm a porn artist, a sexual deviant, and Greg hit me because I deserved it."

"Pretty much. Though she wasn't too happy with him either, once she realized he was going to sue her." He pressed his lips together in a thin line.

I hope he sued the crap out of her for years. Greg was very good at using the court system for his own purposes and his lawyer loved to get paid. "Not all of it is true." I cleared my throat. "I mean he hit often enough and sometimes I hit back."

"But he wasn't violent with you in bed?"

"No, never." I shook my head. "Greg was more interested in destroying my self-esteem than anything else. He considered himself quite a lover and he used sex to control me."

He stood from the desk, walked around, and held out his hand. "Come to bed."

Taking his hand was as natural as breathing.

"Take off the robe, turn around, and face the wall," he whispered. "Now the panties."

Hooking my fingers into the sides of the thong, I pushed it down my legs and kicked it aside.

James guided my hands up to rest on the wall. "Don't move."

I sucked in a deep breath as I listened to him undressing. He released the enclosure of my bra and it fell away. Hands moved over my back and down my hips, and then one slid purposefully between my legs.

"God, you're wet." He kissed my back. "Are you wet like this for me?"

I sucked in a deep breath as one finger teased my clit, "Yes."

"How long have you been like this for me?" he asked gently raking his fingernails down my back.

"As long as I can remember," I responded.

James ran his hands down my back and over my ass as he lowered to the floor and unfastened the shoes. I slipped out of them at his urging and shuddered when he turned me around and pressed me up against the wall. I closed my eyes and waited. I felt the heat of his body before he reached for me. His hands moved over my hips, cupped my ass, and lifted me up and onto his cock. I pressed against the wall and wrapped my legs around his hips.

He sucked in a deep breath and buried his face in my neck. "This is has got to be the best pussy I've ever had."

He sank his teeth into my neck and I cried out—the pleasure/pain of that moment was unreal. After a few minutes, he carried me over to the bed and sat down with me in his lap, his cock still buried inside me.

He rolled us over and started to move inside me—slowly and with sweet deliberation. He came quickly and rolled off me with a muted curse. After a few seconds, he rolled on his side, his mouth claiming one nipple as his hand slipped between my legs. He stroked me gently before rolling over onto his back.

"Come here, baby, and sit on my face."

I sucked in a deep breath but did as he instructed. I choked back a sob as I settled my pussy onto his mouth. He gripped me firmly with his hands and began to stroke me with his tongue. After several agonizing seconds, he guided my hips into a gentle motion. When I came, I screamed. He barely gave me time to recover; he laid me down on the bed and slid into me. I was amazed that he was hard again, amazed and thankful.

He kissed my mouth, then, his tongue sweeping against my teeth and mating with my tongue. I loved the taste of us, him and me.

He raised his head, "Talk to me." He demanded.

I moaned a little, and a small sob escaped me as he thrust into me hard, "Ah, God, do that again." I demanded arching my back as he stroked into me.

He laughed softly, "Did I find a good spot?"

"Oh yes." I whispered as he slid against me again. "Harder." I raked my nails down his back. "Harder." I pulled him tightly to me. "Baby, please."

"Do you like it when I fuck you?" he asked softly against me mouth.

"Yes, it's perfect."

"And if I need more?" James demanded.

"I'll give everything you need." I sucked in a deep breath as he filled me with his cock. "Everything."

"What about the things that I want?"

"Everything." I promised, my breath catching with each thrust of his body into me.

"You'll lay yourself out for me and let me lick your nipples and suck your clit you until you pass out from the pleasure of it?" he asked, his voice rough with demand and pleasure.

"God, yes."

"You'll suck my cock until I can't stand it anymore?"

"With pleasure," I whispered. I was so close to coming I could barely keep my eyes open.

James pushed my hands into position above my head. "You'll let me turn you over and fuck your ass? You'll beg for me to fuck you hard?"

"Yes." A sob wrenched free from my mouth.

"One day," he started as his pace quickened. He gave me four deep bone-jarring strokes, and then he paused and started to rock inside me slowly. The head of his cock rubbed my G-spot with each push. "One day, you'll let me give you my baby?"

"God, Jamie!" I came hard and fast, wetness gushing between us. The hot spill of his seed inside me caused me to clench around him and hold him as tightly as I could. "I love you."

He lifted his head, his gaze connecting with mine in the darkness of the room. "I won't let you take that back."

"I won't." Pulling his head back to mine, I moaned against his mouth when he shifted against; his still-hard cock finding my G-spot with astounding skill.

"I've loved you for years," he whispered as he tucked his face against the side of my neck. "I can't believe you're finally mine."

I lay beneath him shaking and totally at the mercy of my own heart.

Explore the
SINS OF THE NIGHT
with Devyn Quinn!

On sale from Aphrodisia!

# Prologue

---

*Warwickshire, England—1906*

Adrien Roth wasn't sure what awakened him. Perhaps it was the sinking of the sun, the gradual darkening of the chamber already shrouded in shadows by heavy velvet drapes drawn across the windows.

Or perhaps it was dread rousing him from his restless sleep, causing him to twist his wrists against the ropes binding them to the headboard. He cursed the unyielding restraints. No matter how much he writhed, he simply could not free his arms. The skin under the ropes was badly chafed and raw. Struggling only delivered more pain. He ignored it, his hands balling into tight fists to fight the ropes anew.

Helplessness consumed him. A wild-voiced cry echoed through his head.

*They're coming. . . .*

His eyes slipped shut. Silence hung, the lack of sound even more disturbing than a scream or the sound of ominous footfalls on the hardwood floors. His heart hammered in his chest, beating against his ribs with a fury threatening to steal his breath away. He gasped, running his parched tongue over dry, cracked lips.

Opening his eyes, he focused on the dim light behind the drapes as though it were a beacon, the only source of illumination in the world. He silently prayed to God without ceasing. Without allowing himself to think of what was to come, or of how it would end, he vehemently cursed the source of his misery. When more thoughts of torture invaded his mind, his gaze clouded over and his lower jaw trembled. The wait was excruciating.

Minutes dragged like hours. All hope faded with the last precious rays of day. As the wing of night spread over the land, misery and horror was given fresh birth. Fear became more intense.

He did not *hear* them, but *felt* them, the way one would become aware of a spider crawling across one's skin.

His eyes widened when the door swung open and two figures, a man and a woman, entered silently. He knew them both. The man was Devon, Lord Carnavorn, seventh Earl of Hammerston. Tall, well over six feet, his features were strong and commanding; piercing gray eyes, sensual but cruel mouth, tousled brown hair. The outfit of dove gray trousers, white silk shirt, and silk vest of a lighter gray well fitted his muscular frame.

The woman . . . Oh, blessed virgin and tainted whore. She was his angel and his demon, savior and tormentor; appropriately named, for she would consent to lie beneath no man.

*Lilith.*

Her name was a whisper on the lips of pious men, the screech of a night owl, the shimmering frost on the accursed north wind. In one slender hand she carried a gold-gilt candelabram. The flame guttered as she walked. She was a lovely creature to behold through the wavering light. Clad in a white silk dressing gown, the sheer material whispered around her legs. Open at the neck, a glimpse of her sumptuous breasts hinted of untold delights. Black hair cascaded around her shoulders, falling nearly to her waist. Silver-flecked crystal blue eyes, a pert nose, and a pouting little bow of a mouth decorated her oval face. Beyond her beauty was a strange hardness—a hatred lingering in the depths of her eyes and the cruel set of her mouth.

Devon Carnavorn's probing stare raked Adrien's naked form. "I hope you're ready for the coming evening. We have something special in store for you this night." His accented voice was smooth, untroubled, as if all his guests were usually trussed up like a Christmas turkey ready for roasting.

Adrien gave a final feeble tug, wishing the ties would magically dissolve. There was, however, no hope of rescue, and he knew it.

He was afraid, but not for his life. Life was temporary, something he'd been prepared from childhood to sacrifice in the name of the hunt for the creatures inhabiting the night, stalking the weaker human prey. Life was fleeting, easier lost than kept. But what of his immortal soul? No amount of preparation or prayer could sustain a man when eternal damnation beckoned. All he had left was his faith in God and the church. Through the days, he'd prayed when conscious, dreamt that he prayed when unconscious, his time spent in restless sleep refusing to let him find solace or peace.

The beginning of a prayer slipped from his lips. "Our Father, who art in heaven, hallowed be thy name," he said, attempting to wrap himself in the words as if they were a shield. "Thy kingdom come. Thy will be done, on earth as it is in heaven—"

Carnavorn angrily recoiled from the words. A look of scorn colored his face. "Your prayers will not be answered! Your God does not exist here!" Hands fisted in anger, temporarily silenced Adrien with the venom in his voice. Carnavorn recovered his composure and continued in a smoother tone. "I know the old prayers as well as you do. They are meaningless. Nothing."

"You mock the words of my faith, demon!" Adrien spat back.

Dark brows dropped into a frown. "They say the devil can quote scripture for his own purposes," Carnavorn countered icily. "That itself is true enough. I certainly have one that perfectly fits our, ah, situation. Something you may recognize, about an eye for an eye and a tooth for a tooth."

A shiver clawed its way up Adrien's spine. His guts turned to liquid. "If you're going to kill me, do it. I've no fear of death." How many days had he been held captive? He wasn't sure. He only knew that he was growing weaker, resistance fading each and every time the demonic pair descended.

Carnavorn laughed, mouth curling up in a half smile of disdain. "Kill you? Death is too good for you, *Amhais*. As the shadow-stalkers have hunted us, so must we of the Kynn return the favor." He turned to the woman. "Are you ready, my dear?"

An eager smile crossed Lilith's red lips, showing a flash of white teeth. "I have a special surprise for you." Her voice was a combination of warm honey on sharp gravel, throaty and sensuous. She set the candelabra aside.

Adrien shook his head. Hunger, exhaustion, and his weakening body were all making a play on his senses. The faces of those he'd slain drifted to the front of his mind. Their corpses rose to grasp at his legs, tug him down into the depths of an unhallowed grave.

He wanted to cry out, deny this evil in the name of all that was holy. Instead, only feeble words escaped his lips. "No . . . please . . . not again . . ." To beg was demeaning, but he had no more to give.

Carnavorn stepped behind Lilith. Hands on her slender

hips, he maneuvered her to the bed. Reaching in front of her, he untied the sash of her gown and slid it off her shoulders. Underneath, she was completely naked. Her figure was well arranged: full breasts, slender waist, flat belly, and legs that went on endlessly. Beautiful and feminine, hers was a body made to entice, tease, and please. A thin silver chain hung around her neck; a pendant nestled in the hollow between her breasts. Of Celtic origins, the design was that of a circle interwoven with three sharp-edged eyelets that formed a triangle around the circle.

Carnavorn's hands lifted, his fingertips grazing her temples. "Beautiful, is she not?" His fingers continued their trek, tracing the contours of her high cheekbones, the lines of her jaw, down her neck to the hollow of her throat. Eyelids lowering, she tipped her head to one side.

"We have a gift to share with you, Adrien." Carnavorn's head dipped, nuzzling the soft curve of Lilith's neck. His hands found her breasts, cupping their weight. She made a soft sound; half gasp, half moan.

"I don't want your damnation." Adrien's sputtered words were strained.

Devon Carnavorn's gray eyes narrowed, hard and flinty. "I don't recall that you were given a choice. Did you show Ariel any mercy when you put that stake through her heart? She was everything to me, and you took her away with the darkness of your hate and prejudice against our kind. There are truly more things in heaven and on earth than humankind will ever be able to understand. Your mind is too small to comprehend that. But your eyes will be opened, and then you shall see all."

Adrien fought his bonds. "I sent her back to the devil that spawned her. Just as I will send you to hell right after her if I ever have that chance!"

Carnavorn only laughed. His hands found and teased Lilith's nipples, giving them renewed erectness. "I won't let you go, Adrien. You're going to pay for what you did, not once, but again and again and again. You've only gotten a glimpse of what we really are."

He ran his palms over Lilith's hips, then her belly. A low moan escaped her throat. She hovered in a state of sexual arousal, the air around her scented from the sizzling heat of raw desire. His hand found the tender slit between her legs, that velvet treasure every woman possessed. Delving past the soft curls of her Venus mound, he stroked her clit.

Carnavorn dipped one finger inside her depths. He brought it to Lilith's mouth, tracing her lips with honeyed nectar. Her moist tongue snaked out to savor her juices. "You want to taste her." He grinned, feral and unpleasant. "Admit you are as weak as the next man and that lust is ablaze in your heart."

"No—"

Lilith looked at him from under a fall of long lashes. "But it is, my darling." Her gaze traced his nude body, settling on his flaccid penis. "How well I know." Smiling, she began to finger her silver charm. The edges of the triangle were sharpened and could slide through flesh like a razor. The charm had meted out a lot of pain and would deliver still more. The agony itself was not nearly as great as the apprehension of pain to be inflicted. "You belong to me now, beloved."

Adrien winced, his eyes drifting downward. A series of cuts crisscrossed his chest and abdomen, his skin red and swollen, part of the bondage and bloodletting ritual his captors had inflicted.

Devon gave her a gentle push. "Take him."

Lilith flicked her hair off her shoulders and stretched out on the bed. The feather mattress was thick and soft, covered with a warm down comforter.

By day, Adrien was chained in a damp, windowless cellar. When night neared its fall, two silent male servants would bring him to her bedchamber. He was too weak to protest or try to fight his way to freedom. Through his long captivity he'd been given no food and very little water.

Propping herself on an elbow, Lilith trailed her palm over his chest, tracing his dusky male nipples. Her nails were long and sharp. Her touch was chilly, as if no blood flowed through her veins. Her skin had a strange opalescent opaqueness, reminding him more of stone than of living flesh.

Sexual hunger exuded from her like an exotic perfume. Lust pummeled him in a series of gut-wrenching kicks. Adrien caught a quick breath. When she was so close, every breath he took sent his need soaring. He ached to touch her.

Lilith's hand moved to one of the small cuts marring his abdomen. Her fingers felt like silk against his skin. "Don't you like what I do to you?" The wounds were deep and wide enough to draw blood, but do no serious damage. They seemed to mark him as hers and hers alone. Dipping her head, she circled one of his nipples with her liquid-silver tongue, flicking the little nub until it grew as hard as a bead. Her breath caressed his chilled skin as her searching hand rubbed over his bare chest in sensuous circles.

Adrien closed his eyes, trying to fight her alluring touch. A growl rumbled deep in his throat, but he was barely aware of it. "Please—don't—" His voice was hoarse, wavering with desperation. As if to betray his words, sweet inertia washed over him.

Devon sneered. "Words Ariel said. Words your men ignored."

Lilith jerked off her necklace, snapping the thin chain. "Tonight, I will close those mortal eyes of yours." She drew the sharp edge of the charm across his skin, just below his navel. Crimson welled to the surface, and her head lowered. She soothed away the brief sting with her tongue, licking hungrily. Low snarls escaped from her throat as she drank, the way an animal would growl when its food was in danger of being snatched. She made two more cuts, going lower with each, licking and suckling his skin.

Adrien shivered when she wrapped her fingers around his growing erection. His thick, jutting cock pulsed, alive under her touch. A drop of semen leaked from its head, glistening in the candlelight. What she was doing appalled him. It was against his will, but it also fascinated him on a deeper, more primeval level.

"You will pay for murdering my sister in cold blood," Lilith murmured. "As you took Ariel from the collective, you'll replace her."

Adrien's senses spun away when Lilith spread her long hair across his torso. Eyes alight with anticipation, She flicked out her adept tongue. Wetness swirled over the tip of his penis. She suckled in long, deep strokes that stole away his breath and tightened his balls.

Anticipation ran riot through Adrien's veins. Lilith's teeth scraped, a bit more pain to feed his deep-seated erotic desires.

He wasn't willing, but he could be persuaded.

Appalled by his excitement, Adrien was also secretly intrigued by this strange world of sexual vampirism. Fantasies he'd never believed would be fulfilled were bursting into a painfully carnal kaleidoscope of sights, sounds, and sensations. Sex was suddenly not just something to have or have done. It was sustaining nourishment drawing from the very core of energy that could create life itself.

Still, he desired it even as he despised it. The conflicting ideas were plunging him deeper into confusion. Sanity was slowly turning to madness as the carnal desires harbored in his heart took seed and sprouted. The devil had laid a feast before him, and even though he should turn away and embrace the famine, he was a man of desires unfulfilled.

He hungered.

And he ate.

Watching from the edge of the bed, Devon Carnavorn grasped the bedpost, leaning closer. "Show him no mercy, Lilith. Take him in the most painful way."

The malicious words drew Adrien from his enjoyable apathy. "I was sworn of an oath to erase your kind from this earth," he replied. "I will not stop, no matter the hell you send me into."

Despite his words, he was completely under the domination of these foul beasts. The ache to possess Lilith completely worsened. Fiercer than his own disgust at his weakening will was the unquenchable desire to dominate her the way she was controlling him.

Devon chuckled. "Heaven is just a sin away, my friend. Your lips say no, but your body betrays your piety. You can't resist the needs of the flesh, so give in and have the benefit of what is so generously offered."

The shackles of repression were easily cast aside.

*I'm too weak*, Adrien thought.

Pleasure took control.

Bracing his head on the pillow, Adrien moved his hips, savoring the way Lilith flicked her tongue over the tip before taking him deeply. His mouth felt incredibly arid, his lips tender from his hot breath rolling over them. He longed to be kissing her, holding her; he needed to be inside that tight, velvety cunt, feeling her smooth belly against his as she writhed under his body.

Just as he was about to explode, Lilith drew back. She shifted and moved onto her knees, straddling his body. She lowered her hips to his in a smooth motion, guiding his erection into her welcoming depths. He could feel her thighs tightening against his hips. Her sex clenched his cock, soft as rose petals and strong as steel bands.

Lilith dug her nails into his shoulders, bringing a fresh pain of the most exquisite kind. Leaning forward, her mouth captured his in a long, suckling kiss. He tasted his blood on her lips, a sample both forbidden and thrilling. Even as she kissed him, he could feel the strange ripples drawing away his sexual essences the way her lips had drawn in his life's essences. She quivered violently when orgasm ripped through her.

Adrien's own arousal was simmering at a heat threatening to boil over like a volcano disgorging molten lava. Straining against the ropes tying his wrists, he thrust his hips upward, driving deeper into her slick, silken channel.

Face framed with a tumble of dark hair, white teeth sinking into her lower lip, Lilith slammed back, grinding down on his cock. Bracing her hands on his shoulders, she rose a little, then back down, meeting his upcoming thrust with perfect synchronicity. The power of their joining was more erotic than anything he'd ever experienced.

Adrien lost control.

Lust searing his senses, he speared deep in one long thrust. Clenching his teeth, unable to hold back any longer, he felt the pull of his loins releasing. The muscles across his abdomen ridged, then rippled. His brain short-circuited, as a quake of pleasure thundered through him. Hot semen jetted. Lilith's inner muscles rippled around his cock in long, blissful waves.

Adrien moaned, struggling to master his breathing. He was woozy, dizzy, feeling as though his very soul had been drained away.

Sleep would be welcome. Food even more.

The offering he was to receive for nourishment wasn't what he anticipated.

Bodies still joined, Lilith retrieved her charm. Lifting her hand, she slashed through her palm.

Warm blood dripped onto Adrien's chest, the droplets falling like shards of ice in a winter storm.

Lilith reached out and grasped his face. Her nails dug into

his skin, the pressure at his jaws forcing his mouth open. Fierceness blazed behind her gaze. "Drink." She positioned her bleeding hand over his mouth. "Drink of me, and shed your mortal shell." Foul blood dribbled past his lips.

Gagging, Adrien twisted his face to one side. "No . . ." Stomach lurching, he spat her blood back at her.

With a little laugh, Lilith righted his head. Digging her fingers into his mouth and wrenching down his jaw, she fed him more of her blood.

Adrien renewed his efforts to refuse her offering, gagging and gurgling sickly through his efforts not to swallow even as his lungs burned from lack of air. He had to breathe to live.

He had to swallow.

Gasping, he reluctantly swallowed. The strange, sweet taste coated his tongue, sliding like cold lead down his throat. When the chill hit his stomach, he could feel the exotic organism enter his veins, slithering through his body like an evil snake.

Adrien's vision dimmed alarmingly as an unfamiliar euphoria overtook him. An unearthly and wholly incredible energy was burgeoning inside him, spawning outward like a child fighting to be birthed. He could not speak, he could not move. His flesh tingled as though consumed by an inner fire, feeling dry and papery. He could feel the energy pulsing, conquering, consuming . . .

His soul was being swallowed by the black entity stealing his mortality away.

Darkness rose.

Helpless, a mist shrouded his brain, spreading a strange numbness over his senses. Then unconsciousness claimed him, and he knew no more.